Y0-BSL-255

AUTHOR'S NOTE

This book contains themes of disordered eating, pregnancy loss and a parent with cancer. Some of it is based on my own experience, but I have used sensitivity readers for the other issues. I have tried my best to handle them with care, but readers who are sensitive to these themes may still find them triggering.

Please read with care.

This is a work of fiction. Similarities to real people, places, or events are entirely coincidental.

THE SEMI-ROYAL

First edition. February 7, 2020.

Copyright © 2020 Fiona West.

ISBN: 978-1-952172-01-4

Written by Fiona West.

West, Fiona (Fiction wri
The semi-royal /
2020.
33305249483003
cu   03/25/21

MAP

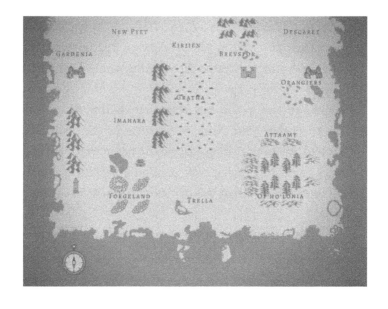

PROLOGUE

EIGHTEEN MONTHS EARLIER

Lieutenant Arron James woke in his hospital bed in Briggin, trying to breathe through the pain. The medication wasn't cutting it again. Monitoring machines beeped and clicked at him in the darkness, as if chiding him for being awake at this hour. Saint was sitting in the chair next to his bed, his head resting against the taupe walls. He had his black sweatshirt on backwards, hood up, trying to block out the ambient light that was constantly present in the hospital room.

"You can push the button," said a soft voice from his other side, "if it hurts. There's no shame in it."

"I thought you went back to the rental house." He let his head flop to his left to see her better. Woz, he loved her. Her smooth skin the color of a walnut tree, her hundreds of tiny dreadlocks, the glimmer in her eyes when she was teasing. Her body was perfectly proportioned except for her long legs; to call them long was like calling his hair "a bit messy." But her body was only surpassed by her mind, her generosity, her poise. Her absolute royalty. He still couldn't believe she'd come all this way. "You should be asleep."

"So should you," Rhodie said, closing her laptop.

"And yet here we are, hanging out with the mice."

She grimaced and he laughed, even though it hurt like Jersey.

"I haven't actually seen any, don't worry."

"That's a relief," Rhodie said, placing her hand over his. "My preference for interacting with mice is in a lab situation, firmly caged. Those I'll treat humanely. All bets are off for mice found in the wild."

"Caught one once. Kept it as a pet in a box under my bed." He shifted to try to adjust his pillows, and she jumped up to help him. He mourned the loss of skin-to-skin contact with her.

"Really?"

"But he got out one day. Poor Ringo. Trap my mum had under the sink got 'im. Still amazed my sisters never ratted me out . . ."

Her lips twitched as she sat back down. "Mice are not rats, but I approve the pun attempt."

Cautiously, he reached for her hand again, and they wove their fingers together. Something about the darkness, about their aloneness, was opening her up for the first time. She'd always bantered with him and seemed to enjoy it, but whenever anyone came around, it broke the spell and she went cold again. He'd made a stupid joke earlier in the day—*Well, I can't lie around all day, so what shall we do this weekend? Rock climbing? Skydiving? Spelunking?* She'd quickly excused herself and then gone to the house Edward had rented for them, and he knew he'd made her cry.

"About my joke earlier . . ." How could he explain that joking about this horrible situation was the only thing holding him together? That sounded pathetic. And he should've known better; she was obviously more attached to him than he'd realized if she'd come all this way.

"It's all right." She added her left hand, sandwiching his hand between both of hers.

"I didn't mean to upset you."

"I know."

Saint shifted in the squeaky chair, and he squeezed her hand tighter before she could pull away. He held his breath until Saint sighed and his breathing became deep and even once more, and then he loosened his grip on her hand . . . a little, anyway.

"Are you in pain?"

"Is that what this strange feeling is?" *Pain* didn't start to describe it. *Pain* was a nothing word for slivers in your foot and papercuts and bee stings. This felt like being ripped apart every time he took a breath; this was a living thing in his chest, hot and pulsing, like a lava flow. He'd never felt anything like it in his twenty-two years.

"Just push the button."

"I'm fine."

She pursed her lips. "Yes, Edward told me you didn't want me monitoring your pain. Stop being a tough guy. You'll heal better if you get more sleep."

Wrong. I'll heal better if I stay up all night and hold your hand and talk to you. You're my cure, love. I push that button, and I'll pass out again. And you'll sneak away . . .

He grunted his displeasure. "Rhodie, I . . ."

"Arrondale Percival James, if you won't push it for yourself, push it for me. I abhor seeing you like this. I need you to get well."

Well, if that didn't spear him through the heart, he didn't know what ever could. With his right hand, he sifted through sheets until he found the button and lifted it up so she could see him click it.

"Thank you," she whispered. "It's for your own good." Rhodie lifted his hand like she was going to press a kiss to the back of it, but she paused when her gaze snagged on his. He started to ask her what that look meant, what all of this meant, why she'd come. But it was already happening; his thoughts were thickening, his eyelids heavy, and he had to let them slide shut as she untwined their fingers. The waves of pain began to slow, his breathing came a little easier.

"Sweet dreams, Arron," she murmured. He was awake enough to hear her, not awake enough to reach for her again, to ask her not to let go.

When he woke the next morning, both Saint and Rhodie were gone and Edward and Sam were in their places. Edward appeared to be on some kind of conference call, and he grasped the built-in microphone of his headphones.

"All right, mate?"

"Yes," James lied. The pain was back. He hit the button as he turned to Sam.

"Did my princess leave?"

His friend raised a skeptical eyebrow. "First of all, I can't see how she's yours in the slightest . . ."

"And yet you knew exactly of whom I was speaking." James grinned, and Sam rolled his eyes.

"Secondly, she went back to the house. Your mum and your sisters arrived late last night and are currently on their way here."

"Okay," James murmured, still looking at the door as though she were about to walk through it.

"We thought we'd take off when they got here. This is a very small space."

"You don't have to. Mum will want you all to stay. She'll feel she's displaced you. We Jameses are used to small, crowded places."

"Good to know. I'll start thinking of a reasonable excuse now," Sam declared, and Arron smiled. He had no doubt Sam was telling the truth. He always did, perhaps to his own detriment. It made him a good friend. Sam always gave it to him straight.

"How's the house?" asked Arron, smoothing his sheets over his torso. "Is Rhodie comfortable there?"

"The house is extravagantly large, well protected and well suited for *all* its occupants," Sam said pointedly, and Arron tipped his head to concede the point that he should care about all his friends and family, not just the one who made his heart beat fastest.

Someone stopped in the doorway, and he looked up to see his mum with Ivy, Cora, and Cora's partner, Brighton. His mum's eyes were shining with tears, but she was smiling broadly, trying so hard to hide it.

"Mum, don't cry in the hallway. Cry in my room like a proper human being."

All his family members started crying then, tears coursing down their pale cheeks even as they laughed.

"That's my Arron, all right," said Aideen, coming forward to kiss his cheek. "How are you, love? Are you hurting?" She grabbed his hand and squeezed it, and the pressure on his IV line made him wince.

"I'm all right," he mumbled, feeling emotional to see his indomitable mom so wrecked. Ivy and Cora kissed him, too, and Brighton did an awkward wave, which Arron imitated.

"Don't let him fool you." Rhodie's voice floated forward from the back of the group, making his heart skip a beat. "He's not using his pain button nearly enough."

"Her Highness was at the house, and she was kind enough to offer to come along and help explain all that's happened to you. I hope that's all right," Aideen said, fussing with his bedding, covering him up even though he was already too warm.

"I'm always happy to see Rhodie," he said, giving her a long look, which she broke almost immediately. Out of the corner of his eye, he spotted his sisters exchanging a knowing glance.

Sam stood up suddenly. "Edward and I are going to do some sightseeing, as I have never been to Briggin before. Isn't that right, Edward?"

"Oh. Yes, unfortunately, Sam and I can't stay." With light amusement, Edward excused himself from the conference call and closed his laptop, hurrying to follow Sam out into the hallway. "Apologies. We'll see you back at the house."

"That one's not subtle," Cora said, tossing a thumb over her shoulder toward Sam's retreating form.

"Neither are you, loudmouth," Arron responded, and she stuck out her tongue at him. "And he saved my life, so maybe cut him some slack for his lack of social niceties."

"I've had Dr. Pasqual paged," Rhodie said, coming back in. "She should be here soon."

"He's going to make a full recovery, isn't he?" Cora asked softly, her face pinched, and Arron saw her reaching for Brighton's hand.

"He's awfully pale," Ivy whispered.

"I can hear you, actually, girls," Arron said in a forceful whisper. "I was shot in the chest, not the head."

His sisters snorted, and his mum pursed her lips in disapproval.

"I am very optimistic that he will make a full recovery," Rhodie offered, standing at the end of his bed, looking at his chart again. She thought it made her look smart, he'd wager, holding that chart. She wasn't wrong. He yawned, his brain starting to go foggy again.

"I thank Woz for that," Aideen said, kissing his forehead and ruffling his hair. "You can get some rest, love. We'll be here when you wake."

"Unless we're eating off the feast Edward's chef is making at the house," Cora added. "I mean, priorities, right? That thing was massive."

"I think he was preparing a boar," Ivy added, rubbing her hands together.

"Good morning," Dr. Pasqual said in her lilting accent. "You must be the lieutenant's family. I can see the resemblance." His family smiled at her, and like moths, they floated over to her to get the whole story on his condition. Rhodie stayed at the end of his bed, watching him, clipboard clutched to her chest, and he felt awash with gratitude to her for making this easier on his family.

"Thank you," he mouthed.

She replaced the chart and adjusted her glasses, glancing at the doorway, before mouthing back, "You're welcome."

CHAPTER ONE

A FEW DAYS AFTER CHRISTMAS, Princess Rhodo-dendron was catching up on research and writing out reports at her reserved desk in the castle's main library. An unexpected noise—a giggle?—reached her ears despite the classical music streaming through her headphones, and she pulled out one earbud. The headphones had been malfunctioning lately; she'd been meaning to take them to one of the castle's magic users to have the magic re-associated with the device, but she just hadn't had the time. Veil Technology was largely fairly reliable: the network that kept their devices humming through magical association didn't often fail. She was going to miss that reliability on her expedition . . . The Unveiled. Wild magic. It wasn't so easily swayed into cooperation.

From somewhere behind the tall oak bookshelves, the soft giggle came again, and Rhodie sighed. She should've realized her brother and sister-in-law were also here, given that she had seen two security personnel just outside the library doors. But when one saw guards posted at every doorway, soon, they all started to run together. How was she supposed to remember which was which? Honestly.

Suppressing an eye roll, Rhodie replaced her earbud and went back to her work. A few minutes later, Abbie left first, subtly adjusting her shirt, running her fingers through her already incurably untamed hair. Rhodie had caught a glimpse of the title pressed against her chest: *Wild Beasts of the Bulvian Tundra*. Wild beasts was right. For goodness' sake, they had their own quarters, didn't they? Edward stayed longer, waltzing by her desk a few minutes later.

"Hello, Second Brother," she said, without looking up.

"Hello, Rhodie. Working late?"

"Yes. And you?"

Edward removed his slightly crooked glasses to clean them on the edge of his shirt. "In a manner of speaking, I suppose I am." She chose to ignore his lascivious grin and the fact that he had no books or work materials of any kind. She would rather die than admit that she knew anything of what had just happened in the ancient history section. "Planning for your trip to Trella?"

She shook her head. "Still finishing up my Alzheimer's study. Soon, though."

"Are we still on for lunch this week? Tuesday?"

"That would suit my schedule."

"Excellent. Have a good night."

Rhodie preferred relative detachment, even with Edward, of whom she was genuinely fond. It just didn't do for things to be too informal; one never knew who might be watching or listening. They were Browards. One didn't maintain a dynasty through careless conversations.

Though she couldn't admit it just then, she was also still just the tiniest bit angry with her brother for planning to send his friend Arron James on her expedition. He was her friend, too, of course; well, more like an acquaintance. At least, she'd considered him an acquaintance until last year, when he was shot.

She had to take a deep breath just thinking about it. Eavesdropping was a terrible habit and very improper; she hadn't meant to overhear her parents' discussion. But some-how, the impropriety of her actions had barely registered when she heard "Lieutenant James" in the same sentence as "crossbow bolt to the chest." She'd come as close to begging as she ever had in order to convince Edward to let her accompany him to Briggin.

Her brother did not know, of course, that she and James had been corresponding for months. Did one refer to text messages as correspondence? No matter. She still would. It was nothing inappropriate, nothing unseemly . . . She'd just needed his help during the war almost two years prior and happened to have his number. For completely normal reasons, not because she'd looked it up in his military personnel file.

Her phone lit up, and she reached for it. *Speak of the devil . . .*

Lt. James: HELP.

Dr. Broward: Help with what?

Lt. James: I'm at a very boring party and wish to leave. Call me so I can make an excuse.

Dr. Broward: Why me?

Lt. James: You're the only one still up. Besides the people who invited me, that is.

Dr. Broward: My brother is available.

Lt. James: Really? He didn't answer my texts.

Dr. Broward: Yes, well . . .

Lt. James: LOL. At it again, are they? Glad they're not my housemates.

Dr. Broward: You've no idea.

Dr. Broward: Are there no lovely young women at this party who've caught your eye? I should think they'd be throwing themselves at you because of your medal.

Lt. James: Oh, they are. And yet here I am, texting you . . .

Lt. James: What does that tell you?

Rhodie felt her cheeks heat. Lord, he was such a flirt. She wouldn't encourage him by responding to it. Not that he seemed to need encouragement.

Dr. Broward: Are you coming to New Year's at Bluffton?

Lt. James: That's classified.

Lt. James: I'll need to confirm your identity first.

Dr. Broward: Very well. How do you propose to do that?

Lt. James: How do you talk to a giant?

It had been her favorite joke as a child. It had stunned her that he remembered.

Dr. Broward: Use big words.

Lt. James: How do you know the ocean is friendly?

Dr. Broward: It waves.

Lt. James: Very good. Last one. What did the banana say to the dog?

Dr. Broward: Lieutenant . . .

Lt. James: Wrong! He said nothing, because bananas can't talk.

Lt. James: Princesses are so silly.

Dr. Broward: I repeat: are you coming to New Year's?

Lt. James: You're not going to call me, then? Just leave me here to fight off these lusty ladies? Fine, but I believe some light recompense is in order.

Dr. Broward: You were quite resourceful when you wanted to leave the hospital in Briggin.

Lt. James: Haven't forgiven me for that yet, eh?

Dr. Broward: I've never had a patient try to make a break for it while under my care before. It left quite an impression.

Lt. James: Temporary insanity. Had nothing to do with you, I'm sure.

Insanity was right. He hadn't been there a week when he attempted to put on his street clothes and go for a walk unassisted. Getting caught had prompted a display of anger that she'd only heard described previously; the books he'd thrown across the room testified that his red hair certainly did come with a temper. That level of agitation made her wonder about PTSD.

"Have you spoken to the psychiatrist yet?" she'd asked.

"I'm still in the hospital, Princess. I think it's a bit premature . . ."

"You have a long recovery ahead of you," she'd told him.

"Yes. I'll need all sorts of special care, I imagine, from a beautiful, royal, qualified professional."

"Nice try," she'd replied, giving him half a smile.

"Come on. Haven't you always wanted to know what's under my uniform? Now you've got your chance, guilt-free."

"I know exactly what you look like under your uniform," she'd said, unwinding her stethoscope and placing the tips in her ears. "Deep breath, please." He complied several times, as she shifted the chest piece around until she was satisfied he didn't have any fluid building up.

"You haven't seen my third nipple, though." He'd waggled his eyebrows.

Rhodie tipped her head. "You have no third nipple."

"Are you certain, Dr. Broward?"

"Well, no, I suppose not *certain* . . ."

He'd leaned closer, dropping his voice. "I do. I do have one, it's a secret." He'd looked deep into her eyes. "And now it's a secret we share."

"Never fear," she'd whispered with mock sincerity. "I shall divulge it to no one." She heard her brother and his friends returning to the room, and she let her gaze fall to the chart on his bed. James reached out and gave her hand a tiny squeeze just before they entered the room. Her face heated as she turned toward the door. When Edward, Sam, and Saint finished with their handshakes and gentle back slaps, she simply picked up her bag and walked out. She didn't do goodbyes.

Lt. James: I can't make it on New Year's. James family tradition says that I must ingest caramel corn, drink beer and play board games with Mum, Cora, and Ivy until midnight.

Dr. Broward: I'm sure Edward will miss you.

Lt. James: Not if he's making out with Abbie behind a statue of King Peter IV.

Dr. Broward: Good luck with your ladies, lusty or otherwise.

CHAPTER TWO

RHODIE ROSE EARLY A few mornings after her uncomfortable library moment with Edward. As was her custom, she used the facilities and then stripped and weighed herself. The number was satisfactory; she'd allow herself breakfast today. She scrubbed her body in the shower like it was a pair of tongs in the lab, not lingering to enjoy the hot water, and dressed in the clothes the maid had laid out for her. She walked into the family dining room with her quiet appraisal; she could see her father through the doorway, sitting at his customary place at the head of the table.

"You made an appointment to see me," he said, not looking up from his tablet.

"Yes."

He took off his reading glasses and set them on the table, giving her his gaze. "Why?"

"I wish to discuss a matter of some importance."

Ignatius chuckled. "Yes, I gathered that, daughter. But you know my door is always open to you. You needn't make an appointment through my secretary like a common supplicant wanting a royal boon."

"Honestly, I had my assistant do it. I've been busy and haven't had time."

"Tea?" He lifted the pot to refill his own cup, and she shook her head. "Mum would have me remind you that breakfast is the most important meal of the day."

"The science doesn't support that."

He smiled at her, pride suffusing his face. She loved that look. That look said so much more than words ever could. She knew her father approved of her career, but in moments like these, she felt it as well. It made some of the pain worth it. After all, why should she let a failure at age twelve define her? Her body had betrayed her future, but it was no reason to let it spoil everything in her life. There was plenty of good left, even if she never married.

She smiled back. "Maid, I'll have some plain yogurt, no fruit." The woman gave her a nod and scurried off.

"Everyone else has come and gone, if you'd like to discuss it now."

She glanced over her shoulder. In truth, she would prefer the privacy of his office, but the convenience factor outweighed, since they hadn't been able to find a mutually agreeable time until late in the week. "Very well." She sat down, and the maid poured her some water. "I would like you to speak to Edward for me. I wish to leave Bluffton and live on my own."

"I take it from your comment that you believe the king would deny your request."

She nodded. "He is still very protective after what happened with Heather and Lincoln. I think he believes Bluffton is the safest place for me."

"Bluffton *is* the safest place for you; that's a fact, daughter."

The maid returned with her breakfast, and she took a small bite of the tart, creamy yogurt. The problem with eating was that it just made her hungrier. "It is also a fact that it often takes me over an hour to get to my lab each way. It is very inconvenient for me."

"I don't think that's it . . ." He folded his arms across his chest and leaned back in his chair. "I think there's something more going on."

I knew I should have asked Mum instead. Her mother seemed to understand her desire not to talk about things better than her father did. They were made much the same way; emotions, intentions, motives were private and better not put on display. Most of the time, they were irrelevant anyway.

"I'm going to be twenty-six in a few weeks. That's a factor as well."

"Twenty-six-year-olds can't live at home?"

"Certainly they can. But this one does not want to."

Her father's eyes narrowed. "Is it Abbie?"

"What? No, of course not. Abbie's wonderful, she's lovely." That much was true: on her own, Rhodie enjoyed Abbie's company more than she'd anticipated. She didn't regret inviting her to book club, nor did she mind taking the occasional meal together at home. It was rather nice to have a woman around her own age.

Ignatius grinned. "I see. So it's not Abbie you object to specifically, just your brother and his wife pawing each other in every dark corner of the palace."

Rhodie did not give him the satisfaction of seeing her react. "Their antics can be somewhat . . . trying."

Ignatius chuckled. "Give them time, daughter. They'll likely settle down in a few months."

She took a sip of her tea to cover her embarrassment over the topic of conversation. "Until then, they're giving me ulcers."

"Rhodie," he teased, shaking his head. "I never knew you were such a prude."

"I'm not a prude," she snapped. The tightness around his eyes and the way his beard twitched said she'd overreacted to the joke. He wasn't going to help her; he thought it was *funny*.

"You're rarely here anyway. Why do you need to move out?"

"If I were married, I'd live elsewhere. What's the difference?"

Ignatius leaned forward. "For one thing, in this instance, you'd be living alone."

She waved a careless hand at him. "I'd still have my security. Next objection?"

"It's more than that, love. Mum and I both think you work too much. We like being able to keep tabs on you. We'd never hear from you nor see you if you moved out. There's value in having others nearby, even if it's just to pass a pleasant breakfast with."

She stood up. "So you won't help me?"

He smiled as he picked up his tablet again. "I am afraid not. Sorry, love. Try Mum, she's a good egg. Or here's a novel idea, though one I know you won't try: perhaps try speaking to Edward directly."

"Have a nice day, Father."

"And you, my dear daughter," he said, replacing his glasses. "And you."

RHODIE ARRIVED AT HER lab ninety minutes later. Two of her graduate assistants were waiting for her at the door like paparazzi, which she'd also had to dodge outside. How long would the agar plates last once they were poured? (Two weeks, so go ahead and prep them now.) Thoughts on how to keep them at 4 degrees Celsius? (Still working on it. Dry ice, maybe?) How would she like the glass beakers and test tubes transported? (Order new ones and keep them in their original packaging, bill it to the lab.) And that didn't even cover their questions about the ongoing experiments they'd be managing for her while she was away. Three months was a long time to be gone, but they were both capable and resourceful. Their classes didn't allow them to go with her, much to her chagrin and theirs, but she'd found a few former students who'd jumped at the chance to put a research expedition with the renowned Dr. Broward, youngest biomedical researcher in history, on their CVs.

Not that she was infamous. Notable, maybe. Her notoriety certainly extended beyond the borders of her own nation—most royals chose not to work in anything except politics. But she didn't associate with many other royals. It hadn't been intentional. Her parents had hired them tutors at home for the first years, then sent her on to boarding school, which had been an unqualified disaster. She'd come home at Christmas and vowed not to go back. It had been three months of the worst teasing, tormenting and ridicule she'd ever endured. Some of the others were just curious about her motivations, but most were downright cruel. And it wasn't limited to her interest in medicine and intention to become a doctor. Her stuck-out ears, her short dreads, her collarbone. Yes, they teased her about her collarbone, because apparently, it shouldn't stick out that much; she still remembered her mother's confused face when she told her. She'd been perfectly happy to go back to tutoring at home with the younger children, and she'd had her brothers and their friends for built-in companionship. Since she could then move at her own pace, her acceleration towards medical school had increased two-fold. University at fourteen, medical school at seventeen, and her residency at twenty-one, which she finished in two years flat. Moderation was for people without ambition.

Between meeting with Dr. Nuñez about the protein synthesis crossover research that involved both their labs, doing the reflex and reaction protocol on the rats they were using to test out a new nerve stimulant, taking a quick lunch with one of the new doctors doing her residency at the university hospital who'd asked to meet with her, and doing more groundwork for her Trella expedition, the day flew by. When she checked her watch, she found she was already late for book club. Luckily traffic was on her side, and she managed to get to her friend's apartment in record time . . . not that it helped.

"I'm sorry I'm late again, Carlie," she sighed, air-kissing both her rosy cheeks, as her security, Trosen, took up his place by the apartment door.

"You're only ten minutes away," Carlie teased. "One of these days, we're going to start without you."

"Mari's leading. She'll wait." Rhodie smiled. Mariona's questions were always humorous, even if they were sometimes painfully personal. That artistic temperament wasn't always the most tempered. Abbie waved at her from across the room, her pale face beaming, and Rhodie smiled as she waved back.

"I loved it!" Mari gushed as they took their seats and Carlie brought Rhodie a cup of tea.

"Of course you did," Bridgette said. "It was about a painter."

"That isn't the only reason."

"I found it problematic," Rhodie added, "but I thought the symbolism was just gorgeous."

"I didn't really get it." Carlie frowned. "Why did he not take the boat with the others?"

Mari pulled out the discussion questions she'd printed off as they started to debate the point. It was just the five of them tonight, which Rhodie greatly preferred; a few other members had come and gone over the last three years, but the group was blessedly small at the moment. She disliked the greater noise level with more women and the general feeling that she couldn't be herself with unknown acquaintances. She'd made friends with Bridgette at a pre-med conference during undergrad, and her friendships with Carlie and Mariona had come through her.

"I didn't care for his casual relationships with women," Rhodie put in.

"Agreed," said Abbie, flipping her hair over her shoulder. "Not a lot of respect there."

"Royals," said Mari, rolling her eyes. "Specifically, Orangiersian royals." That comment landed right on Rhodie's chest like someone had tightened a screw clamp around her heart. Mariana preferred her own culture's carefree way with relationships; she couldn't hope to understand the pressure she and her siblings were under to find appropriate mates. Not that she hadn't failed at that already.

"Think whatever you like," Rhodie said, sipping her tea, careful not to let her true opinion show on her face. "We have an image to maintain. No one's going to contract with us if we have a reputation for running around with every John, Blake, and Danny from the docks, or wherever."

"There's nothing wrong with our royals just because they're a bit straitlaced," defended Carlie, patting Abbie's knee. She knew better than to touch Rhodie: it was rule #1.

"Straitlaced? I don't think Rhodie's concerned with fashion whatsoever," teased Bridgette, and Rhodie smiled to cover the sting.

"You married ladies just think relationships are the answer to everything," she replied. "Some of us have wider pursuits."

"Hear, hear," said Mariona, lifting her wineglass in salute.

"Isn't there anyone you're even interested in?" Carlie asked. She'd been with her boyfriend, Dan, for three years, and they were expecting him to propose any day.

"Not in the slightest," she said, shutting her book too hard, since the conversation had now veered away from the topic. To her surprise, she felt a pang of guilt. No one needed to know about her text conversations with James. That was private, and it wasn't going to lead to anything anyway—it wasn't possible. Not for her. She glanced at her sister-in-law, who probably knew more about her interactions with James. James was a blabbermouth; another reason they'd never work.

Abbie was close with Edward's friends, but she wasn't making eye contact with anyone. If she knew anything, she wasn't making it obvious. *Good*. Rhodie couldn't abide a knowing look at her expense right now. "Is there more tea?" she asked, rising.

On the way home, however, in the dark of the carriage, she pulled out her phone.

Dr. Broward: Have you read *Oils and Ink*?

Lt. James: Painter who doesn't leave the sinking island, right?

Dr. Broward: Yes. Did you like it?

Lt. James: Parts of it. Not as a whole.

Dr. Broward: And why not?

Lt. James: His choices didn't add up. If his health was so bad, he would've left; he expressed a will to live, but then acted against it. And his family, who pressured him to do everything, was silent on this point? Too important for that.

Dr. Broward: Agreed. At least someone has some sense tonight.

Dr. Broward: I did enjoy the symbolism, at least.

Lt. James: Yeah, the author had a way with theme. Just not plot.

Dr. Broward: The others didn't see that whatsoever.

Lt. James: Oh yes, it's book club night, isn't it?

Lt. James: Are you drunk, then?

Dr. Broward: Afraid not, sorry.

Dr. Broward: Though I may be next week. It's a romance next.

Lt. James: If you want to come to my place, I'd console you afterward.

Dr. Broward: Unnecessary, thank you.

Lt. James: Sweet dreams, my princess.

Dr. Broward: You too, Lieutenant.

CHAPTER THREE

"THANK YOU FOR COMING, Dr. Broward. I would've come to you. I know how busy you are." Tezza Simonson shut the door of the security office behind Rhodie and motioned for her to sit. "Can I get you anything? Tea?"

Rhodie shook her head. "No, thank you. My mother said you wished to speak to me about my upcoming expedition, is that correct?"

The dark-haired woman nodded curtly. "I understand that you'll be in the Unveiled, in Trella, for part of the time. You're starting off near Belicia, then moving further inland toward the Toki-Tokana range, near the coast."

"That's right." Though her mother would be appalled at her posture, Rhodie leaned back in her chair, her back tired from a long day of bending to look into electron microscopes.

"And Lieutenant James will be your security?"

"Edward has deemed it so, yes." It came out frostier than she meant it to; she didn't really resent Edward's decision any more than she resented the warm looks James was always giving her. The ones that made her stomach flutter like the scarlet tiger moths that frequented the tree outside her office window—*Fraxinus ornus*, she thought. She'd been meaning to look it up.

Tezza's eyes narrowed. "You don't want him to accompany you? Dean and I have the final say on the security staffing, not His Majesty. If you're unhappy . . ."

"No," Rhodie said quickly, regretting that she'd let her mind wander again, letting the silence linger too long. "It's fine. If Edward will feel better with one of his friends protecting me, I can be flexible." Truthfully, she didn't mind having James along. He was just a good friend, nothing more. No matter, she could keep her emotional distance, even if their physical proximity would be impossible to avoid. She'd been ignoring his harmless flirting for years; she was practiced at it by now. Though she hadn't observed him enough around other women to be sure, he was probably like that with everyone.

Tezza opened a manila file folder and paged through its contents. Rhodie resisted the urge to crane her neck to see what she was reading.

"Your current security is Greg Trosen. How's he working out?"

"Fine."

"No complaints?"

"No." He did sometimes stand rather close to her in elevators, but that was understandable due to the limited space.

"Why isn't he accompanying you to Trella?"

"He doesn't wish to leave his wife for such an extended period of time. They've just had a child two months past."

"I see." Tezza grimaced. "Here's my concern: Lieutenant James has no magical aptitude. Trosen does. Being in the Unveiled will open you up to magical influence. Untamed magic can be . . ." She looked at the ceiling, as if searching for the right word. "Unpredictable. I would feel better with someone with magical aptitude on your detail, especially at night. Someone who can ward your tent, sense malicious intent from other users, things like that. I'm going to send Sergeant Graeham and Sergeant Petros with you as well; both have basic magical defense skills, and I would like you to make use of them, especially when you're in a high-density magic situation."

"That's fine."

Tezza was staring at her so hard, Rhodie was surprised it wasn't leaving a dent on her face.

"Do you know what you're getting into, Highness?"

Rhodie waved her hand as if shooing a fly away. "I imagine I'm in for some disturbed sleep due to mosquitoes, some hot days. A different cuisine."

"That's not what I mean."

"You're referring to magical anomalies? Technological inconveniences?"

"Yes. What's the purpose of your expedition?"

Rhodie crossed her ankles under the hard office chair. "I'm examining the local flora and fauna both inside and outside the Veil, hoping to analyze how they compare and whether one might have greater medical advantages over the other."

"You'll forgive my bluntness, but why can't you do that here?"

Rhodie was wearing her reading glasses, and she adjusted them to stare over the top of them at Tezza. "I can, and I have. My findings, however, were inconclusive, because only a very small portion of Orangiers is Unveiled. I'm also interested in what kind of indigenous remedies I might be able to uncover for biomedical research."

Tezza's face gave away nothing of her thoughts, and it made Rhodie a bit uneasy. It wasn't like the woman had the power to keep her in Orangiers, but based on her line of questioning, she wasn't happy about it.

"I don't want to try to tell you how to live your life," Tezza started, and Rhodie couldn't help thinking, *Then you're the only one.* "But there are some types of magic and some cultures that do not like outsiders. They don't like being examined. What you see as harmless, they see as intrusion. Trellans may be happy to welcome tourists and take their money, but they may not be so happy to have you poking around in their business on a less casual basis. Some knowledge is considered sacred."

Rhodie nodded slowly. "I appreciate your concern. I have been in contact with Saint Teresa University, so I do have some professional contacts I can utilize if I run into trouble. They're eager to collaborate."

Tezza's gaze was still as sharp as a new scalpel. "Let me tell you a story. I'm from Op'Ho'Lonia, which is more like Trella than Orangiers. My Aunt Pollonia used to make these corn cakes—they could make a grown man cry, they were so good. She made them every holiday. One night, her house was robbed, and the recipe was taken. She and her family did a house-to-house search of the town for the recipe, and when it was found, the thief was run out of town on a rail. That's how closely secrets are guarded there, Your Highness. They kicked him out over dessert." Rhodie's face must have showed how unimpressed she was by the story, because Tezza sighed again. "Well, let me leave you with this advice: when dealing with unfamiliar magic and unfamiliar magic users, don't trust your eyes or your ears. Trust your gut. If it doesn't feel right, it probably isn't. Intuition can be as valid as any other sense. Don't ignore it."

Rhodie stood. "Thank you for your concern, Ms. Macias."

"It's Mrs. Simonson," she corrected politely. "I remarried last month."

"Oh, that's right. Forgive the error; I know Sam, and I should've known better. How is newlywed life treating you?"

It was the first smile she'd seen cross the woman's face. "It's good, ma'am. Thank you for asking."

Ma'am. The word made her stomach pinch, a painful reminder that she'd lost her young woman status before she'd gained the relationship that most people had achieved by now. Rhodie forced a smile, happy to let the conversation end there, rather than tease Tezza about "popping out children," as she'd heard her lab colleagues do to one another, or imply that her parents must be relieved to have her coupled again, as her mother might do. She would let the woman just have her happiness.

"Have a good voyage, Highness."

"Thank you, Mrs. Simonson. I will do my best."

CHAPTER FOUR

JAMES WAS IN THE SHOWER when the doorbell rang. It was a pleasant chiming doorbell, soothing and serene. He hated it. He missed the screechy electronic doorbell from his mum's flat that made you jump. This doorbell made him feel like a poser. He opened the frosted glass door of the shower and poked his head out, trying to hear over the noise of the water. He heard nothing. Maybe if he just ignored whoever it was long enough, they'd go away. His friends had a nasty habit of dropping by early on weekends. But given that Saint and Sam had saved his life in Op'Ho'Lonia, he felt he should grant them some leeway.

When his bathroom was steamy, as it was now, he sometimes remembered what it had felt like to look down and see the crossbow bolt sticking out of his chest, the air dense around him in the muggy forest. He could still smell the nearby bog and the water lilies. He could still feel the blood, slippery under his fingers, as he touched his chest. He could hear the cicadas who went right on singing, and the shouts of Lincoln's men in triumph and retreat, the fear in his friends' voices as they called for help. But the military psychologist had said it was normal to experience some flashbacks. They didn't bother him particularly, just as Saint's hostile brand of rehabilitation hadn't. No, the anger bothered him more than the actual memories. Anger at himself for not being more cautious, at Lincoln for rebelling against his family. Sam wore his heart on his sleeve, and Saint smothered his feelings through gruffness, but James twisted his into something that scared him less.

The doorbell sounded again, and he sighed. *8:05 a.m. Really?*

"Coming!" he shouted and shut off the water, wrapping a towel around his waist. James hurried out of his bedroom, scratching his surgery scar on his chest, which always seemed to itch in the morning. He threw open the front door and came face-to-face with a stranger.

"Who are you?"

The liveried footman's navy-blue coat with gold trim and shiny black shoes made James think he could be from Bluffton, but that made no sense; Edward had his number. If he wanted something, he'd just text him.

"Arrondale Percival James?"

"No, that's *my name*. What's yours, Stranger Mc-Strangerton?"

He held out a thin box, and when James took it, he was surprised at how heavy it was for its size. "What've you got in there, stranger? Lead? Plutonium? Gold? It's gold, is it?"

The man cocked his head, giving James a wary side-eye stare tinged with confusion, and held out a clipboard. "Sign please, sir."

"Do I look like I've somewhere to keep a pen in this outfit, mate?"

The man pulled a pen from his leather briefcase. "Here."

James signed and quickly closed the door, then ripped into the box.

Dear Son,

James blinked. His mother wouldn't send him something like this. Aideen was a warm, curvy, rosy-cheeked broad who liked to tease him and ruffle his red hair, even though it already resembled a bird's nest, and sigh about how hers used to be the same color before her children turned it gray. She didn't send nondescript cardboard boxes full of paper. If she wanted to say something, she sent a handwritten letter or note. If she had a present, she dropped it off herself in order to receive copious hugs and kisses for her trouble. He was going to need pants for this, whatever it was. James jogged to his bedroom and came back in a T-shirt and jeans before snatching up the strange letter once more.

Dear Son,

I regret that we have not yet had the chance to meet in person. This may come as something of a shock, but you are next in line for a very powerful dukedom, which I hope you will take up with relish. I have stage-three pancreatic cancer and need to name a successor quickly; I would like to bequeath it to you, as you are my only male heir. Though I have not publicly claimed you, that situation can be remedied. Your mother forbade me from it, fearing that you would have no normal life, not understanding all that your title could give you, the doors it could open. I have tried to provide for you in my own way, through your trust and recommendations I wrote to the military academy on your behalf . . .

James choked on air. He'd seen enough of *that* letter, the rest of which appeared to be a long list of regrets his father had concerning his paternity. He'd let someone else catalogue the man's absolution; he had zero interest in it. *A duke? My father is a duke? And not just any duke, an extremely pow-*

erful and influential duke, who apparently helped me get into the school of my choice. James needed to sit down at this revelation. He set the letter carefully aside and whistled low at what came next. An inventory of what his holdings would be, their current estimated worth, their projected value in the next quarter, the next year, the next ten years. Spoiler alert: they were all increasing, some exponentially. He stared at the steep growth curves, his heart pounding harder with every page.

Someone knocked. James jumped. "What? Who is it? I'm not being made king of anything, am I?"

"Kinda doubt it," came a thickly accented female voice. "But anything's possible."

Cora? What was his sister, who lived two hours away, doing here so early? He looked down, the papers suddenly feeling almost slimy in his hands. "Um, hang on, love. I'm coming." He shoved the box into an unused drawer in the kitchen.

"Hustle up, Arron, the other residents are thinking I'm about to nip off with their valuables."

James chuckled as he jogged to the door. He grinned at her, and she grinned back, her ivory face bright with delight to see him, her short cerulean hair curling around her ears.

"Blue this week?"

"Aye, since it's my last proper dye job for a while, I wanted to go out with a bang." She glared at her partner, who stood next to her, rolling his eyes.

"Woman," Brighton chided, "do you want a baby with the proper number of limbs or not?"

Cora rubbed her growing belly fondly. "I think the baby would appreciate having a mum who hasn't abandoned her sense of style while she's being gestated."

"Good grief, Cora, I said you could get highlights. I said you could use henna."

"Tea, loves?" James moved toward the stove before they could reply.

"Yes, please, but make it quick, we've got to be down there when they open or we'll have to wait for hours, and my overly kicked bladder doesn't relish the thought of that."

"Where are you off to, then?"

The couple beamed at each other so hard, James wondered if he should leave the room and give them some privacy . . . and it was his house.

"Hello?" He waved his hands. "Earth to Cora and Brighton. Where are you off to?"

"Here I thought the hair would be a dead giveaway," said Cora, easing her large body into a metal chair at his modern kitchen table.

"So did I," said Brighton, smirking. "Let's give him another clue and see if he can get it. He always was a bit daft." He cleared his throat. "Might we borrow your camera for a thing we're doing today?"

"So the clues are blue hair and borrowing my camera?" James tapped his chin. "Are you doing a pregnancy shoot or something?"

"Yes," Cora deadpanned, "we've gotten up at the butt crack of dawn to take *photographs*."

James smiled and took a breath to tell her that one of the principles of outdoor photography was called "the golden hour," the time just after sunrise, when the light was the warmest on the spectrum, but snapped his lips shut again. His family had strong thoughts about him being a well-read know-it-all, so he kept it to himself. "What was I thinking?"

"I don't know," said Brighton slowly, "but you weren't thinking that we were getting hitched today."

James's heart doubled in size. "Really?"

The couple grinned and nodded, and he propelled himself across the kitchen to crush them both in the tightest hug he could manage.

"You guys, that's fantastic!" He bent to Cora's belly and cupped his hands around his mouth. "You hear that, little one? Your dad's making an honest woman of your mum! You won't be a bastard after all!"

They laughed, as he knew they would. Honestly, he couldn't care less whether they were married; they were committed to each other, but it did make things easier for taxes and property law. Though they'd been living together for several years already, it made him happy to see them make it official, for their kid's sake, if nothing else. He did like to see them settled.

The kettle sang, and he was forced to let them go as he moved to set out mugs and jars of loose-leaf tea that he'd gotten at an organic co-op downtown. He knew his family was about to give him grief over eating and drinking like a fancy-pants rich person . . . but he was just glad they were here. It hadn't been easy on his sisters when his absent father (who was not *their* absent father) had given him his loft and trust fund. But once they got over their resentment for something that was out of his control, they'd been happy for him. *But what would they say about the paperwork in those drawers?*

He couldn't think about it then. Just like he wouldn't think about the fact that his sister was yet another person in his life joining the ranks of the married . . . Edward had gone first, then Sam. He was running out of single friends, and frankly, it was hard not to be jealous. At least he knew Saint would probably never abandon him for matrimonial bliss: he loved the single life. Meanwhile, James would only consider settling down with one person, and half the time, it seemed like she didn't really want him around. He sighed without meaning to.

"Feeling all right, love?" His sister ruffled his unruly red hair as she picked her mug, and he nodded.

"Of course."

"Good, because we're hoping you'll come with us to the courthouse. Mum and Ivy are coming down on the train."

He smiled. "I wouldn't miss it. I'll bring the rice."

Cora tsked. "No one throws rice anymore, big brother. It makes birds explode."

Brighton threw an arm around his neck. "You're lucky to have us around, dummy."

He slurped his tea. "Can't argue with that. Can I bring a date to this thing?"

CHAPTER FIVE

BUDGETING REPORTS. They were the last thing Rhodie wanted to be doing on a Saturday morning. Not that she minded working, but the lab was quiet and dark. She preferred a little bit of people noise, just the feeling that she wasn't alone. She'd pointedly ignored her mother's huffy disappointment when she'd skipped family breakfast that morning, opting instead for a hard-boiled egg and a bran muffin in the carriage on the way. Her phone dinged.

Lt. James: I'm going to a wedding. Come be my date.

With no one around, Rhodie didn't need to hide her smile, so she let it break across her face without reservation, the way she always wanted to when she saw his name. Still, she should play it cool. He was a flirt and her brother's best friend. It didn't mean anything.

Dr. Broward: I don't know, I'll have to check my schedule.

Dr. Broward: When is it?

Lt. James: About thirty minutes from now at the courthouse downtown.

Lt. James: Don't dilly-dally.

Her mouth fell open and she scoffed loudly. *What? Thirty minutes?*

Dr. Broward: I would've liked a bit more notice . . .

Lt. James: I only got twenty minutes more than you did, and I've spent that recovering from shock.

Dr. Broward: Who's getting married in thirty minutes?

Lt. James: My sister Cora.

Dr. Broward: She's the middle one, isn't she? The one who came to Briggin?

Lt. James: They both came, thank you very much. I'm adored by one and all.

Dr. Broward: I meant the one who brought her partner.

Lt. James: Brighton. Yes, he came as well.

Dr. Broward: I believe he challenged me to a game of chess back at the house. I beat him soundly.

Lt. James: My princess is so smart.

Lt. James: Come on, hustle down here. Time's running out.

Lt. James: It'll be a fun surprise. Please?

Rhodie hesitated, staring at the piles of spreadsheets and graph paper on her desk, and felt they were staring back at her, judging her for not processing them in a more timely manner.

Dr. Broward: Fine. I will come. But not as a date, just as friends.

Lt. James: ::RAISES BOTH ARMS IN TRIUMPH::

Dr. Broward: You're making too much of this.

Lt. James: I don't think so. Cora will be pleased.

Dr. Broward: There may be photographers. Will she care?

Lt. James: Care? She'll be thrilled. She just dyed her hair to match one of those puppets on that kids' TV show.

Still snickering, Rhodie grabbed her purse and texted Trosen to get the carriage. She'd just take a quick break. Being Saturday, traffic was light, and the carriage was able to drop her right out front so she could duck inside without drawing attention. She found James's apple-red head from the back, and she resisted the urge to call to him across the marble foyer, to watch him turn and grin when their eyes met. Woz, she was pathetic. Maybe she shouldn't have come. She caught the moment Cora, Ivy, and Aideen noticed her approaching, and chuckled inwardly at their identical disbelieving stares. She thought the bride might drop the grocery store bouquet of daisies she was holding.

"Dr. Broward?" Aideen gasped. "Is that really you, love?" His sisters had been rendered speechless, but his mum had always been a talker under any circumstances.

"Hello, everyone, it's so lovely to see you again. I just wanted to come and offer my congratulations on your nuptials and wish Cora and Brighton—"

"I invited her," James interrupted. "I get credit for this. Me." Rhodie pivoted to give him a disapproving glare, but then she noticed his clothing—he'd dressed for the occasion. He had a black jacket slung over his shoulder on two fingers, but his pinstriped dress shirt was obviously tailored to his lithe form, as were the pants she'd already admired from the back.

It isn't proper to take note of other people's bodies, she felt sure her mother would say. But when presented with that handsome freckled face, those teasing hazel eyes, how could she not?

"Well, I'm shocked down to my socks," Cora said, pressing an exuberant kiss to his cheek, making him blush. "Thank you, big brother. This is a fun surprise."

"Didn't I say that? Didn't I say this would be a fun surprise, Princess?"

"You did," she agreed, and she noticed his sister Ivy bouncing her gaze between the two of them, her eyebrows furrowed lightly.

"So does that mean you two are . . ." She pointed back and forth between them meaningfully.

"Yes," Arron deadpanned at the same moment Rhodie said, "No."

"Lieutenant," she started, but he just laughed.

"Fine, fine. No, we're not. I know you all became close over my bonus chest hole, and I thought it would be appreciated if I invited her."

His mother and sisters all shared a matching grimace at his description of his wound, and Rhodie felt the need to move the conversation forward, but at that moment, a clerk with a clipboard called out, "Cora James and Brighton Prosper?" The group migrated toward the open double doors, the excitement building, and Rhodie was suddenly grateful to be included. She was never impulsive like this, but she found it somewhat infectious. Rhodie felt an arm thread through hers as they went into the judge's chambers, and she stiffened before she saw that it was his mother's, not James's. He couldn't be touchy with her like that here—or anywhere, really. People would talk.

"Hello, dear," cooed Aideen. "I haven't seen you since Briggin. How've you been?"

"Oh, just fine, ma'am. Working hard on my research."

"Well, we appreciate you running down here at the last minute to join our little celebration here. Cora and Brighton really wanted to do it spur-of-the-moment. If it were me, I might've put a bit more planning into the moment, seeing as you only do it once, Woz willing, but you know how young people are. And there's no money for such things, by and large, what with the baby coming and Cora being between jobs . . ."

"Mum," James said gently, "the judge wants to start."

"Oh!" She slapped a hand over her mouth, her cheeks reddening. "So sorry, don't mind me. Just running at the mouth again." Her children and soon-to-be son-in-law were grinning fondly at her, and even the judge seemed charmed by her easy self-deprecation.

"Who do we have here?" he asked, coming around from the bench. "I like to stand down here for weddings, give you the full experience . . ."

The group chuckled and chattered excitedly. "I'm Cora, and this is Brighton. We want to get married today."

"Sure you're not going to surprise me with one more family member as a witness, are you?" he teased, cocking an eyebrow as he looked suspiciously at her bulging belly.

"No, sir," Cora said, reddening. It seemed to be a family trait: it didn't take much embarrassment for them to show it all in their cheeks.

"Well, then." The judge gave the couple a short speech about the responsibilities and rights of married couples under the law, which they seemed to mostly be ignoring as they gazed into each other's eyes. Rhodie couldn't help but smile. Aideen continued to lean on her, but when Cora passed her bouquet to Ivy to hold both Brighton's hands and say their vows, Rhodie heard Aideen sniffling.

It wasn't a surprise, really, but Rhodie considered herself the worst comforter in the world. She pulled her arm away in order to pat Aideen awkwardly on the back, and she shot a panicked look at James where he stood a few feet away, just next to Brighton as best man. *"Moms,"* he mouthed, rolling his eyes, grinning. That was no help at all. She stood next to his mother stiffly, trying to focus on the judge's familiar words, Cora and Brighton pledging to be together through storms and still water. When the judge pronounced them husband and wife, Aideen started crying in earnest, much to Rhodie's dismay. This was the worst way bodies acted, as far as she was concerned, and just another example of why they couldn't be trusted. It was a reflex, but it was so undignified; she avoided it at all cost.

"Would you like a tissue?" Rhodie whispered, digging in her purse for a handkerchief, but Aideen shook her head.

"It won't help, love. When you get to be my age, the tears just come whenever they want. I used to be a tough broad. Now I've gone all soft," she said, gesturing down at her round middle and chest, "in all sorts of ways."

Rhodie patted her hand. "My own mother would be in the same state, if it helps. I thought she was going to flood the sanctuary at my brother's wedding."

Aideen squeezed it. "Thank Woz you were here, love. I'd have had no one to hold me up. I'm so glad you came." She sniffled as she wiped the tears from her cheeks with both hands.

"I now pronounce you husband and wife," the judge intoned, and Aideen surged forward, arms out to embrace the happy couple.

Rhodie waited at the fringe as they shook the judge's hand and thanked him. Aideen's words about them having no money were hanging over her head. When they turned toward the exit, she spoke up. "Since I've come empty-handed, I would like to treat you all to lunch wherever you like." To her surprise, no one balked at the offer . . . but they also picked a cheap diner so Cora could get blueberry pancakes, which were the baby's favorite food, apparently.

James put a light hand on her lower back as they headed for the doors. "I'm glad you came," he whispered, and she let herself look deep into his eyes as they descended the steps.

"Me too," she whispered back.

CHAPTER SIX

"YOU KNOW YOU WANT THIS . . . ," James said, waving a bottle of beer under Edward's nose. "Just a taste."

"No. Thank you." He lifted his glass of water to his lips with a smirk, then reached down to pet Saint's dog, Buster. They were at Saint's house to give Edward a chance to get out of Bluffton for a change. Plus, he had a nice garden: variegated ivy clung to the brick wall between his house and the next, and he'd planted topiaries around the edge of the neatly manicured lawn.

"Come on, a little sip."

"Do you want my dynasty to continue or not?"

"Honestly, I couldn't care less either way." James sipped the beer instead of taunting Edward with it.

"You should," Saint called from the doorway, coming out with a platter of uncooked sausages and burgers, slapping them onto the sizzling grill. "Your doctor-princess will have to marry someone royal if he doesn't produce someone stat."

"On second thought, have some cabbage, mate," said James, pushing the coleslaw toward his friend.

"What's the basis for this diet?" asked Sam, who was munching on carrot sticks himself.

Edward sighed. "The perinatologist says it'll increase my virility and motility. It's not so bad. Fewer refined carbs, more seafood, no alcohol, no sugar."

"Well, not *your* motility," James teased, grinning. "A bit of you, perhaps. Little tiny king bits."

Edward elbowed him, and James knew he'd embarrassed him, but he didn't care. Even kings needed someone to tease them once in a while. He'd done far worse to him as his roommate in school.

"Game's on," Saint said, as he went back inside. Sam and Edward started to follow him, but James caught Sam's sleeve. His friend turned to look at him, and James motioned for him to stay quiet with a finger to his own lips.

"You guys coming?" Saint called.

"In a moment, just cheer louder in our absence," James called back, closing the glass patio door quietly.

"I need your advice." There was no sense in beating around the bush with Sam.

He crossed his arms over his chest and widened his stance. "Okay. Go ahead."

"I got a letter, and it says I'm the next Duke of Greenmeadow Downs."

"Pardon?"

"I am the next Duke of Greenmeadow Downs."

Sam's face contorted with confusion. "One more time."

"I can't figure another way to say it, mate. I can say it backwards if you like. Downs Greenmeadow of Duke next the am I."

His friend's stormy expression didn't clear. "That's . . . a shock."

James laughed without amusement. "You're telling me, mate."

"Greenmeadow Downs, like the rolling, verdant mountainside community north of here? The most coveted dukedom in the nation?"

James nodded. "That's the one."

"How . . . how did that . . . happen?"

He tugged on one earlobe. "My absent father, the current duke, slept with my sweet mother on the sly, and apparently, I was the only male offspring he produced. I knew my mystery progenitor was wealthy, based on my trust, but I had no idea . . ."

"Did you bring the letter?"

He pulled the first several pages out of his back pocket. Sam began to read, his eyebrows high on his forehead. He let out a low whistle as he turned the page. "Manors, estates, a real estate company, agricultural ventures, a blimp, a huge art collection, a charitable foundation . . . This is massive."

"I'm sure I wasn't his first choice. Or rather, I'm certain I won't be, once we've actually met in person, rather than just through the cold exchange of DNA."

Saint would've made a joke about the exchange likely being pretty hot for those involved. Edward would've pulled out statistics and stories about other people this had happened to, where everything turned out fine. But Sam just skimmed the letter again, then stared off into the distance. "Do you want to be a duke?"

James paced out deeper into the garden, and Sam followed him. "How can I say no? My poor mum, all this time, scraping by."

"You can't share with them from your trust?"

He shook his head. "It all has to be for my direct benefit; the trustee, that solicitor, Mr. Reynes, he makes me submit receipts for everything. My housing, my schooling. I haven't been able to do a thing for them except what's from my military pay, until now. My mum could retire; she's already in her sixties. Think of my sisters; Ivy can quit that awful job at Crumbel's and go back to art school, where she belongs. Cora and Brighton can buy a decent house for their baby instead of renting that cesspool with walls. Jersey, I could give them a manor if I wanted to; there's eight residences," he said, tapping the paper for emphasis. "Eight. I can give them anything they want if I take this."

"But it doesn't seem like the lifestyle you'd prefer. Or rather, it doesn't seem like the social circle you'd prefer."

"I'll admit, the idea of that much wealth gives me hives. I can barely tolerate my trust, and this is substantially more. I want to earn what I have; my mother's worked hard her whole life. Being handed a fortune just because of who my father is . . ."

"Uncomfortable."

"Yes. And I'd rather get a root canal in every tooth than be forced to associate with snooty rich people all the time."

"But would you be that miserable? You wouldn't have to hang out with them, would you?"

"You've seen the kind of expectations people push on Edward. How he has to deal with the spotlight constantly; these foundations, these business dealings, who do you think that's with? I wouldn't do well with that. You know how my mouth does its own thinking sometimes . . ."

"Not to mention your temper."

"That too." He ran a hand through his hair, sighing. "Don't tell anyone, all right?"

Sam scowled. "Don't be insulting. I'm not you."

"Fair point." James sat on a low brick wall. "What would you do?"

"Who does it pass to, if you don't take it?"

He sighed again. "Does it matter?"

"You asked what I would do. I would gather more information before making a decision. Inspect the offer from all sides. You're still one of his heirs; it might be possible to inherit something apart from the titled lands and properties." Sam pulled a silk handkerchief out of his pocket and wiped his sweaty brow. "Could we not have discussed this inside, in the air conditioning?"

"We're in the shade, Mr. Particular. Besides . . ." James paused.

"Besides what? You don't want Edward hearing?"

"Not Edward. Well, yes, I don't want Edward hearing, but mostly because I don't want it to change things with . . ."

"With Rhodie?" Sam bounced lightly between his spread feet. "Are things that serious with you?"

James laughed. "I've been serious about her since I met her. She's yet to be serious about me beyond answering most of my text messages, then frequently ghosting me for days or weeks at a time."

"But she did come to Briggin when you were wounded."

James took a long pull on his beer and chose not to mention her presence at the wedding for the time being. "Yes, she did. But I still don't know exactly what that means." A good deal more had happened there than any of his friends knew about. Just because he had his hopes up didn't mean anyone else should.

"You didn't ask her?"

James grimaced. "It isn't that simple, mate. Rhodie . . . Rhodie's a very private person. If I push her for too much, I'm afraid she'll turn away. I can't scare her off."

"Well, being together for the next three months should be fun, then. And by fun, I mean difficult. The duke hasn't named you as his successor yet?"

James shook his head slowly as he took a long draw on his beer. "Not officially. He said he'd wait to hear from me."

"How long do you have to decide?"

"He didn't exactly say. He's got cancer, I guess."

"That's sad."

James scoffed, looking away. "I can't bring myself to mourn him. Spent my whole childhood doing that."

"Hmm." Sam rubbed his smooth chin thoughtfully. "What does your mum say?"

"Haven't talked to her about it. I'm more than a little upset that she never told me, never warned me about all this." He'd tried to put his anger aside at the wedding, but it had gotten harder and harder as the day went on. He'd finally begged off dinner by claiming he had a headache.

"You have to admit, it would probably help your chances with a princess if you were a very wealthy duke."

James pointed at his friend's face. "That. That's exactly what I don't want. I don't want them to say, 'Oh, he was nothing, she didn't know his name until he became a duke. Then he was good enough. Before? Not so much.'"

"Them?" Sam asked. "Who's them?"

James stood up, pacing. He felt like flexing his fingers, a sure sign that his temper was flaring again. "The papers! The aristocracy! The thalassocracy, the meritocracy, the plantocracy, whoever! All the '-ocracies.' I don't want anyone thinking she chose me because of my title. If she chooses me, it's for love. When she chooses me, it's for *me*."

"I worried that Tezza was just choosing me out of convenience, so I empathize with the feeling. But I think you're oversimplifying the issue. The dukedom just makes it easier for her to choose you for you, more socially acceptable. That's important to Rhodie; she's by the book."

James clenched his jaw. "Maybe I'd like to see her throw the damn book out for once."

"That's asking a lot from a woman like that. You know how Edward is. She's the same way. It's drilled into them from the time they're small; rules and regulations and traditions matter more to them."

Both men fell quiet, and James looked up at the clouds, feeling unmoored.

"Is *plantocracy* a real word?" asked Sam.

James chuckled. "Yes. Let's go inside and find a drink. I'll explain it later."

CHAPTER SEVEN

"I'LL HAVE THE POACHED salmon with steamed broccoli and a side salad, no dressing."

"I'll have the fettuccine Alfredo with chicken."

Interesting. She didn't want to pry, and she certainly didn't want details . . . but as usual, curiosity proved more enticing than discretion.

"You've given up on the fertility diet, then?"

"I'm not sure it was working, anyway," he replied. He'd always been a terrible liar. Edward leaned back, stretching, then let his hands rest behind his head, looking out at the sea. He looked . . . relaxed.

"Mmm. Well, it was worth a try. I admire your commitment."

He shrugged. "I try to do my part. You know, besides actually doing my—"

"Stop. For Woz's sake, Edward. You'd think you were raised by pirates."

"Sorry, Doctor," he chuckled. "How did your Alzheimer's study turn out?"

Rhodie snapped her napkin open and laid it in her lap. "Frustrating. We didn't get the kind of results we were hoping for. I believe many of the study participants had a more advanced condition than their caregivers realized. Since they don't often self-report, it makes it that much more difficult."

"I fear for Simon. It would break my heart to lose him that way."

"Well, we won't give up," she said. She refused to acknowledge the catch in his voice. "Despite the high comorbidity with trisomy 21, you needn't fear yet. His caregivers are better trained than most. I'm confident we can get better results on the next round." It was a lie. She did plan to conduct another study, but she had no idea if it would yield anything different.

He was watching her carefully.

"Do you have something to say, Your Majesty?"

Edward shook his head and reached for his water. He was clearly hiding something, clearly had something on his mind. She knew all his tells.

"Don't be shy. You could always have me exiled if you regret sharing your mind." Pain flickered across his face, and she immediately regretted her choice of words. The loss of their oldest brother had been difficult to face; it still was, in many ways.

He leaned forward. "I suppose I'm wondering if there's anything you do fear. You project this constant assurance, this boundless optimism. I admire it, but . . . everyone's afraid of something." That was a good try, but it wasn't what he'd been thinking about, she was sure of it. And yet, when she considered the question . . .

Dying alone. Losing my lab. Coming upon you and Abbie copulating in the hallway.

She gave him her best reassuring smile. "I'm sure that's true."

Edward laughed. "A political answer if I ever heard one."

"I'm not crazy about spiders; does that count?"

"I meant more on the emotional spectrum, but I'll take that one. I expect you'll see some large ones on your expedition."

"I can't say I'm looking forward to that part of it, but there's no reward without a few risks."

"I'm sure Lieutenant James will take very good care of you." She felt her face growing hot at the mention of James's name. She held her tongue as the waitstaff set their plates in front of them. "Yes, I wanted to speak to you about Lieutenant James . . ."

"Oh?"

"Would it be possible to send someone else?"

"Why? He's known you for many years. I trust him entirely. Don't you?"

She nodded slowly. "Yes, of course, he's a trusted friend. But is he really ready to return to active duty? The shooting was only a few months ago."

Edward twirled his fork to fill it with pasta. "Dr. Broward, it was over a year ago. He's been checked out by his doctor."

"And the psychologist?"

"You know I'm not privy to that information."

"I'm just concerned about him. It's nothing to do with me."

Edward's lifted eyebrow said he had doubts about that. "Why haven't you visited him? He's been asking for you."

She'd tried; she'd even gone to his penthouse . . . then lacked the courage to knock. She'd wanted to. It was easier to hide behind busyness, easier to think up snappy comebacks via text message than in person. He had the quickest wit of anyone she'd ever met, and she frequently felt dull by comparison. It had nothing to do with the glowing way he smiled at her . . . or her stomach's answering acrobatics.

"What reason would I have to do that?"

"What reason? He's not discreet about it." Edward wiped his mouth, pulling out his phone. "And speaking of indiscretion, it is my unfortunate task to inform you that you two were photographed together last weekend." Rhodie's body locked up with tension as she stared at the screen he turned for her to see; they'd caught the moment he'd put his hand on her back, the moment she'd let herself stare deep into his eyes. They both looked like lovesick teenagers. *I knew this was going to happen. I should never have gone to that wedding. Now there'll be gossip and prying questions and . . .*

"They're not going to run it," Edward continued, "but they did let me know about it, in case someone else had a copy." She let the breath flood out of her tight chest with relief.

"He's not discreet about anything, but it means nothing. I attended his sister's wedding as his guest. You said it yourself; life's a joke to James."

"I don't know how to break this to you, Rhodie, but I don't think he's—"

"How's Abbie adjusting to life in the palace?"

Edward pursed his lips, clearly displeased at being interrupted. "She's adjusting well, thank you for asking. Having some friends through your book club has helped immensely. Thank you again for taking it upon yourself to invite her; it meant more than if Mum or I had asked you to do so."

"My pleasure."

"I wasn't so sure," he said, nudging the vegetables away from his pasta, "whether you'd warmed to her, after what you'd said about her when she and I were . . . in conflict."

And by 'in conflict,' I assume you mean when you left her in Gratha because she had the nerve to call you out on the toxic anger you have toward our godfather . . .

"I am a Broward. When you announced your decision to fulfill your marriage contract, she became one of us. I would never make your life more difficult with a pointless family feud."

He nodded, a secret smile stealing over his face.

"Edward."

"Mmm?"

"Out with it."

He looked embarrassed. "Out with what, precisely?"

"Oh, come now. You have something you are dying to tell me."

He looked pained. "I can't. I will, soon. I promise."

Thankfully, Rhodie knew from experience how to break her brother: silence. Keeping her face impassive, she took a bite of her perfectly cooked fish, her eyes on her plate, pretending to savor her food. In truth, the stress of that photograph was ruining the experience for her entirely . . . The press loved speculating about her dating life, given that she was the only adult Broward without a marriage contract. The spinster doctor? Out on a Saturday? Everyone seemed ready to believe that their innocent contact was something juicier. It was the last thing she needed, especially when she and James were leaving together on an expedition in a few days. The military contingent would certainly have a few members willing to sell a picture of them for a few bucks. She was not going to let that happen. She'd just give him incentive to keep his distance, that's all; she had the prickly princess routine down pat by now.

After a few minutes, Edward huffed, "Fine, I'll tell you," as if she'd been cajoling him. Rhodie smiled inwardly; her mother would be proud. "There's going to be another Broward joining our family soon." His excitement was barely contained; he looked like he wanted to leap out of his chair and shout it over the balcony for all the world to hear. It was no wonder; they'd been married a year now, and this was their first.

"How wonderful," she said softly, grinning, conscious to keep her voice down. Despite her annoyance over their behavior, she was very pleased. *Also, perhaps they'll tone it down now.* "A boy Broward or a girl Broward?"

"Too soon to tell, but my money's on a boy. She's been craving salty food."

Rhodie tsked. "Old wives' tales. We shall wait until the medical verdict comes in." She laid her napkin over her half-finished food. "Has she been very nauseous?"

He nodded. "The doctor says it's good. I'm trying to trust him."

"You should. Dr. Teegan is excellent."

"We're not using Teegan; it's Barber. Douglas Barber."

"Really?" Her mind latched on to the fact and wouldn't let go. "Who recommended him?"

"I'm not sure. I believe Abbie got a referral from one of her doctors in Gardenia."

"Hmm. I don't believe I've had the pleasure of meeting him. I shall rectify that immediately. My niece will have the best care available."

He grinned, beaming. "Thank you, Doctor. He's a perinatologist, which was recommended for a high-risk pregnancy, due to her prior conditions."

Edward, she'd noticed, was always careful not to speak the word *lupus* in public, whether they appeared to be alone or not. He wasn't sure if that was for Abbie's benefit or his own; so far, they'd been able to keep her illness a secret. Not that it was anyone's business but theirs, of course. Rhodie supported the decision entirely. Still, it couldn't be easy to tiptoe around it when explaining Abbie's absence.

"What names do you favor?"

"Do you know, I haven't even thought about it yet. I've just been so excited and nervous. She's not far along, there's plenty that could still go wrong."

She patted his hand. "We will not think that way. When will you tell the rest?"

"We thought to wait until twenty weeks."

She nodded approvingly. "And how far along is she?"

"Just eight."

"Well, when I return, I'll be able to rub it in all their faces that you told me before anyone else."

"I think Ginger and Dahlia have a pool going regarding who would know first; you were a safe bet last I knew."

She chuckled quietly. "Yes, they have a pool going on many things, including whether I shall ever marry. The outlook is not as promising."

He blinked. "Are you interested in marrying?"

"Not at the moment. I could perhaps be persuaded by the right man, but I am content in my career." It was on the tip of her tongue to keep going, to ask him if she could move out, to explain why it was important to her . . . but she looked into her brother's still-glowing brown eyes and decided not to ruin their lunch with business.

"Share a piece of cake with me?"

Her look reproved him. "Do you not know who I am?"

"I do." He grinned. "I just thought perhaps I could entice you in a spirit of celebration."

"I do not eat dessert, but thank you for the offer."

"Why is that, anyway?"

"I simply do not care for it," she said, signaling the waitress.

"Not any kind?"

"No," she lied.

"Not peach pie? Tiramisu? Chocolate chip cookies?"

"No, none of them."

"Blueberry crisp?"

"No."

"Raspberries and cream?"

"Edward . . ."

"I am not satisfied. I will find a dessert you like."

She gave him a flat smile and he laughed.

CHAPTER EIGHT

"A PROPER ORANGIERSIAN feast for my sojourning daughter," Ignatius boomed, lifting his glass in a toast toward Rhodie. "May we share it with her again in three months' time!" The table was spread with every kind of seafood imaginable: oysters, shrimp, lobster, crab, salmon, and her favorite, scallops. Rhodie lifted her wineglass in acknowledgment as her family cheered and echoed his toast.

"I hear there's loads of cute guys in Trella," Dahlia said, "so keep your eye out."

"First Sister, you know that's not an appropriate interest for women of our station," Rhodie chided gently as she pushed food around on her plate with her fork. Her mother had filled it for her, and it was far more than she could possibly eat, but with food this good, she'd managed to eat more than she usually did.

"Still," said her twin Ginger. "If something happens, we want pics."

Rhodie's shoulders shook as she laughed silently. "Pictures or it didn't happen?"

"Exactly. You're away, you could make up anything. We'll need hard evidence."

She cleared her throat. "It must be a serious wager if we're establishing stakes now."

The twins exchanged a look. Their frequent bets weren't exactly a secret, but they didn't often reveal what they'd wagered. They were getting more creative as time went on, becoming bored with just betting money, apparently, since they both had more than enough.

"Loser does the winner's foreign-language homework for a week."

She adopted a somber persona. "Well, one of you is going to be busy."

"You're so lucky," Andrew muttered to her.

"Oh?"

"Yes. I'm dying to get out of here, and there's no hope for me."

"That's a bit melodramatic, Third Brother. I would've taken you as my assistant if school weren't in session."

"We're *tutored*, Rhodie. School's in session whenever we want it to be."

She wiped nonexistent food from her mouth with her linen napkin. "Be that as it may, Mother and Father felt that you shouldn't fall behind."

"I'm nearly an adult. I think I can manage my own affairs."

"I'm sure it does feel that way," she said, patting his hand affectionately. He scowled at her good-naturedly.

"Rhododendron." Her mother wasn't asking for her attention so much as commanding it, and she looked down the table at her. "I want that plate clean. You're going to waste away over there. One good bout of illness, and you'll shrivel up and blow away in the wind."

"I shall do my best," she said. She was trying to mask her resentment by looking down at her plate when she realized that she barely had any more freedom than her fifteen-year-old brother. Her meager appetite suddenly faded entirely, and she took one more bite for appearance's sake before tossing her napkin over the plate.

THE NEXT MORNING, EDWARD and James were chatting quietly in the hallway outside Rhodie's suite. She couldn't hear their conversation, but based on James's bright smile and the strong, back-thumping embrace they shared, she would've bet anything Ginger and Dahlia wanted to wager that Edward just spilled the beans about his baby to his best friend.

They noticed her and Edward approached her, attempting to help with her luggage.

"You told him, didn't you?"

He shrugged one shoulder, embarrassed. "He's going away for a long time. It's better done in person."

"Uh-huh." She smiled. "And you're as bad about secrets as he is."

"He'll keep this one. I know he will."

"I certainly hope you're right," she said, digging in her satchel for her passport.

"Well, goodbye, Dr. Broward. Safe journeys. Love you."

"I love you, too," she muttered, still digging. "See you in a few months."

"All right. Call from time to time, will you? I don't want Mum and Dad hounding me for vicarious updates. You know how they are."

"Yes, I do." She smiled, finally finding her passport.

"Is my name being taken in vain?" Her father grinned, and her mother was already crying. She wouldn't get a good send-off from them. Edward understood her ways.

She gave her mother a one-armed hug, and her father took it as an invitation to sandwich her between them. *So much touching all at once . . .* She tried to breathe slowly, but a strong discomfort was rising inside her, and she was about to push them away when they parted from her willingly.

"We love you," her mother whispered, wiping her tears with a handkerchief. "Be good. Please write to us. Lieutenant, watch over our girl, won't you?"

"Is that why you've sent me along? Now that I consider it, I'm not sure I'm fit for the task . . ."

Lily lifted an eyebrow at him as she swiped at her nose, and he grinned.

"Yes, I will, of course I will. No need for motherly disappointment. I can't live with that. It's fatal to my carefree disposition."

They loaded themselves and their things into carriages and wagons and headed for the port just as the sun began to rise over the ocean. She'd forbidden the family from coming to the docks in order to prevent more public crying; it was just ridiculous.

Most of Rhodie's research supplies were already on board the massive ship; only her personal trunks and suitcases remained. It would be a three-day voyage. Thankfully she wasn't prone to seasickness.

The metal military monstrosity before her was sending a message, of course: don't mess with us. But it was practical too, because the hundred or so soldiers she and James were accompanying would be training the Trellan military in exchange for a base on Abbie's new territory, the Lesser Wandering Rooster Islands. Their first base camp would be entirely for her benefit: it was outside the Veil, the magical network that allowed their electronic devices to work reliably. Leaving the Veil had her a little bit nervous; she liked to know what to expect, and the Unveiled felt . . . untamed.

Rhodie leaned on the railing, looking out over the ocean as the ship set sail, and James quietly appeared next to her.

"Excited?"

She nodded, keeping her eyes on the water.

"Me too." He stood with her in silence for a long while, then wandered away.

CHAPTER NINE

JAMES KEPT HIS DISTANCE, more or less, the next few days on the ship. As she'd been sailing since before she could walk, she didn't have any trouble adapting to life at sea. But she did notice that he was never too far away . . . She'd be studying in the cafeteria and look up to find him a few tables away, just watching. He hadn't tried to text her, either, which was a little unusual. Did he feel weird about their conversations now that they were sort of working together? Legally, she was obligated to follow his orders, but realistically, he served at her pleasure. Maybe this assignment had finally put a little seriousness in his irreverent soul.

When they dropped anchor in Belicia, several customs and immigration officials lined the docks. They walked all the passengers into an area that reminded her of an open-air mall: it was breezy, with palm trees growing up through openings in the concrete roof, but based on the fences, she was fairly sure they were not yet free to leave.

"Wait right here."

The customs agent walked toward the enclosed, air-conditioned area with their passports while everyone else waited, sweltering, outside. Apparently, no one had told them that Rhodie was a royal; perhaps they hadn't wanted to separate her from the rest of the group or try to accommodate the whole contingent in the VIP waiting area. Either way, she was stuck where she was. Rhodie resisted the urge to sway, to shift her weight. Showing anxiety was a family no-

no. She tried to focus on her surroundings; small duty-free shops with colorful locally made gifts, alcohol, and packaged food lined the open walkway. The one closest to her had an assortment of warm-climate clothing out on racks: swimsuit cover-ups, sun hats, sundresses, kid T-shirts and onesies.

Rhodie tried to be subtle as she looked them over. She didn't shop much, and buying a onesie would be socially unacceptable, as none of her friends were pregnant, and she didn't want to spark speculation about Abbie. Some of the sayings were crass, regarding bodily functions; some were cute and destination-oriented. But some of them had puns.

It was yellow, an appropriate color for either gender, and in neat white block letters, it said "I'm glad to be out, I was running out of womb." The blue one next to it had a forty-five-degree angle on it, and it read "I'm acute baby," and that was tempting as well, but she found her fingers trailing over the yellow one. Lieutenant James was nearby, talking on the phone, trying to keep people from stacking her trunks too high and damaging the contents. In his uniform, with his dark sunglasses on, his red hair rumpled, the sun shining on his freckled skin . . . she had to admit that there was a physical appeal to the man. She signaled him, and he hung up and came over.

"You rang?"

"Despite the fact that you are the most indiscreet person on the continent, I would like to ask a favor."

"Name it."

She couldn't see his eyes through his dark sunglasses, but he sounded genuine.

"You are fit for the task?"

He scoffed, then stopped. "Is this going to disgust me? Is it . . . ?"

She covered a laugh by clearing her throat. "No, you needn't fear bodily fluids." She turned away from the store and pretended to be looking at the palm trees. "I'd like to purchase this yellow onesie behind me, but I can't do so without arousing suspicion. If you purchase it for me, I will pay you back tonight."

James looked around subtly, and when he spotted it, he snickered. "Out of womb? Clever."

"I thought so, too. I thought I might know someone who would also appreciate it."

"I'm your man." He lowered his sunglasses to wink at her, and she allowed herself a small smile before she walked away from the store toward the vending machine to buy a water. A few minutes later, the customs agent came back, clearly scanning the crowd for her, relieved when he found her.

"Your Highness, I want to apologize," he said in Common Tongue. "No one notified us that you were part of the contingent."

"Please think nothing of it, Agent Ogando," she replied in perfect Trellan. "I am here in a professional capacity, not as a diplomat."

He smiled and continued in Trellan. "Our medical examiners are on their way to check your group's nostrils for squealing nose malady; would you like to wait here or in the VIP lounge?"

"I can wait here if it won't be long."

Twenty minutes later, their boxes were released from customs and they were able to start loading the utility wagons for the long drive ahead to their first base camp. Unsurprisingly, she did not have to submit to the nose test, unlike the rest of the group. It did not escape her notice that, even with the hubbub of cargo organization, Lieutenant James was never more than a few paces from her, and she wondered if that was Edward's doing or his own preference. She dismissed that it could have been a coincidence. Both men were too protective to allow that possibility.

James plopped a paper bag into her lap as he slid into the back of the carriage she was sitting in.

"Is this for me?"

"Yes." He glanced at her, smiling. "Why else would I hand it to you?"

She opened the top. A burger and fries sat inside, its oils putting dark circles on the paper bag.

"I don't think so," she said, setting it between them.

"Rhodie, you've gotta eat. I'm sorry, but the pickings were so slim here, they rivaled your waistline."

"We need not discuss my waistline."

"Look," he said, hauling the bag over, "ignore the greasy peasant food on top, that's for me. Your salad is at the bottom." He pulled out his food and nestled it between his thighs. James passed her back the bag.

"I decline to eat in a moving vehicle, thank you. It's a sure way to stain one's clothes."

He nodded soberly. "Yes, I'll wager that's so. But it isn't moving yet, so do me a favor and take a few bites, eh?"

Rhodie scowled at him and pulled out her salad, popping off the clear plastic top.

"That's my girl."

"Do not patronize me. I am a twenty-five-year-old woman with an IQ of 161, and I am no one's girl."

"It's just an expression," said James, munching on a french fry, his gaze tender. "Also, psychologists now believe we should actually measure three different kinds of intelligence, so one number is kind of meaningless." He stuck his hand in the paper sack. "Ooh, bonus fries!"

"When did you read that?"

"A few years ago."

"You can't be more specific?"

He grinned. "I read it in the *Contemporary Journal of Acutely Obscure Psychological Research*, published by Barrowdon University in the Tenth Month of the year 511 AB. Can't remember the author's name, though. Dr. Thakur, maybe?"

Rhodie stared at him. "How can you recall all that?"

"I have a good memory. Eat your salad, Rhodie."

"It's Dr. Broward," she said, taking a bite of the white iceberg lettuce with her plastic fork. "Do you know your IQ?"

"Yes, I do. But as I already told you, it's a massive oversimplification of human intelligence, and therefore not a good indicator of my mental capacity. Intelligence should really be assessed on short-term memory, reasoning, and verbal recall." He took a big bite of his burger and spoke around it. "You're losing points on verbal recall at the moment. Probably because you're hungry."

She wasn't going to ask him his IQ. Not right now, anyway; she was supposed to be maintaining distance, not engaging him. The soldier who had been following her around since they left climbed into the back and promptly curled up against the side of the carriage and closed his eyes. James followed her judgmental stare.

"Princess, don't think such thoughts about our sweet Petros. He needs his beauty sleep if he's going to stand outside your tent all night."

The man gave James the stink eye, then closed his lids again. The carriage lurched forward and she put the top back on her salad, balancing it on her knees. James continued to shovel food into his mouth, and Rhodie was glad for the quiet. She'd intended to sleep as well, and she leaned her head to rest on the back of the velvet bench seat.

"You can lie down and use my lap, if you like."

"I hardly think so."

"Rhodie," he laughed. "Who's going to see? Who's going to care?" He clearly wasn't getting her telepathic messages to play it cool. It was time to firmly remind him of who she was.

"It's Dr. Broward. And I care," she said, curling a coat into a pillow shape before she jammed it under her head.

"Why?"

"I should not expect you to understand." She shifted around, trying to find a suitable angle. "All it takes is one photograph, one person with a cell phone who sees my head on your leg from the wrong perspective, and my reputation would be damaged." *Like it almost was a few weeks ago when I impulsively accepted your invitation.*

"So we'll leave the curtains closed."

"Oh, certainly," she said dryly. "Let's make it appear I have something to hide. That makes perfect sense."

"Perhaps I can tell you a bedtime story, then." James cleared his throat dramatically, and Rhodie was glad her eyes were already closed. The urge to roll them was nearly irresistible.

"Once upon a time," he started, "there was a beautiful princess with an immense vocabulary and an unreasonable amount of scientific knowledge insider her fantastic brain."

"Woz preserve me," she muttered, and he shushed her.

"The princess was going on a long journey, across tempestuous seas, over green mountains, to explore the deepest secrets of the Unveiled. 'Who,' she wondered, 'shall I conscript to accompany me on such a dangerous journey?'"

"You were hardly conscripted, Lieutenant."

"Who's telling this story?" He cleared his throat. "Luckily, the princess had a brother who had a strong, handsome friend with some free time on his hands."

"You mean him?" she asked, pointing at Petros. "I do not recall him spending much time with Edward, but I do spend considerable time at the lab; perhaps he was present in my absence."

Petros grinned, but didn't open his eyes.

"Don't encourage her, mate. As I was saying, the princess's brother had this friend. A man who had known her for a long time. In fact, one summer, they presented her father with a plan to allow fourteen-year-olds the right to vote."

Rhodie's cheeks heated. She'd forgotten about that. That had been a terrible year. A downright horrible year. And the distraction of drafting impossible legislation had been entirely welcome. James and Edward had both volunteered to help her, but Edward had lost interest fairly quickly, while James was still poring over books with her in the treehouse when they were called to dinner.

"While he commends his past self for his progressive stance on the matter, he also now regrets his participation, having met more fourteen-year-olds. Also, I was only twelve. Why did I care if you had the right to vote?"

"You'd have had it in two years. I think the time expenditure was warranted. That's not an unreasonable wait. "

"I suppose not. You know, I nearly pursued a law career because of that summer."

"Really?"

"Really, truly, sincerely."

"What changed your mind?"

"I decided that reading was too precious to me to be tainted by work." He paused. "Surely you could put your feet on my lap, even if your head is too scandalous."

"Oh for goodness' sake," Rhodie grumbled, and she turned to put her feet up on his legs.

"And a foot massage is a given?"

"Don't you dare, Arron James." Rhodie burned with embarrassment. How did James always manage to make her feel like a child again? *You are a cultured, fashionable, articulate woman; there's no need to debase yourself with such expressions.* She opened one eye, and he was grinning at her as he reached into the bag at his feet and pulled out a thick book. Thick books were intriguing; it had nothing to do with him.

She'd always been drawn to them in the way that some people craved chocolate.

"What are you reading?" He turned the cover so she could see, and she read it aloud. "*Notable Graphic Novel Artists of the New Century*. Is that an interest of yours?" She hadn't thought his interests to be so pedestrian.

"Would I read it if it wasn't?"

"I just didn't realize."

"Have you ever read a graphic novel?"

"No. It isn't my style."

"But if you haven't read one, how do you know it isn't your style?"

"Because I see the type of people who read them. I have nothing in common with them."

James snapped shut his book. "Based on what? How they dress? Their vocabulary? Their related interests?"

"Well, yes."

"But I don't fit that mold. You and I have plenty in common as far as interests go. One outlying interest doesn't preclude the possibility that we'd connect in other ways, does it?"

Rhodie didn't want to argue with him—not in front of the guard, anyway. "You're probably right."

He lifted an eyebrow. "You're conceding? I despise easy victories," he said, reopening his book. He left her alone then, and though she would never have admitted it, she did sleep better stretched out flat on the seat.

Their arrival was just as chaotic as their departure from the ship had been. Rhodie hurriedly put on her shoes and ducked out of the carriage to oversee the unpacking of her equipment and supplies. She was surveying the camp as James approached her.

"We're planning to set up a temporary hut for your lab equipment. It'll have insulated metal walls and a self-sealing roof."

"Yes," she said, digging in her bag for her sunglasses. "So Weathers said. Will it have a locking mechanism?"

He nodded. "But we'll put a guard on it as well. And you'll have a rotating night guard on your tent, too. In order to afford you privacy, we put you in a tent of your own rather than force you to share, as the rest of us will, in sweaty solidarity."

She smiled. "Thank you." She would accept their special treatment in this instance, more because it suited her temperament than because she felt she deserved it or needed it.

"The second base camp will have cabins and a lodge with rooms, and you've been reserved one of the lodge rooms because it's easier to secure."

"Sounds fine." She blinked as she looked into the forest to the west. "What on earth . . ."

"Oh, that."

"What is that?"

"That's the edge of the Veil."

"From the wrong side? That's what it looks like?"

"My anthropology professor would have me correct you and say 'the other side' rather than 'the wrong side,' but yes, it's not the side you're used to seeing. Have you noticed your skin?"

"What about it?"

He rolled up his sleeve: he *sparkled*.

"I've heard about this," she said, pulling his sleeve up higher for a better look and moving her fingers over his skin. "Fascinating. The domesticated magic from the Veil is clinging to your skin; it recognizes you and your devices as familiar to its environment. It's avoiding mixing with the Unveiled magic by staying close to you, like a child who's afraid. May I take a sample of your skin?" Without waiting for him to answer, Rhodie started digging around in boxes for a kit to gather some of his epithelial cells. "I want to see if your cells are denatured in any way by a closer proximity to the domesticated magic. Some people posit that our close quarters with the magic is what's increased cancer rates . . ."

She glanced up momentarily for his reaction and got caught in his smile. It was the gentle kind, the kind she usually got from people who'd known her a long time, who were aware of her quirks. His gaze was warm, and his hazel eyes laughed.

"Yes, you may certainly have a sample." He leaned closer to her, his elbows propped on a metal box. "Sample as much as you like, any way you like."

His proximity and innuendo made her tongue-tied for a moment before she collected her wits. "Just this bit will be sufficient, thank you," she said, finding the kit she was looking for and turning back to him.

"You should examine it soon; I'm told the effect is fairly short-lived, depending on the person. I know it's not what you're here to study, but it's a nice bonus."

"Yes, I will," she said, steadying his forearm, letting herself enjoy the feeling of his muscles under her fingers. She scraped the underside of it gently so as not to remove his hair. "Now do me."

He recoiled. "You want me to scrape your arm?"

She nodded once. "For comparison. Here," she said, wiping off the razor blade with an alcohol wipe, "just hold the slide for me and I'll do it myself." Rhodie did so efficiently. "Next, I need sterile water."

"What, ocean water's no good? You don't want seaweed in your samples?" He looked around, still holding the slides, his face red from the heat.

"No, it's got too many other organisms in it. Your canteen's contents will have to do."

He pulled it out, and she took a small amount with her pipette.

A gruff voice behind her chuckled. "Couldn't wait to get started, eh, Doctor?"

"Oh, Colonel Weathers, good. Here, give me your arm. It will be better to have two samples with approximately the same amount of melanin." She ignored his perplexed look and began rolling up his sleeve when her research assistant passed by. "Oh, Joline, could you please get me the methylene blue so I can stain these slides? Thank you."

CHAPTER TEN

WHEN SHE LOOKED UP from her work a few hours later, she'd taken ten samples, wet mounted them on slides, examined them at intervals for varying levels of denaturing or decay, and James was still there, watching her work.

"Can I get you something?" he asked.

"Oh. Um . . . no. I'm fine. But I should probably unpack."

"And eat."

"Yes," she agreed. "Has my tent been erected? I'd like to freshen up."

He led her to the doorway of the hut and pointed to a green canvas tent on the other side of an open central area: the tents were arranged in concentric circles, with hers near the middle—and flying the royal standard out front, of course, because what could be less conspicuous? Its blue-and-white flag shouted to all passersby that someone famous changed her clothes and occasionally voluntarily lost consciousness inside these canvas walls. Kidnappers, come one and all; she's in *this one*. Rhodie shook her head. No one was going to get past Petros or his daytime counterpart, Graeham, she felt fairly confident of that. Her safety was not in question, at least not during daylight hours. She went to grab her satchel, but James had it already, and he gestured for her to go first.

The inside of the tent was fine. Nothing fancy, though she noticed that someone had thought to bring a real mattress instead of a cot, and she appreciated that. She'd need someone to hang her mosquito net, but that could be arranged. She didn't have electricity, but she didn't really need it; she could check her email and charge her phone at the lab during the day. She turned around to ask James where the latrines and showers were and found him carefully entering the tent with a candle to light her lamp, one hand sheltering the flame from the breeze. The glow illuminated his freckles, making them look like stars; he had so many of them, she found his face fascinating to look at, but she was always trying to connect them like constellations in her mind.

"What is it?" he asked. "Did you not want me to come in? I apologize for not knocking at the post, but I lacked an available hand . . ."

"No, no," she said quickly. "It's nothing. But you don't have to play servant for me, you know. I'm capable of lighting my own lamp."

"I know that. I just thought I'd try to make you more comfortable."

She wished she had something to hug against her chest; his thoughtfulness was getting to her. Or perhaps it was just the long travel day they'd had. Yes, surely that's what had her thinking such sappy, sentimental thoughts about her brother's best friend.

Once the lamps were lit, he puffed out the candle and set it on her desk. "I'm off duty now; the guard will change at 0800 and 2000 daily unless you need us to shift that for some reason."

She shook her head. "That sounds reasonable to me."

"Good." He clapped his hands softly. "Then as it's 2145, I'll say good night."

A pang of guilt made her stiffen. "Lieutenant, you didn't have to stay."

"I wanted to see you settled first, make sure your accommodations didn't present any problems." Shifting his backpack to the side, he pulled out the plastic bag that held her gift for Edward and gave her a knowing wink. She allowed a small smile in a silent show of gratitude, and she opened her trunk to shove it to the bottom where it wouldn't be found. Something leggy and black scuttled into the corner and she stood up quickly. He was almost out the door when she grabbed his backpack strap.

"Whoa!" He stumbled backwards. "Rhodie, what the—"

"There's an insect. A large insect. You kill it." She pointed to the corner.

"So all that business about not playing the servant was just—"

"It doesn't apply to large insects, obviously."

He sighed. "Can you at least supply me with a weapon of some kind?" Scooting just close enough to the trunk to push it open, she carefully pulled out one brown flat and slammed it shut again.

"A shoe? I was hoping for a crossbow, but I suppose I can make do with—"

"Less talking, more smashing," she said, shoving him toward the shadows. "It's going to get away and then I'll never fall asleep."

He grinned as he shuffled forward, getting out his phone for a flashlight. "Well, we can't have that, can we, Princess?" James swiveled his head, trying to see into the tight space, and then quickly stepped. "Holy—I didn't know they came that big."

"I did," she said, "but only in theory. Get in there and make it history."

"Suddenly, I feel I'm being underpaid . . ."

"You can have a raise. A big one."

"I feel some light recompense . . ."

Frustrated, she reached for her shoe, but he held it out of her reach. "All right, all right." He skulked into the corner, aiming, then brought down the shoe with a mighty whack.

"Ooh, he's fast," he said smashing again and again, each hit moving closer and closer to where she was standing. "Got it!" He stood up and showed her the smashed guts on her expensive leather shoe, and she grimaced.

Something caught her eye on the other side of the tent. "There's another one!" she said, pointing, and James got it on the first try this time. They searched carefully and found no more, and he took her shoe outside and carefully wiped it clean on the grass before returning it to her.

"Don't let me forget," he said, reshouldering his backpack, "I brought that book for you. Dr. Raggio, *My Practice, My Promise.*"

"Oh, excellent. I didn't bring any light reading."

He chuckled. "Right. Okay. Well, sweet dreams."

"You too," she said, silently wishing he could guard her all night, too. For security and insect-smashing reasons, of course.

CHAPTER ELEVEN

RHODIE WOKE TO THEIR first morning in camp and stretched. She'd slept well, but she was anxious to start. She'd been waiting months for this. She opened the tent flap and examined her skin first: the sparkle was gone already. She couldn't wait to get to the lab and see if the samples were in the same condition. Rhodie dressed quickly and slipped on her sturdy leather hiking boots, just as the sun was peeking over the hills. She checked her phone as she crossed toward the makeshift lab, and her night guard (what was his name? She couldn't remember) trailed after her.

"Take them down! You cannot use that here." A female voice made her look up. A young woman with warm sepia skin and wavy chestnut hair down to her waist was standing at the edge of the camp. Her lack of a uniform—just loose tan capri pants and a black T-shirt with a white cat on it—indicated she was not part of the Orangiersian contingency.

Rhodie looked around: three junior officers appeared to be setting up the portable magic enhancers she'd requested, large umbrella-like stands that encouraged their devices to work more reliably. The men had stopped to stare at the Trellan woman who stood at the edge of the camp, her fists shaking with rage.

"You're in charge here; do something," the woman shouted at Rhodie, and she felt taken aback that the woman apparently knew something of who she was and what her role was here.

"Will you join me for breakfast?" Rhodie asked as they neared her position. Trellans valued hospitality above most other things; it might be a good way to smooth things over.

"Your devices are unnatural. Take them down." *Or perhaps not.*

"I'm Dr. Broward. May I ask your name?"

The woman slid her jaw to one side, and her voice was cold. "I am Yautia."

She's named after a tuber? Though really, Rhodie mused, it was no stranger than her being named after a flowering bush.

"We need them to do our work," Rhodie explained. "To do our research. To find out more about the environment here. How to care for it, how to use it to advance medical treatments . . ."

"It's not wanted. It's not needed. I will engage the magic on your behalf, to help power your devices. Just please, take them down."

Rhodie didn't need more than a few moments to consider the woman's offer: her relationship with the magic here would be more useful anyway. It would take the Orangiersian magic users days to be able to convince it to perform even simple functions.

"Very well," Rhodie said. "I apologize. We didn't realize they would be offensive. We will disable them for now." She wanted to settle the woman down, but she didn't know how her touch would be received, and frankly, she didn't like using her body that way. "Take them down," she commanded, and the men moved to obey.

"You'll put them back up when I leave, though," Yautia muttered. "As if I wouldn't notice my own magic being sucked away."

"Would there be a better place for them?" Rhodie asked.

"Yes," Yautia said. "In your country."

Rhodie felt her shoulders drop. She certainly didn't want to offend anyone. "Won't you join me for breakfast? Our cook is a local man, and his food is good." She'd only had his dinner last night, but she assumed the rest of it was good as well. Yautia gestured for her to lead the way.

Rhodie led her to the tent that served as the mess hall and watched as she politely interacted with the soldiers who served her eggs and fruit.

"Your soldiers do not know how to cut up a mango," Yautia observed, squinting at her plate.

"There's a right way to cut up a mango?" Rhodie asked. The other woman then turned her scrutiny on the doctor. She must have decided she was sincere, because she nodded.

"This way, it's still stringy. If you cube it, the strings won't stick between your teeth. Not all varieties, but this one."

"How many varieties are there?"

"Hundreds."

"Interesting." Rhodie led her to a table near the exit. She was about to ask Yautia whether different varieties had different magical applications when the woman beat her to a question.

"You don't use magic in your lab." Well, it wasn't so much a question as a mild accusation.

Rhodie cleared her throat. "Well, we do, but simply to power our instruments. They don't run our processes for us. I am interested, however, in the effect of magic upon the plants and animals here."

"You don't heal with magic?" Yautia asked, an edge to her voice. "I know there are practitioners in Orangiers. I have corresponded with them before."

She shook her head. "There are, but I don't believe it's the best course of treatment; it leaves too much to the whims of the magic. Other health-care providers may see it differently, of course, but that's my opinion."

Yautia snorted, coughing. She took a sip of orange juice. "You mean, you can't study its work, can't reproduce what it does, so you don't trust it."

Rhodie leaned back in the folding chair. "I wouldn't say that I don't trust magic. I use it to power my phone, clean my clothes, keep my food cold . . ."

"Using something and trusting it are two different things. When you use technology to power your devices, it requires no investment, no relationship. You claim the low-hanging fruit, but won't climb higher for the rest of it. But I don't expect someone so young to understand."

Rhodie eyed the Trellan woman; they appeared to be about the same age . . . Perhaps her relationship with the magic was preventing her body's aging process. Edward had said the Warlord-in-Chief of Gratha also appeared much younger than he truly was. Yautia caught her strange look and laughed.

"Give it another hundred years, dear." She wiped her hands on a napkin. "I know you are anxious to check your skin cell samples; you were muttering under your breath, and the magic heard you. I can work with the devices in your lab first."

CHAPTER TWELVE

ASIDE FROM THAT INITIAL confrontation with Yautia, the first week in the camp went swimmingly. James had seldom been so happy. The dukedom was still troubling him when he thought about it, but he got to follow Rhodie around all day. He could stare at her as much as he wanted to, and no one thought anything of it. It went swimmingly, that is, until he started throwing up. He tried to hide his illness as well as he could, but by the time he went off duty, he was well and truly sick. When he slept through his phone alarm the next morning, they sent someone to check on him and arranged an alternate guard. He did, however, hear his phone when it rang.

"Hello?"

"Hi, mate. Can I use your flat for a thing?" It was Saint.

"What kind of a thing? A sex thing?"

His friend was silent. "What do you—what? Why do you assume it's a sex thing?"

"I don't know, you were the one being vague. Is this a noble cause? What do you want it for?"

"My relatives are coming to town and we need more space."

"Oh, that's fine, then. Sam's got a key."

"You sound weird. What's wrong with you?"

"Sick. Caught . . . something."

"That's too bad. Things going okay with the sister?"

"Yes, going fine."

"So you haven't told her how you feel, then?"

James groaned. His stomach was sour, and it was impossible to get comfortable on his cot. "No, I haven't."

"Your issue," Saint drawled, "is that you're trying to be her jester, when you should be her knight. That's your problem. That's what's wrong with you."

"Preposterous. There's nothing wrong with me. Nothing that prescription medication wouldn't solve, anyway."

"Jesters make jokes."

"Don't try to change me, Saint. Love me as I am."

"Joke."

James smiled a little. "What about you, what's new in your life? Attracted any new lady friends in the park with your four-footed chick magnet?"

Saint snorted. "Lame attempt to change the subject. Also: joke."

"All right, fine. I get it. You're suave and cool and manly, and I'm a punch line with hair."

His friend chuckled. "You've got a knight side, mate. I've seen it with your sisters. You just need to, you know"—he paused—"channel it. Channel your inner knight."

"Channel my inner knight," James echoed, rubbing his stubbled chin.

"Channel it. That's what you've got to do. Channel it."

"I'm going back to sleep now. Have them take their shoes off, I love those floors."

"Mate, they're Imaharan. You couldn't pay them to leave their shoes on."

HE WOKE TO FIND RHODIE sitting on the edge of his bed, and he quickly pushed himself up to sitting. "What are you doing here?" he rasped. "Get out. I'll infect you."

"Good morning, Lieutenant." She reached for his forehead. James tipped his head away from her hand, grunting at the pain in his belly when his abs flexed.

"I mean it, Rhodie. Out. You don't have permission to be here."

Forget steel: she was leveling him with a gaze that was much harder than that. Titanium. Diamond, maybe. "You forget yourself, Lieutenant. I don't *require* permission to be here," she said.

"These are *my* quarters," he muttered, wishing his head would stop spinning. Wishing he wasn't soaking up the comfort of her presence, wishing he wasn't relieved to know that she was here to take care of him. But he couldn't let her get sick because of him.

"I outrank you in this instance," she said.

"You actually don't. You don't have a military rank."

"Well, perhaps I don't care . . ."

"I'm not happy with you right now," he said. "I lack the strength to fight you, but I'm not happy." He slumped back against the metal bars at the head of his cot.

"Noted," she said, but the distracted note in her voice told him that she'd already started examining him. "Take off your shirt."

"What? Why?"

"I want to see if you have a rash."

"I don't."

She reached for his forehead again and he dodged her touch again. With a small sigh, Rhodie took off her reading glasses and folded them in her lap.

"Lieutenant James, what do you know about brain bender fever?" Her voice was polite, but her piercing brown gaze was making it clear that there were a number of ways she'd like to punish him right now for his lack of cooperation.

"Not much," he admitted. He was lightheaded. He wanted to lie back down, but he didn't want her to know how bad he felt, and besides, she was a royal. You didn't laze about in front of royalty, no matter how much you felt like a steaming pile of compost.

"It's caused by a parasite that embeds itself in your liver—not your brain, interestingly. Once it matures in your system, your liver starts to shut down. Then your kidneys. If it spreads to your brain, you will form micro-hemorrhages that will cause your brain to swell. You will have seizures, you will fall into a coma, and you will die. Is that what you want?"

Ashamed, he shook his head.

"I didn't think so. So despite your anger, you are going to cooperate with me. You will allow me to treat you, and I will take every precaution not to become infected. It is transmitted by blood, so unless an infected mosquito bites me or you become the source of a blood donation that I can't see needing, there is little risk to me. I am wearing an insect repellent so powerful, it will probably give me cancer. Now lie down."

He complied.

"How did it start?"

"My stomach hurt last night, and I was fatigued . . ."

"Are you sure it wasn't just the uniform?"

"What?"

"They're called fatigues, you said you were—sorry, never mind."

"Dr. Broward, you just told me I was going to die if I didn't cooperate, and now you're making jokes?" He shook his head slowly. "Ridiculous."

"I apologized, did I not?"

"You did. But I'm still irritated."

"What other symptoms? Vomiting?"

"Yes, I threw up once last night. Just thought I ate something dodgy."

"What did you eat?"

"Rice and beans, and those little starchy hockey pucks, and some kind of cabbage relish."

"The pressed plantains?"

"Could be. I don't know." He covered his mouth as he yawned. He wanted to go back to sleep.

"Does your chest hurt?"

"No."

"Are you coughing at all?"

"No. I just feel cold and my . . ." He sighed. "My muscles hurt, and I'm nauseated."

Rhodie pressed her hand to his forehead, and he didn't try to shift away, even though he still wanted to. "As I suspected, you're burning up. I want you out of these clothes."

"How I've dreamed of those words . . ."

"And here I thought this tent was a joke-free zone," she said primly, and despite how awful he felt, he smiled. "Where's your trunk?" she asked.

"At the end of the bed."

She turned toward the door. "Guard, take this trunk to the quarantine tent."

"Wait, what?" James sat back up too quickly, and his stomach lurched. He grunted. Chance's eyes were big, and he knew he must look as bad as he felt.

"What's the problem, Lieutenant?"

"You didn't say anything about moving me. You said I had to cooperate with your treatment . . ."

"And part of my treatment is ensuring that you will get a good night's sleep. That's much easier to do when you're alone, isn't it?"

"I suppose so . . ."

"How big of you. Get up, please."

James cleared his throat. "You'll have to step outside first . . ."

She crossed her arms. "Why?"

"You can't imagine any scenario where I might want privacy as I'm getting out of bed?"

"Oh, for goodness' sake, I've seen you go swimming at King's Beach plenty of times."

"It's significantly different than that, thank you very much. I don't know why you're giving me such a hard time," he grumbled, his teeth chattering.

Rhodie pursed her lips. "You're right. I apologize. Perhaps you're not the only one being too familiar lately." Reaching down to the end of the bed, she handed him his trousers and then stood with her back to him. He shoved himself into each leg and zipped them up, the movement like a fat rubber band that wouldn't stretch. His muscles felt atrophied, stiff. He pulled on a second shirt for appearances. She pulled the blanket off the bed and settled it around his shoulders.

"Can you walk unassisted?"

"Yeah," he muttered, jamming his feet into his untied boots. "I think so." He noticed that she didn't stray far from his elbow as he shuffled across the central yard. "Where am I going?"

She stopped in front of her quarters.

"Oh, no. No way, Rhodie. I'm not taking your tent from you."

"That's right," she said, gently pushing him forward into the tent as he dug in his heels fruitlessly. "You're not taking it from me, I'm lending it to you for a short period of time."

"No."

"I'll spend a few nights with Joline and the other research assistants."

"*No.* I'll just go back to my quarters." He pivoted to do just that, when he heard her dialing. James turned slowly back to her, afraid of what he would find.

"Hello?" Edward's deep voice came through the speaker.

"Hello, Second Brother," Rhodie said cheerfully. "How are you?"

"Fine, thanks. You?"

"Well, I've been better actually. One of the camp members has fallen ill, and he's giving me a hard time. He's resisting my treatment."

"I am *not*," James said, shuffling over to stick his head where the camera could pick up his face, "resisting her treatment. I'm resisting *special* treatment, especially when it displaces my protectee from her . . ." His stomach lurched, and he felt all the blood drain from his face. "Oh Woz, I'm too sick for this." He sat down hard on the edge of the bed.

"Mate, you look like death warmed over. Why am I involved in this? Listen to Rhodie."

"Fine," he bit out. "But I think ganging up on me when I'm sick is very unfair, and you're going on my list."

Edward chuckled. "Your 'most awesome friends' list, I assume?"

"No, Your Majesticness. Quite the opposite."

"I'm off, then. Feel better, James. Rhodie, keep me posted, please."

"Yes, I will. He's going to sleep now."

"Only because I have no other option, not because you told me to . . . ," James muttered, crawling under the covers. Even though they were clean, they were slightly damp from the oppressive humidity. He didn't care.

"Frame it however you need to, Lieutenant," she said, pulling the covers up under his chin and patting his shoulder through the thin blanket.

"Your mattress is softer than mine," he said, his words running together a bit as he began to drift off.

"I don't doubt it. I'll be back in a bit with medicine," he heard her soft reply, and then he was out.

WHEN HE WOKE AGAIN, he thought someone was shaking the bed. "Knock it off for Woz's sake, Cora," he muttered . . . then realized he was the one shaking the bed. He tried to sit up, but his abs hurt. Everything hurt. His head was pounding, his throat was dry. *Water.* He looked around, but saw none within reach. His tent—*her* tent—was pitch black; he stumbled toward where he thought the door was, only to find solid canvas. James cursed softly, and the tent flap opened behind him.

"Why are you out of bed?" Rhodie chided, lighting the lamp on the bedside table.

"Have you just been sitting out there?"

She shrugged. "It's as good a place as any to read."

"No, it isn't. It's not safe." He tried to lick his dry lips. "I need a drink."

"I'll get you one. Lie back down, please."

He did, but he wasn't happy about it. *I should be serving her, not the other way around. Damn those bugs.*

She came back with medication as well as a clear glass bottle of ice-cold water.

"What is it?"

"Just an antiviral. I wouldn't try to poison you now; there would be no sport in it. I agree with you that easy victories aren't as sweet."

His brain was fuzzy, too fuzzy to spar with her, and despite her teasing, he saw how that worried her. "I'm okay, Rhodie. Go to sleep. Stop sitting outside my door."

"You're off duty."

"So?"

"So I don't have to listen to you."

He snorted as he knocked back the water and the meds in one go. He rolled over. "Put out the light, will you?"

He slept hard for a few hours, and then it turned fitful. Someone rubbed his back through his sweaty shirt, and when he rolled over, someone put a cool cloth to his head. When he whimpered, someone put the water bottle to his lips again. When he threw up, someone emptied the bucket. Someone added another blanket to the bed when he shook. Around dawn, he felt hot and kicked the blankets off. When someone tried to cover him back up, James finally gained enough consciousness to realize who that someone was . . .

"You're still here?" He couldn't keep the incredulity out of his voice.

Rhodie smiled, and he noticed the lines around her eyes. "You asked me not to sit outside. You didn't say anything about sitting inside."

"What about royal appearances?"

"What about them? You're sick. I'm a doctor."

"You're gonna be dead tired . . ."

"I dozed when necessary. I don't need a lot of sleep. Less than most, I believe."

He nodded, then rubbed at his face.

"Is the light too much?" She'd moved it away from the bed to the desk, where she had five different texts open.

James shook his head. He didn't want her to turn off the light; he wouldn't be able to see her.

"How do you feel?"

"Bad," he mumbled. Sleep was right there. It wanted him again. "Rhodie."

She came over to his side. "What is it?"

"I'm sorry."

She leaned back. "For what?"

"Getting sick. Being troublesome."

"Nonsense."

"It's not. I came to take care of you, not the other way around."

"Quite honestly, this is the easiest you've ever been with me. You're far more trouble in your normal state. I feel certain that once you resume your normal duties, you'll more than make up for it. Now stop worrying over nothing. Do you want food?"

His stomach launched a violent protest at the suggestion that nearly resulted in him expelling whatever was left in there, and he shook his head slowly. James rolled away from the light, letting sleep claim him again. His dreams were uncomfortably strange, as if his mind could sense the issues happening to the rest of his body: He dreamt that his father came to the camp and demanded he "come home." Rhodie wouldn't allow him to be released from her care, so his father set up a tent and stayed, planning to take him home when he was better. In his dream, he hoped he'd never get better.

When he woke again, it was afternoon. He felt . . . not as bad. Better wasn't quite right, but at least he was hungry. Rhodie was asleep at her desk, her arms pillowing her head, her glasses still on. He touched her back gently, feeling it rise and fall in deep sleep. With his pointer fingers, he slipped her glasses off and set them safely aside before he went in search of food.

CHAPTER THIRTEEN

A FEW DAYS LATER, RHODIE was packing her bag when James strode into the lab, wiping the breakfast crumbs from his shirt, running a hand through his already-sticking-up hair. *That hair.* It drove her a little bit nuts that he never tried to do anything with it. Surely some kind of gel could tame it. Other men did such things. He was already glowering; that had been his permanent expression since he'd received a text message yesterday afternoon.

"All right?" he asked in greeting, and she nodded.

"Just getting ready to go out with Yautia."

"You trust this woman?" He crossed his arms over his chest. "You don't know anything about her, except that she offered to help with our magic."

"Which is working perfectly, by the way," Rhodie added, pulling the pack onto her shoulders. "Better than in Orangiers."

James grunted, but must not have disagreed, because he said nothing.

"Did you sleep well? You're feeling all better, aren't you?"

"I'm fine."

She paused by the doors of the lab, curiosity getting the better of her again. "What's eating you, then?"

"Me? Nothing."

"You're awfully grumpy."

"I'm not *grumpy*," he snapped, then softened by degrees. "I don't like you hanging around people without background checks. It's my job to protect you. You make it impossible, adding strangers to a situation already fraught with unknowns." His words reminded her of Tezza's warning, but Rhodie hadn't sensed any danger from Yautia. She'd been nothing but helpful. She wasn't one for gut feelings over her mind's analysis of a situation, but this seemed fine.

"Well, she's been a wealth of information in our interviews. My research assistants have more leads than they know what to do with. Joline was practically giddy this morning."

More disgruntled grunting. Lovely. He was going to be an enchanting companion today as they marched through the jungle, dripping sweat. That was unlikely to improve his disposition.

Yautia was waiting for them under the canopy again. Rhodie had noticed that she rarely left the cover of the jungle, and when she did, she seemed slightly nervous about it. She'd shown them a small grove not far into the forest, and they'd dragged a few chairs up there so she'd be more comfortable. There had been some disappointment in Rhodie's research so far: in Yautia's opinion, there was no difference medicinally between plants grown inside or outside the Box, as Yautia called the Veil. But time would tell. They would move inside the Veil in a few weeks, and then she'd know for sure.

"Here." Yautia passed her a steaming cup of amber liquid, housed in the lid of her battered plastic thermos.

She sniffed it; the faint scent of basil and cinnamon wafted toward her. "What's this?"

"Villania tea. It will help you see it."

"See what?"

"Magic."

Rhodie felt her eyebrows shoot up. *Really?*

"Give me that," James said, snatching the cup from her fingers, sloshing the liquid. "You're not drinking that."

Rhodie's temper flared, but she tamped it down, wiping the tea off her shirt instead of yelling at him. "Villania grows everywhere here, and it's not poisonous."

"Even so. It's not worth the risk."

"Lieutenant," Yautia pressed, "have your magic user examine it. You will find nothing harmful in it. I promise you."

"I really would like to test its properties, James," Rhodie said. "What reason is there that the other guard can't just check it first?"

"His name is Sergeant Graeham, and he's otherwise engaged." James brought the tea closer to his face and sniffed it skeptically. "It's probably just a common hallucinogenic."

"I want it tested." This was too important to back down from, no matter what had his panties in a twist. He glared at her, his hazel eyes silently snapping at her. She glared back, hands on her hips.

"Fine," he growled. "But you have to come with me. I can't leave you here alone."

"Fine," she replied evenly, but his behavior was still troubling her. This wasn't like her happy-go-lucky friend to be all bent out of shape. *PTSD,* her mind whispered. *Yes, his shooting was a long time ago, but look where he is now: in a deep forest again, in a foreign country. It could be. It could.*

"Your irritability is unusual."

"Come off it, Rhodie," he growled as he led them across the camp.

"PTSD can happen anytime, you know. It doesn't have to be immediate, it can—"

James stretched out his legs to quicken their pace. "I don't have PTSD. I'm allowed to have personal problems you don't know about. I'm allowed to have a bad day."

She said nothing as they passed Joline and Grace, on their way up the hill to meet with Yautia. "If you say so." *What kind of personal problems?* It wasn't like they were close enough for her to ask, but she wanted to. There were reasons, real reasons, sensible reasons, that they weren't closer . . . but the tension in his shoulders and the pinched expression on his face now made her want to grind those reasons under her boots. She wanted to help him.

He came to a sudden stop near the latrines. "Can you hold this? I burned myself, and I don't feel like searching the whole camp for Chance when I can just text him."

She took the thermos cup from him gingerly. "There's a med kit in the lab. Perhaps he could meet us there."

James muttered something, then typed out the message with more force than necessary. The response came quickly. "He'll meet us at the lab." James moved to take the tea back from her, but she pivoted away from him, starting slowly toward the building.

"I've got it."

He pointed at her, following. "If you drink that before he examines it . . ."

"I'm not going to," she said quietly. "I promise. I want to, but I won't." She smiled at him over her shoulder. "Don't you trust me?"

A begrudging smile played at the corner of his mouth, and she caught a tiny sparkle in his eye before it disappeared. "I do trust you. I probably shouldn't, but I do."

Rhodie was torn between wanting to go slow, lest she also burn herself, and going quickly, in order to treat his injury. She ended up splitting the difference; not much of it spilled. "If this works, if we can *see* magic, it would change the outcome of the whole trip." She wanted him to understand that she wasn't trying to annoy him or make his life difficult. It was strange; she'd never felt the need to reassure Trosen of her motives.

At the entry to the lab, he tried to reach around her to open the door for her, just as she shifted to open it herself, and they bumped into each other. His strong hands were on her elbows, stabilizing her, before she knew what was happening.

"Sorry," he muttered, staring into her eyes, his hands lingering.

"Well, you know what one tectonic plate said when it bumped into another . . . ," she quipped, then smiled at the very skeptical look on James's face, based on the cocking of his eyebrow.

"No, what did it say, this miraculous talking tectonic plate?"

"My fault." She grinned.

James closed his eyes and shook his head. "Terrible." He let go of her elbows and opened the door, motioning her inside. Sergeant Graeham was already waiting for them. "Hi, Chance."

"Good morning, Dr. Broward, James," he said, as he reached out and took the tea. "I assume this is the tea you want tested?"

"Yes, Sergeant, if you don't mind." Rhodie let her hip lean against the metal table as she watched the two men.

"Why would I mind?" he asked, amusement in his voice.

"Lieutenant James indicated that you were otherwise engaged..."

"I'm never too busy for you, Doctor."

James snorted. "Just test the tea, Chance." His friend grinned at him as he ran his fingers around the edge of the cup.

"Well, at first glance, there's nothing magical about the cup or its contents. There's magic lingering nearby, but I believe it's either residual from Yautia's influence or simply curious about what's happening here." He closed his eyes then, and Rhodie watched, fascinated. She'd always been just a tiny bit jealous that she hadn't inherited any magical aptitude. She probably could've worked to develop it, but she'd never had the time.

After a few moments, his eyes fluttered open again. "Seems fine to me." He took a sip. "And it's delicious as well."

"That's not for you," Rhodie chided, stealing back the cup carefully. "Satisfied, Lieutenant?"

James nodded. "If Chance says it's safe, I trust his judgment."

Tentatively, Rhodie took a sip of the villania tea. *How much should I drink? How long will it take to become effective?*

How much magic will I be able to see? Trace amounts, or does it need to be a more condensed amount? How long will it work?

Hard plastic clattered to the ground, startling her out of her thoughts. James was reaching down to pick up the med kit he'd knocked off the table while trying to treat his wound.

"Oh, I'm sorry," she said, putting down the cup. "Let me help you."

"I'm fine," he grunted, trying to get a sterile bandage out of its packaging. "Go back to your musing."

"My musing?" she asked, smiling, arms crossed over her chest.

"Yes," he said, distracted by his own fumbling. "You get this far-off look in your eyes when you're thinking hard. You had it just now. You do it in the lab, mostly."

"I think I can put off my musing for a while," she said, scooting closer to him and gently taking the supplies from his hands. He held still as she rolled up his sleeve and examined his burn, holding his freckled arm lightly, like a baby bird she was afraid of crushing. "It's only second-degree. Let's just add some antibiotic cream to it and leave it open to the air," she said, reaching for the tube without waiting to see if he agreed. "If it starts to blister, we can talk about additional treatment . . ." She had the cap off and was about to squirt it on his arm when the villania tea kicked in. She thought it was a shadow at first. The electron microscope next to James was edged in purple, like someone had taken a marker and outlined it. Rhodie couldn't believe her eyes as she took in her lab: a fine violet mist was circulating like an air current, but most of the purple rested on the equipment and samples.

When she looked closer, she realized the mist was actually made up of tiny particles spiking out from the surface of the objects, like metal shavings attracted to a magnet.

"Rhodie?" James's face was full of concern. "Are you just musing again, or . . ."

"I can see it," she whispered. "I can *see* magic." She quickly rubbed the cream into his arms, ignoring his wince of pain. "Let's get back to the forest. I've got so much to do . . ."

CHAPTER FOURTEEN

THE NEXT WEEKEND, JAMES walked down the noisy jungle road with Chance and Petros; being Rhodie's night guard, Petros didn't get many nights off, so they'd wanted to make the most of it. Rhodie had been spending every day in the jungle with her research assistants and Yautia—a good chunk of the nights as well—since she'd first tried that villania tea . . . they'd more than earned some downtime. Chance and Petros were singing and laughing about something a girl had said. James was vaguely surprised the other two hadn't brought her back to camp with them, but maybe they didn't want Weathers's attention. That cranky old bastard's attention wasn't something he was eager to attract, either. Most of the evening was a blur; he'd played pool, he knew that, but he didn't know how many pints he'd consumed or how many girls he'd danced with. And he'd texted with Rhodie . . . It was easier, somehow, when she wasn't right there with him.

Lt. James: Why don't scientists trust atoms?

Dr. Broward: Is this a joke?

Lt. James: Yes, Princess, a joke. A funny. A ha-ha.

Dr. Broward: Because they make up everything.

Lt. James: You ruined my punch line!

Lt. James: I believe some light recompense is in order . .
.

Dr. Broward: More recompense?

Dr. Broward: Fine, I'll tell you a joke, then.

Dr. Broward: Did you hear about the depressed rabbit?

Lt. James: No . . .

Dr. Broward: He didn't carrot all.

Lt. James: GROAN.

Dr. Broward: What was wrong with my joke?

Lt. James: That's a dad joke.

Dr. Broward: A dad joke? It's just a pun.

Lt. James: No, it was a bad, bad dad joke. The kind old men tell to make their children laugh.

Dr. Broward: Since I'm not a father, does that mean I've committed a faux papa?

Lt. James: STOP IT.

Faux papa. That's hilarious. He didn't bother holding in a chuckle.

Dr. Broward: Going to bed now.

Lt. James: Sweet dreams.

Chance had nudged him in the ribs. "Come on, mate, you spend all day flirting with her. Play pool with us."

He must have won, because he was in a jovial enough mood to sing with them as they tried to avoid the puddles the late-afternoon rain had made.

Chance and Petros had just started into another bawdy song; "I'll go to me parents and confess what I've done," they bellowed, "and I'll ask them to pardon their prodigal son . . ." Purely out of habit, James glanced over toward Rhodie's tent.

"*Sonofabitch.*" He'd broken into an unsteady run before Chance or Petros even turned their heads to look at him. *Asleep.* The guard in front of Rhodie's tent was asleep, slumped against the post, even with all the noise they were making. Her light was off; she'd said she was going to sleep as well. *Unconscious. Vulnerable. Alone.* There weren't any other thoughts in his head; it was only looking back later that he realized how completely enraged he'd felt.

He did not stop to identify the guard. He asked him no questions. He must have been mad to grab a fellow soldier by the collar and break his nose with his fist. The man's blood sprayed his shirt, and the guard fell to the ground.

"You jacking stupid sonofabitch," he slurred, "I'm gonna kill you!" But there were two of the man, and he wasn't sure which was the real one. James took a swing anyway and missed entirely.

That missed connection allowed Chance to push between James and his shouting victim while Petros wound his arms through James's and grabbed him behind his neck, holding him tight, forcing him down to the ground. Private Tracy, his victim, was holding his face, writhing on the ground.

"You broke my nose!" Tracy seethed. "What the jack is wrong with you, Lieutenant?"

"Is that a joke? Is that a jacking joke, you jacking stupid piece of shit?"

Petros apparently decided that they should not be together, and he hauled James to his feet and dragged him away from Rhodie's tent toward their side of the camp. James continued to hurl insults at the injured man over his shoulder.

"Clam up, James, you're going to wake the whole camp."

"Good!" he shouted. "Let them wake, we can lynch him together. I offer my bedsheets in the service of His Majesty's justice. Get off me, Petros!" James fought against his friend; he still hadn't been inside Rhodie's tent to be sure she was okay.

"Not until you calm the jack down," Petros growled.

James needed to know, he needed to see with his own eyes that she was safe. But Petros had the advantage of both greater size and greater sobriety.

"Knock it off, mate, or you're going in the trough."

James eyed the water trough sitting by the stables. It would be cold. He did not want to go in there. He could hear his mother telling him to take a deep breath and count to ten, ruffling his red hair, a constant reminder of his temper. He was fairly sure he'd have to count to ten thousand before he'd feel calm again.

Petros let him go when they got to their tent, but wouldn't let him leave.

"You go then," he told Petros. "Just go check on the princess. Make sure she's all right. Anything could've happened while that dumb shit slept."

His friend considered this, then stepped outside the tent. He borrowed a sentry's radio; apparently he didn't trust James to keep his word and stay put. After a brief conversation, he ducked back inside.

"All right, here's the scoop: The princess is fine. She didn't even wake. She—"

"What if she was poisoned?"

Petros held up his hands. "She's not poisoned, mate. She's fine."

"She's my responsibility, I'd better go see." He stood up, and Petros pushed him back down.

"She's all of our responsibility, and she's awake now. Everything is fine." He paused. "Amendment: everything is fine unless you are Private Tracy, and you're now the proud owner of a broken nose."

"He deserves more. He deserves a hundred."

Petros snickered. "Don't think that's possible, mate."

James put his head in his hands and threaded his fingers into his hair.

"Do you need treatment for your hand?"

"My what?"

Petros gestured to his right hand, and he put it out in front of him. "The pain must be swimming upstream against the alcohol."

"If I go get ice, will you stay here?"

James nodded. By the time Petros came back, he'd passed out on his bunk, still in his fatigues.

AS IF THE VOMITING and pounding headache weren't enough, Arron James also woke to a summons from his commanding officer. Wincing, he quickly washed the booze-scented sweat off and changed his clothes. He crossed the camp, flexing his sore hand; his knuckles had turned a nice shade of purple overnight. Colonel Weathers was already in his office. Tracy sat across from him.

"You wanted to see me, sir?"

"Sit, Lieutenant." James sat next to Tracy, ignoring him completely. "You want to tell me what happened last night?"

"Yes, sir. Sergeant Graeham, Sergeant Petros, and I were on our way back from town around 0100."

"Intoxicated." It wasn't a question.

"Yes, sir. I noticed that Private Tracy was asleep at his post guarding Dr. Broward's tent. I woke him up."

"With a fist to the face?"

"Yes, sir."

"Woz-condemn-it, Lieutenant. There's a chain of command for this kind of thing. You can't just go around busting open the faces of junior soldiers." He leaned forward. "I realize that you're used to a certain amount of latitude because of your friendship with His Majesty, but this kind of behavior isn't going to fly with me. I'm aware of your record: this isn't the first time you've solved problems with your fists. The only reason your ass isn't on a transport back to Orangiers tonight is that you acted in the princess's best interest, but you need to get your shit together."

James nodded and immediately regretted it; the pain was terrible. He wished he felt guilty about what he'd done, wished he could show contrition on his face . . . but it wasn't there. He was so angry, and his flare-ups had been worse lately. The duke's demands weren't helping his already hair-triggered temper, nor were his mother's lies of omission. And he was angry with Lincoln, angry he'd been shot trying to capture him. Angry he hadn't seen it coming.

The colonel turned to Tracy. "You fall asleep again, and I'll have you court-martialed."

"Yes, sir," Tracy said, sitting up straighter. "It won't happen again."

"You're both on desk duty until further notice. Report to Reese at 0900."

They both saluted and exited the tent. Just outside, James grabbed Tracy by the arm.

"Forget the court-martial; you'd better pray Edward never finds out you fell asleep while guarding his sister. You're never subbing for my team again."

Tracy shook him off and stormed toward the mess hall. Chance sidled up next to him.

"So," he said.

"Don't start," James groaned, massaging his temples.

"Think I have to, actually. You still don't know who you assaulted last night."

James started toward the mess hall, and Chance followed. He waited until James had food in front of him before he continued.

"That's no lowly private you struck in your booze-fueled wrath last night. That's Patrick Tracy, the Duke of Lower Rivermoor's nephew. He's set to inherit a boatload in a few years, but the duke felt he needed to toughen up, serve our country first. This is his first tour."

"And it's going to be his last tour if he doesn't figure out how things are around here."

"You don't need some duke coming after you for abusing his successor. You need to let this go."

James stabbed at his eggs with more force than the task required. *No worries, mate, I've got a duke in my corner as well.*

"I hadn't gotten the memo that he was here for toughening up; here I was, tenderizing him. I'll try to change my tactics."

CHAPTER FIFTEEN

"LIEUTENANT JAMES, I require your assistance."

James looked up from his punishment paperwork. He'd been slogging away at it for several hours, and he'd barely made a dent in it. Why in the world did the government need so much pointless information, anyway? But Rhodie could take precedence over anything else . . .

"Of course, Dr. Broward. What can I do for you?"

"I would like to collect more fungus samples. And I would like you to accompany me."

He hesitated . . . Did she know he was in trouble with his CO?

"My commanding officer . . ."

"I have spoken to Colonel Weathers. He agreed to allow you to put off your paperwork until later."

He breathed a sigh of relief, not only for the break, and grinned at her.

"You've broken me out of detention. I'm forever grateful. When do we leave?"

"Immediately. I have water for you. Can you navigate back to those caves you found?"

"Is my hair red?"

"As a fire hydrant."

He suppressed a grin and followed her out, ignoring the dirty look Tracy was shooting him.

"Do you require any special equipment for collection?"

"I shouldn't," she said, her mind obviously elsewhere. "As long we don't ingest them, there's no danger." She glanced at him. "Immature as you are, however, I guess I should never discount the possibility that you'll try to put things in your mouth."

James grinned. "Excellent burn, Dr. Broward. You're learning my ways well. Let me carry that," he said, pulling the pack from her shoulders.

"I'm capable of carrying my supplies, thank you," she said, hauling it back up her shoulders.

"I beg your pardon. I didn't mean to imply you were weak . . ." His eyebrows waggled. "I'd hate for you to over-power me just to prove a point."

Rhodie shook her head slightly as she led the way down the path. "Isn't this what you were reprimanded for?"

He blinked. "Pardon?"

"I asked Colonel Weathers why one of his most capable officers was doing paperwork instead of his regular duties, and he informed me that you'd been reprimanded for con-duct unbecoming an officer . . ." They were walking single file down the narrow path, but she glanced at him over her shoulder. "I assume he disapproves of your casual manner with me."

"Among other things." *She thinks I'm capable? Buried the lede on that one, beautiful.*

"What other things?" Her question was quiet, despite the fact that they were alone.

"It's mostly the flirting. Also, a bit of drinking now and again." *And when the drinking happens, a bit of assault as well. Good thing she's a heavy sleeper.*

"I see." He expected a volley back, a prod of some kind . . . not this disappointed silence. It made the air seem even heavier in the humid undergrowth. Still, he didn't owe her an explanation, and she was likely too polite to ask for one.

"You're not usually an intemperate person."

Classic Rhodie. Just fishing for answers instead of asking . . . "You haven't seen me when Edward cheats at cards. It's rapiers at dawn."

"Edward doesn't cheat."

"He does when he plays strip poker with Abbie . . ."

"I do not wish to hear the details, thank you. This trip has been a welcome respite from that subject." They came to a fork, and she stopped.

"To the right. Do you think they'll tone it down now that they're pregnant?"

"One can only hope. Across the river?"

"That's right."

"Is there a bridge?"

"Unfortunately, there is not. But the rocks are fairly large." He drew up next to her in time to see her eyebrows draw together in thought. "I'd be happy to hold your hand . . ."

"I was sure you would be."

"Or I could always carry you across. You're not heavy."

She let out a sharp laugh. "I would rather build a raft out of fallen limbs than let you carry me."

"And knowing the maritime stock from which you come, I'm sure your craft would be seaworthy, but you'd be expending considerable time and effort that would be better used elsewhere . . . Although, if you name it after me, I'll aid you in your stick collection."

"Incorrigible."

"As ever."

She sniffed. "Take me to the edge of the river and I'll survey the situation from there."

"You're the boss."

"You'd do well to remember."

"Oh, it's never far from my mind, Highness."

"Dr. Broward."

"Sorry, old habit."

She was wearing jeans again. He loved her backside in jeans. If he had his way, she'd never wear those awful pencil skirts again. The woman belonged in cotton. It brought out a softer side of her . . . not that he needed her softness. But it was nice occasionally to feel that she wasn't hiding behind formality, if only on the outside.

"Are your lungs feeling well?"

He cleared his throat. "Yes, I'm fully recovered, as I believe I've mentioned." He paused as she navigated some gnarled roots that bisected the path, ready to reach out to steady her if needed. "But if you wanted to lay your head upon my chest to listen to them, I'd gladly lie down . . ."

"See, there. That's unnecessary. You're just going to get into trouble again."

"Not if you don't tell anyone."

She shook her head. "You're getting the habit, though. You're too familiar with me, too comfortable . . ."

He lowered his voice. "I'm not half as familiar as I'd like to be."

She spun to face him. "Lieutenant, I don't want to see you suffer because of our friendship."

He smiled at her. "Why, Dr. Broward, are you offering to put me out of my misery?"

She tipped back her head to look at the canopy overhead. "Why do I bother?"

"I give up, love. Why?"

"Dr. Broward."

They stopped at the edge of the river, and he put his hands on his hips, lifting his voice to be heard over the rushing water.

"Darling, I've known you for nearly a decade. Do you really want me to call you 'Dr. Broward' when we're in private?"

"We're not *in private*," she said through gritted teeth. "I don't spend time in private with men. That would be highly inappropriate."

"Yes, Woz forbid we do anything inappropriate." He shifted closer to her, and she shuffled backwards to maintain the same amount of space between them. *She doesn't like to be touched, Edward said. I wonder why.*

"Maintain a polite distance, please."

"Is standing close to someone impolite?"

"Of course."

His gaze dropped to her lips. "Even if the closeness is wanted?"

She ignored his question. "Let's see this crossing, then."

He smiled. Her aloofness was so adorable; he'd give her exactly what she asked for . . . "Very well, *Dr. Broward* . . ." He could tell she wanted to glare at him, but she lifted her chin and descended the steep bank to the edge of the river. It wasn't very swift or deep, but it was fairly wide. Someone had placed large flat rocks across it, which could be slippery when wet.

"I'll take the pack and walk alongside you in the water as you go across on the rocks in case you require my assistance."

"That's not necessary."

"In this case, it's not negotiable, I'm afraid. If you want to see the cave, we're doing this my way. I'm already on thin ice with my CO. I don't need to add 'made the princess a dripping, soggy mess' to my list of offenses."

"Very well." She removed her pack, and he sat down to take off his boots and roll up his pants. He could feel her displeased gaze on him, and he smiled.

"I'd like to see you truly angry someday. I bet it's epic."

"Oh, I'm sure you'd love that. You seem to live to antagonize."

"Tease maybe," he said, looking up, "but not antagonize. I rather prefer to style myself as the hero."

He stepped into the water and regretted this plan immediately. The water was remarkably cold for such a tropical climate, and he had to clamp his mouth shut to keep from making loud, ridiculous noises, lest she know he was uncomfortable. *There's no other way,* he thought. *She'll slip and fall on her backside if I'm not next to her, proud creature that she is.* The rocks underwater were slimier as well, and he found himself sliding his feet along the uneven bottom, as if he were on ice, lacking the desired traction. He kept his eyes on her, but wasn't at all sure that he could keep her from falling without losing his own balance if she slipped. It wasn't long before the situation was tested: the stones were a bit too far apart, even for her long legs, and she had to take a bit of a leap to get to the next one. Her arms windmilled, and she tipped back on her heels precariously. In the split second he had to help her, he managed to get his hands on her hips and shift her center of gravity farther forward again.

She made a little grunt of acceptance, then pushed his hands away without so much as a 'thank you.' Not that it surprised him; they'd had to train Edward to thank them for things as well. It wasn't that they were an ungrateful bunch; they just assumed people wanted to help them and therefore did not require acknowledgment.

They were most of the way across when a large parrot suddenly took flight from the canopy and his focus slipped . . . and then so did his foot. His right foot shot forward and wedged against a bigger rock, leaving him doing an awkward split, mere inches from the water. He flailed about, avoiding knocking into her so she wouldn't fall, too, surprise seizing him when a strong hand grasped his and stabilized him. Rhodie looked down at him, her eyes wide, her arms straining to keep him from toppling, even as her boots fishtailed on the wet rocks.

"Just let me fall," he said, raising his voice over the rushing water, afraid to pull away, lest he pull her into the river with him.

"Nonsense," she said, and kneeling carefully on the rock, she reached down to grasp his elbow and haul him back onto his feet, a look of smug triumph on her face.

"Rhodie," he growled. "You should've just let me go. When you're under my official protection, you're obligated to obey my orders, and there's no sense in risking yourself for a pair of wet trousers—"

"And what if you'd hit your head on the way down and fallen unconscious? What protection would you be providing me then? It was the logical thing to do." She continued to step lightly across her rock path, her arms out for balance, calling over her shoulder, "And it's Dr. Broward."

He scrambled to follow her, sloshing through the water, irritated that she'd risked falling in and thrilled that she'd broken her touch rules to do so.

They traversed the rest of the distance to the cave in relative silence apart from directions, and he ducked inside to check for any potential security issues before he gave her the all clear. She spread out her sheet and ordered her sample bags as he strolled to the back of the cave, peering into the dark. There were some markings on the wall that looked quite old, and he pulled out his camera to take a picture. Perhaps there were some indigenous peoples who'd used this cave in the past. How far back did it go, anyway? Some of these caves led to water, he knew. He heard her busily scraping away at the rock and turned to find her kneeling on the sheet, her backside high in the air, labeling her sample in her neat cursive.

James looked away. *A jester would make a joke, but the knight would look away.* He kicked a rock down the cave to see how far it bounced. As it bounced away, something shifted behind a rock. His hand went to his machete.

"Rhodie . . ."

"Dr. Broward. Yes?"

"Stand up and back away slowly."

CHAPTER SIXTEEN

"BACK AWAY?" RHODIE asked. "Why?"

"There's a snake."

She sat up, squinting into the darker part of the cave. "Where?"

"Behind that rock. I think it's *Epicrates striatus*, which isn't poisonous, but I'd prefer to check it out without you standing four feet away."

She peered around him. "I can check it out." She'd been hoping for the chance to see one up close; she'd heard that they sometimes carried an interesting microbe that repelled Veil sensitivity, acting in symbiosis with the snake's body. Researchers still hadn't figured out how the microbe benefitted from the arrangement.

"No." His voice was firm.

She dusted off her hands, getting to her feet. "I'm the biology expert here, soldier. I'm more likely to get an accurate identification."

He caught her by the arm before she could pass him. "Dr. Broward, is this why you asked me to come with you? Because you think you can disregard my orders on the basis of our friendship?"

"Your orders happen to be unnecessarily overprotective." She tried to pull her arm from his grip, but he wouldn't allow it. *Ugh. I guess we are in a cave, perhaps the caveman act is appropriate . . .*

"That's your opinion, Dr. Broward. And you are welcome to file a complaint with Weathers when we get back to camp about how I wouldn't let you pet the snake."

Her temper flared. "I do not appreciate the patronizing insinuation—"

"And I want to hear all about how much you don't appreciate it—outside."

"Look." Her gaze was over his shoulder, and he turned. The snake was emerging from behind the rock slowly, and James turned to put Rhodie more behind him.

"Stay calm," he whispered.

"I am calm," she whispered back, trying to keep the humor from her voice. "Are you calm?"

"I'll be calm once you're outside." He began to back away from the reptile, pushing her along with him.

"Look how long it is," she said, pointing over his shoulder. "It must be six feet. All the other varieties are smaller. It must be the boa. It won't harm us."

"You can't be sure."

He was sweating profusely, and the loud, crinkly sound of his feet against the tarp made him jump.

"Please watch your step around my specimens," she said, as if she were advising him that a tile floor was wet.

"Your specimens are kind of the least of our problems right now, Your Highness."

"Lieutenant, you are being ridiculous. There are no poisonous snakes here," she chided.

"I just don't like them, all right? Now we're leaving!" He spun around and caught her around the waist, propelling her outside. She collapsed onto the ground with a log at her back, laughing. He stood watching her, shaking his head, hands on his hips.

"I've thought up thousands of jokes for you over the years, and *this* is what finally amuses you? My ophidiophobia?" She just laughed harder, wiping tears from her eyes.

"I think you'll find it a very common fear amongst those who aren't certifiably insane nature types. And if you aren't careful, you're going to find yourself walking back to camp by yourself, lady." She knew he was genuinely peeved . . . She should stop. But she couldn't.

"Your face," she said, gasping for breath, pointing at him. "Your face was classic."

"Rhododendron Elizabeth Jennifer Jane Ainsley Broward, quit laughing at me or I'll tell your mother."

That did it. She stopped laughing abruptly. "Did you say my mother or my brother?"

He folded his arms. "Which one scares you more?"

She thought for a moment, then slowly got to her feet. "My mother, I suppose."

"For goodness' sake, you're all dirty now," he said, brushing off her back. "Are you all right?" His touch, which had not bothered her whatsoever inside the cave, suddenly felt unwelcome when meant to correct her.

"Yes, I'm fine," she said, sidestepping away from him.

"Right. I'll just go get your things, and then we can leave."

"I'm not finished, Lieutenant."

"You can't be serious," he groaned.

She gestured toward the cave. "Look, your fearsome creature's gone back to bed. If you cease kicking rocks at him,

I'm sure he'll be happy to snooze away the hot afternoon under that stone while I scrape fungi from the walls of his cave." She patted him on the shoulder as she headed back inside. "You can keep watch in case he starts to move again."

"You've got twenty minutes."

"I need an hour."

"Then we can come back tomorrow. I'm serious, Rho—Dr. Broward."

Her eyes narrowed. "A compromise, then. Forty minutes."

He sighed. "Fine."

She gave him a small smile that felt at odds with her earlier out-of-control belly laughter. "Shall I call my friend Sienna to devise an impromptu immersion therapy?"

"No, thank you," he muttered, kicking the ground.

"Shall I hold your hand?" She had meant it to be mocking, but it came out too gently for that, and she felt her face heat as he considered his answer.

He gazed into her eyes, the twinkle of mischief in them unmistakable. "I think it would help, yes."

Time to back pedal. "Unfortunately, I need both hands free to do my work. What a pity."

"Tease," he said, strolling closer.

Uh-oh. He wasn't deterred. "Scaredy-cat."

James crossed his arms. "That's quite a thing to call a recipient of the King's Medal for Patriotism."

"Good thing the enemy didn't employ any reptiles . . . We'd have lost the Brothers' War for sure."

His mouth hardened into a line, and she knew she'd gone too far. James stomped in the woods near the mouth of

the cave and pulled a long stick out of the underbrush, hastily ripping off the vines that clung to it as Rhodie watched
him.

"What are you doing, Lieutenant?"

"Evicting the tenant so you can stay as long as you like."

"You're going to remove a six-foot long snake with a
stick?"

"You, the expert, said it isn't poisonous. You, the expert,
said I have nothing to fear . . ." He marched back into the
cave, looking not half as confident as he had when he'd
marched out of it, and she hurried to follow him.

"That doesn't mean it won't hurt like Jersey if it bites you
. . ."

To her annoyance, he ignored her caveat. "You, the expert, said it poses no danger. So I'm just going to remove the
damn thing." He edged toward the spot where the snake had
disappeared, his hands visibly trembling; if he stabbed the
cursed thing instead of scooping it, she didn't know what it
would do. Rhodie scrambled internally for a way out of this
that didn't sacrifice his pride.

"Well, speaking of danger, one thing I didn't take into
consideration was magical intervention," she said. She made
her voice soft. He turned in surprise when her hand touched
his shoulder, and she felt her own surprise at how easy it was.
James wiped more sweat from his brow; it was pouring off
him like his sweat glands had suddenly somehow doubled.

"Wh-what do you m-mean?" he asked, leaning against
the opposite wall of the cave—probably to keep upright, if
she had to guess.

"Well, it's conceivable that someone enchanted that snake, gave it attributes that it would not normally possess, such as a cursed bite."

James was nodding, his breathing slowing somewhat. "That sounds logical."

"So why don't we just leave the snake alone? You can keep an eye on it while I work near the mouth of the cave, and if it comes any closer or shows any interest in us, we'll leave right away. Agreed?"

He nodded again, flexing his jaw. He dropped the stick and ran a hand through his hair; it was as soaked as if someone had dumped a bucket of water over his head.

"Would you care for some water?"

He chuckled wryly. "I think I'd better, or I'm liable to get severely dehydrated."

"Who would help me back across the river?"

"If I'm already drenched, I can't see how I could do any worse."

He took a long drink from the insulated canteen she passed him, and she felt him avoiding eye contact with her. So she stared at him, wondering how she could bring up this extreme reaction. She'd noticed that he wasn't himself lately. On the outside, he was happy-go-lucky, but she wasn't sure it wasn't compensating for something. He seemed . . . broody? Nervous? They were all classic signs of PTSD. Given his shooting, it wouldn't be surprising if a foreign forest situation was bringing all those memories back.

"Better?"

"Oh, yes," he quipped, "having to pause for a princess to pity you is the epitome of manhood."

It was on the tip of her tongue to ask him, but she opted for honesty instead. "That's quite the tongue twister. And I don't pity you, I feel chagrined that I teased you. I apologize, Lieutenant."

"That's all right. Don't worry about it." He handed back the canteen. "Woz knows I've teased you often enough."

She tapped her chin thoughtfully. "True. I seem to re-member seaweed on my shoulder one summer that you thoughtfully put there for me."

"Well," he said, wiping his brow again, sliding to the ground. "Younger me had just heard wonders about what it can do for your skin. I didn't want to deprive you of that ad-vantage."

"I'm so lucky to have you about, Lieutenant," she said, smiling, as she began to sort her samples again.

As they wove their way back through the humid forest, Rhodie took them on a detour to Yautia's home; she had a gift for the woman, and they were leaving soon, moving on. Her concrete house, painted in bright tropical hues, each block a different color, came into view between the wide palm trees.

"Hello?" Rhodie called at the edge of the yard.

The woman's face appeared in the open doorway, smil-ing. "Doctor. You're leaving? Come in," she said, gesturing for them to open the low wooden gate at the edge of the property.

"Yes, day after tomorrow. I just wanted to give you this," she said, holding out the book. "It's a field guide to Orang-iers, to inspire you to come visit us someday. I would love to repay you the kindness you've shown us."

Yautia's smile grew as she paged through the book. "Thank you. I would like to keep in touch."

"You'd better," Rhodie teased. "I want to see my castle grounds through the lens of those magic tea leaves. Are you sure you won't come with us to the next location?"

"No, my home is here." Yautia's hug was firm, unexpected, and Rhodie heard James take a breath to correct her when she let go.

"And you, Lieutenant. Take good care of your charge. She will need you before her visit to Trella is finished."

"What?" His tone was sharp, and his gaze even sharper. "What does that mean?"

Yautia shrugged. "You'll see."

CHAPTER SEVENTEEN

THE DAY THEY LEFT THE first base camp, James got a phone call.

"Lieutenant James?"

"Yes?" James held the phone with his shoulder as he buttoned his navy-blue uniform shirt, in a hurry to get everything packed and on the wagons.

"My name is Hilda Graves, and I'm your father's private secretary."

"I haven't got a father." It came out without a second thought; he'd been telling people that for so long, it didn't register as a lie until it left his mouth.

The woman cleared her throat uncomfortably. "This is Arrondale Percival James, correct? Born the thirtieth day of Eleventh Month in the year 495? Child of Aideen Charity James?"

"Yes, sorry, that's me. I didn't . . . that's me. What can I do for you, Mrs. Graves?"

There was an annoyed pause before the woman went on. "His Grace would like to know when you're coming to the manor house to transfer the title."

"I'm out of the country at the moment on a three-month expedition, so I'm afraid that won't be possible for quite some time."

"I see. When do you return?"

"I'll have to check my calendar. I believe it's sometime around the fifteenth of Fourth Month."

"Then we'll expect you the sixteenth."

"Mrs. Graves," he said, scratching at his suddenly itchy scalp, "I'm afraid I don't . . ."

"You don't what, young man?"

"That's the thing, you see. I haven't decided whether or not I'm going to accept . . . what's being offered to me."

"I see."

He was all too aware that he might have an audience he didn't realize was listening, so he tried to ask the question that had been burning his mind since that Saturday morning when the courier showed up. "If I chose not to . . . sign, who does the . . . thing pass to?"

"If you choose to reject your birthright, the duke's holdings will be auctioned to benefit the foundation." She spit out the word *auctioned* like it was Marmite. "And one of the oldest family lines in the country will be broken. If you don't mind me saying so, young man, that would be a tragedy."

"And if you don't mind *me* saying so, compared with the extinction of the blue whale, the fifty-year-high rates of homelessness, and increased substance abuse amongst adolescents fifteen and under, it doesn't seem like a *tragedy* to me. Of course, considering every fifteen-year-old I've ever met lies on those surveys to entertain themselves, I'm not sure how accurate that information really is."

"To each his own." The woman's voice was frosty, and it reminded him why he didn't want to spend time with these people. Why he'd rather go down to the pub and throw darts any given night with Chance and Petros than put up with their insufferable condescension.

"Was there anything else, Mrs. Graves?"

"No, Lieutenant. Have a nice day, and we'll see you on the sixteenth."

She hung up without waiting for him to confirm the appointment.

"Who was that?" Chance asked. "You look like someone just spit in your supper."

"Telemarketer," he muttered, stalking out into the yard.

Chance paused for a moment before calling after him. "What did the telemarketer want to talk about blue whales for?"

CHAPTER EIGHTEEN

IT WAS NEARLY 2100, and Rhodie had just finished settling into her second temporary home of the voyage. The new location had the added bonus of a large lodge, built in the style of a log cabin, with several floors of private rooms. The bathroom down the hall was still shared, but she was happy to have a door again, and being on the second floor gave her a lovely view of the ocean. Apparently, this was some sort of failed resort, which afforded them kitchens and even a cabin for her lab—an old arts-and-crafts demonstration room. She hadn't asked how Weathers had found this place, but she was impressed.

Rhodie was doing some reading about fungal colonies in Unveiled countries for context for the samples she'd collected with James when her phone rang; the colonies were growing nicely for her in the lab. She was hoping she could keep them alive long enough to bring them back to Orangiers. She reached for the phone without pausing her studying.

"Hello?"

"Dr. Broward," Edward said.

"Second Brother." Rhodie propped the phone against the shelf built into the desk and waited for him to continue, but he didn't. "Why's your video off?"

"I don't . . . I can't do video right now. How are you?"

"I'm adequate. I found an interesting species of orchid today that I'm excited about. Lieutenant James carried my samples, so I'm not as worn out. I didn't realize trudging through the jungle was going to be so taxing. It's the heat more than the trudging, really."

"Rhodie." There was something in his tone she couldn't read. She put down her book.

"What is it, what's wrong?"

"Are you alone?"

"As ever," she said flippantly.

"Are you sitting down?"

It's the middle of the night there. Why is he calling so late? "Edward, you're worrying me . . ."

"We lost the baby, love."

Although Rhodie had never given nor received such news as a physician, she lunged immediately for her medical persona. "Is Abbie spotting? That's common at the beginning of a pregnancy, so I wouldn't necessarily—"

"Spotting was last week, then cramping. The ultrasound revealed that her heart was inadequately sized."

Her insides were trembling. *Detachment,* she told herself. *Stay detached.* Trouble was that her heart wanted engagement and her mind wanted detachment. Their desires, being polarized, had been magnetized, their opposition creating an attraction that Rhodie could barely fight. And if they touched . . . if they touched, she knew her heart would win out.

"Her?" Her own voice sounded faint.

"Yes. The baby was a girl. Abbie had a D&C this morning."

My lovely sister-in-law had surgery, and I wasn't there. My dear brother lost his baby, and I wasn't there. She pushed the feelings away harder and fought to stay in her mind.

"How's she recovering?"

"Physically, she's fine. Just tired. Emotionally, she's . . . not fine. Nor am I."

Calm, soothing words. That's what she wanted to say. Helpful, older sister wisdom about how these things happen and we must just keep on and this was probably for the best if she wasn't healthy. But her gaze drifted to her trunk, to the tiny yellow onesie hidden there at the bottom, and just like that, her mind and heart snapped into contact.

"Oh, Edward," she said, her eyes filling with tears. "I'm so sorry, love. I'm just so, so sorry."

"Thanks." She could hear him snuffling, his breathing shaky. *That's why he didn't want video. He didn't want me to see him cry. I wouldn't have shamed him.*

"Is there anything . . ." She swallowed down the catch in her voice. "Anything I can do?"

"No."

"Do you want me to come home?"

"No, I just wanted you to know. I knew you'd . . . want to know."

"Yes, I did. Thank you for calling."

"You're welcome." He paused, and she took a breath to ask him if he was going to take some time off work when he spoke. "I have to go," he said, his voice unsteady.

"All right. Yes. We'll speak again soon. Please kiss Abbie for me and tell her I'm thinking of her."

"I will." He rang off without saying goodbye.

Rhodie wiped her tears and stood up, moving to her dresser. She pulled out her exercise wear and changed. *If I don't get out of here, I'm going to lose it and everyone's going to hear.* With shaking hands, she tied her shoes and whipped her door open. The last person she wanted to see right then, Arron James, stood there in sweat-stained workout clothes, apparently in conversation with her night guard.

"Is everything all right, Dr. Broward?" His eyes were narrowed, suspicious.

She nodded curtly, then turned toward the stairs.

"Dr. Broward, you can't go out without an escort."

She pivoted to give them her profile. "Fine. Come, night guard, let's go."

"His name is Petros, as you well know, and he's not appropriately attired for running. I'll go with you."

"No, thank you. Come, night guard."

"Rhodie . . ."

She turned and descended the stairs.

"Rhodie, wait."

She strode out the front door, ignoring him completely. He fell into stride next to her within feet of the front steps.

"Don't run next to me."

"You'd rather I run behind you? Come to think of it, the view is better back there . . ."

"Don't speak, Lieutenant."

"Fine, it's your run, have it your way. I can run silently. I can enjoy the sunset and the quiet and the . . ."

"Lieutenant."

"Sorry." He was pouting and were she less irritated, it would've been endearing.

She made for the beach; the sun was still lingering in the west, and it edged the waves in gold. *My niece. I could've brought her to the ocean. We would've made castles for her to rule. I could've taught Abbie how to twist her dreads if she took after Edward . . .*

"Stop it," Rhodie whispered aloud.

"Pardon?"

"I'm not talking to you."

"Ah. Forgive me for assuming such nonsense, as I'm the only one here."

Rhodie chuckled, but it tripped and got caught up with a sob. James turned toward her sharply.

"Are you having a medical event?"

"A medical event?" she asked, exasperated. "What's a medical event?"

"Less than an emergency, more than an incident. I'm not prepared to deal with medical events."

"Well, that's fine, because I'm not having one," she panted, swiping at her face. *My niece. Maybe she'd have had Abbie's blue eyes and Edward's dark skin. Maybe she'd have had those cute rolls babies get on their thighs. Maybe she'd have giggled when I kissed her belly, called me Aunt Rho. Maybe . . .*

Tears were blurring her vision, and Rhodie swiped at them, bumping James in the process. "Give me some space, will you?"

"Sorry." He grapevined over five feet and yelled, "Is this better? I'm on another continent now. Undiscovered, perhaps. It's lovely here, do be sure to visit me in my new home."

Arron would've played with her, too. Kicked a football on the south lawn, swung her around by her ankles like a wild man. A new thought seized her. *Does he know? Edward will tell him soon, assuredly . . .*

James's phone rang once, twice, three times.

"Aren't you going to answer that?" she called.

"Negative."

"Why not?"

"I can't run and talk."

"You're doing so right now . . ."

"That's different," he said, closing the space between them again. "You don't mind if I'm a bit breathless, which is good because in the presence of your intelligence, grace, and wit, it's a constant."

"You should see who it was."

He blinked at her. "Pardon?"

"See who it was."

She stopped, hands on her knees, and he circled back to her, pulling the phone out of his pocket.

"It was Edward."

"Call him."

"Why?"

She looked into his eyes, knowing all her pain was evident. "Arron, just do it."

His phone plinked. "He's left a message."

Rhodie's heart squeezed painfully. "Please, don't put it on speaker—"

"James, it's Edward," her brother's voice came from the phone. "There's no easy way to say this, mate, but we've lost the baby. I just wanted to let you—" He ended the message, cursing softly. James stared at the phone for several moments, his chest still heaving, then he held it out to her.

"Would you take that, please?"

She did so, watching him warily. "Why?"

"Because if I throw it into the ocean, I'll have to pay to replace it." He paced, locking his hands behind his head. "Are we still running?"

"Do you still want to?"

He nodded, not really looking at her. She started back down the beach at half speed, picking up the pace as her breath came back. Their matched footfalls on the packed sand made an almost crunching sound. He wasn't looking at her anymore; he stared down the beach.

"Not fair," he muttered.

She glanced at his profile. "No, it isn't."

"Do you need to go home, to be with them?"

"He didn't want me to."

"You could anyway. He probably doesn't know what he needs right now."

"Arron." He looked at her. "Why don't you call him?"

"He's probably calling Saint and Simonson."

"I'm sure he'd like to hear from you."

He shook his head. "I wouldn't know what to say. I'm sure to get it wrong."

"Just say that you're sorry. That's what I did."

"I am sorry," he said, his voice cracking. "I'm very sorry."

"Arron . . ."

He cleared his throat. "Stop calling me that."

She slowed to a stop. "I'm not teasing you, I'm being sincere."

"I know, but you're making my eyes water, and I'm supposed to be scanning the horizon for assassins."

She huffed a laugh. "I'm not tender."

"If you truly think that, then I wish we could switch places so you can hear how my name sounds when you say it."

"How does it sound?"

"Like you hurt for me. Like you care too much." He turned his head to give her his profile. "I'm sorry, I can't . . . I'm not fit for duty right now. I'll call you a replacement guard." He held out his hand, and she realized he wanted his phone back. As much as she didn't want him witnessing her tangled emotions, he was the safest option. She certainly didn't want a stranger witnessing them.

She crossed her arms. "How do I know you won't throw it into the ocean? I can't be financially responsible."

His eyes narrowed. "Give it, Rhodie."

She shook her head. "I don't think so."

He dug the heels of his hands into his eyes and chuckled.

"Are you crying?" She was horrified. Yes, she hated her own tears, had been running from them, but she was trying to tease him, make him laugh. Not cry. Never cry.

"It's been a really terrible day, all right?" He said, turning away, his voice torn away by the wind. He wiped his eyes on his shoulders one at a time. "Can we just go back? I'll get it together. I'm sorry."

She wished Edward were here. He was the hugger. Not her. She tried to remain professional and clinical when it came to her body, and hugging fell firmly into the emotional category. But looking at his reddened eyes, the way his mouth quirked and twisted, his heaving chest, his hands obstinately on his hips as if he could ward off tears by looking tough . . . she had to do *something*.

Hesitantly, Rhodie threaded her arms through his, caught him around the waist and brought her cheek to his shoulder. He was a little sweaty, but warm. He smelled like salt and that cologne he always wore, with a hint of citrus. She closed her eyes and squeezed him. That's when it occurred to her that he wasn't hugging her back. His arms had gone out to his sides, hands held high, as if he were being arrested.

"What on earth are you doing?"

"Edward said . . . Edward said you don't like to be touched."

"I don't. But I think I can make an exception for my niece's passing."

His arms lowered until they rested on her upper back. "Niece?" he whispered. "It was a girl?"

She nodded, and her tears would be held in no longer. "She would've been beautiful, don't you think?"

She felt him nod, and he held her more fully, enveloping her in his strength. She shivered.

"Are you cold?" He pivoted them so his back was to the wind, bringing up one hand to her neck to tuck her closer into his, and she stared unseeing at the cloud of freckles on the back of his neck. They stood there, listening to the music of the waves, holding each other, neither acknowledging the tears streaming down their faces until the sun dipped below the horizon.

"For someone who supposedly has little experience, you're alarmingly good at that."

She lifted her head. "At what?"

"Comforting." He shook his head. "But I should've known, because you excel at everything."

She smiled. "I imagine I'm a terrible kisser."

"Oh?" Even in the twilight, she could see his eyes light mischievously. "I'm sorry, but all evidence is to the contrary. I simply don't believe you." His eyes were teasing, warm. "Unless you'd like to offer proof . . ."

"You'd like that, wouldn't you," she said dryly, and he gave a small chuckle.

"Yes, I would." He paused. "If you're terrible, I wouldn't tell anyone." Then he leaned closer, brushing his nose against her earlobe, and his voice dropped to a whisper. "I would tell *everyone.*"

She buried her face in his neck, shaking with laughter. *I love this guy.* She didn't analyze the thought. Her heart was too raw, and he was a balm. She pulled back to see his face, wiping the tears off her cheeks. She took a deep breath, intending to step away from his warmth, collect herself. But his right hand was still on the back of her neck, cradling her, and he began to draw her forward, his expression curious. Her eyes widened, but she didn't stop him.

"Rhodie, may I . . ."

She nodded faintly. *He was just kidding, he won't tell anyone. I'm nearly twenty-six years old, for Woz's sake. I can do this. I can totally . . .*

The moment his lips touched hers, something clicked. It was like someone had pulled the chain on the light bulb of her overactive mind, and it went out. Exited stage right. Left the building. She thought she wasn't sure what to do before they began, yet her fingers were threading through his soft hair, and she was parting her lips to his tongue's polite bid for entry. Even then, he kept it light, teasing, playful—just like him. Even the wind seemed to be playing with them, ruffling their hair, lifting the edges of their clothes. He didn't move his hands at all, just held her still as he explored her mouth, sucking, teasing, licking, never straying from her lips. He pulled back a little, and she somewhat frantically grabbed the front of his shirt to keep him there. He smiled as he came closer and kissed her again. *We both have money enough. We don't need to work. He can just go ahead and do this forever as far as I'm concerned.*

"See," he said, nudging her nose with his, "I knew you were a degenerate liar." She smiled and pulled him back toward her, but he held himself away, grinning, resting his hands on her shoulders. "I know, darling. I'm irresistible, but you must try." He slid his hand down her arm and intertwined their fingers as he led them back down the beach toward the camp. They were well out of sight of the rest, so she let him. Something had shifted, after all.

"We should send them flowers," he said. "Edward and Abbie."

"That's a nice idea," she said, sobering a little. "Do you want to split them?"

His grin was blinding. "Dr. Broward wants her name right next to mine. I knew it."

Rhodie rolled her eyes, but she grinned, too.

CHAPTER NINETEEN

JAMES NEEDED A MINUTE. He sat in the lodge's main-floor bathroom on the edge of the tub, his head in his hands. Unlike Rhodie's mind, before their lips even touched, his mind had started racing and hadn't yet stopped.

She's not stopping me. Holy Jersey, she's not stopping me. Don't freak out.

Am I really doing this? Are we really doing this?

Her first kiss. She's giving me her first kiss. Right this minute.

Damn it, I already wanted to be her first and last everything, but now . . .

Does she like it?

Good thing we're out here and not in my room, or I'd be tempted to comfort her like crazy right now . . .

Am I a bastard for using her niece's death like this?

Don't maul her, James. Just keep your hands still.

What if she's teasing me? What if this is the only chance I get to be close to her?

Does she like it? Is she happy? I should pull back just a bit and see . . .

Oh, the princess wants more, does she? Yes, ma'am.

Woz, her lips are soft.

I wonder if she'd go swimming in the ocean with me . . . without swimming attire.

Uh-oh.

This line of thinking can't happen right now.

Nope, shut it down.
Shut it down, James.
SHUT IT DOWN.

The lower half of his body had not been getting his brain's messages whatsoever, and since he didn't want to complicate matters, he'd slowed things down, made a joke, changed the subject. Or changed it back, rather. Guilt, grief and joy were swimming around together in his head. Would Edward be angry? He'd made it clear that he expected him to behave himself . . . Maybe he should've asked more questions about what that meant, exactly. Would she tell him? They were very close . . . Damn. *It was totally consensual. I'm sure of that, I didn't manipulate her . . . did I? She was feeling pretty emotional. She'd seemed okay when I dropped her off at her room, a little quiet, maybe. Maybe I should make sure everything is okay between us tomorrow.*

This was no blind date, no random make-out session. His dream woman, his Supergirl, she had to be 100 percent okay with this—1,000 percent.

He'd started stripping off his clothes to shower when his phone plinked.

Dr. Broward: Thanks for letting me comfort you.

He stared at the phone. *Write back, you idiot! Time is lapsing!*

Lt. James: Pleasure was all mine.

That wasn't enough. Was she saying that it was just because of the miscarriage? What if she doesn't want more? *Want to comfort me again tomorrow?* No, too gross. *Want to bear my children?* Too commitment-oriented. *Want to try another first with me?* Ugh. He finally settled on attempting to be alone with her regularly . . .

Lt. James: I'm always up for an evening workout if you want company.

Good, that's good. Polite, shows interest, a chaste, joint activity. . .

Dr. Broward: I'll keep that in mind.

What? What does THAT mean?

This relationship is going to kill me.

JAMES RELIEVED PETROS the next morning at 0800. "Quiet night?"

"Mostly."

James narrowed his gaze. "Meaning?"

"Meaning there was a fair amount of video chatting after you dropped her off. Hard not to overhear that."

The momentary delight he'd felt to know that she was excited about what had happened between them the previous night was swamped immediately by fear. "Listen, mate, you can't say anything . . ."

"I'm not you."

"Strange, that's exactly what Sam said the last time I confided in him."

Petros snorted. "Not a coincidence. I'm going to eat."

"All right. Thanks, mate. Sleep well."

If she'd been crying, he probably wouldn't have heard her. It could be either. As soon as he was gone, James knocked softly on her door.

"Yes?"

"Just wanted to let you know I was here," he said through the teak. "I can take you to breakfast or order it for you whenever you like."

"Come in, please."

He hesitated. Was he getting the brush-off already? He wasn't ready for that.

"Lieutenant? Are you there?"

"Yes, I'm . . . here."

"Well?" *No, she doesn't like to kept waiting, does she?* He slowly put his hand to the door and pushed it open. *Be the knight, be the knight.* Rhodie sat at her desk with her glasses off, computer open, books and papers fanned out next to her, rolling one of her dreads between her fingers.

"Could you assist me, please?"

"With what?"

"My hair."

He stared at her for a long moment, and she stared back. "You're serious?"

"Of course I'm serious. It seems I have underestimated how easy this would be to do myself. My mother urged me to bring a beautician, but I didn't heed her advice and now regret it, though I would never admit that to her."

James shuffled forward into the room, leaving the door open. Her comb and pomade were scattered on the table with her books and her glasses.

"Are your hands clean?"

He looked down at them. "They appear to be. Mother would've let me come to the table like this."

"Very good. Go ahead."

James felt his cheeks heat. "Dr. Broward, I'm afraid I'm a bit out of my depth here. You're going to have to help me understand what you want."

She tsked at him. "All that time spent with Edward, and you never learned how to care for dreads?"

"What on earth do you think men do when they spend time together? You think I braided his hair for him?"

Rhodie held out her hand, and he slapped it for a low five. She huffed impatiently.

"Give me your hands, please." *What is happening right now?*

"First of all, it isn't braiding, it's technically knotting, and secondly, it's simple enough that I think even you can manage it." She placed a yellow pencil between his hands and held them between hers, rolling it back and forth between his palms. "See that?"

He nodded, desperately trying not to freak out that—*Rhodie Broward is touching me by choice.*

"That motion, that's what I need you to do with your fingers to the dreads on the back of my head where it's hard to reach. Down at the roots, where the loc is too fluffy. Do you see?"

He nodded hesitantly, moving behind her. Poking through her damp hair, he could indeed see what she was talking about, and he picked up one and began to roll it between his hands vigorously.

"Yes, but between your fingers, and less like you're starting a fire, please."

He hufffed a laugh. "Rhodie, I don't think I can do this, I don't know what I'm—"

His princess turned to face him. "You're doing fine," she said softly. "I got a good start on it, I just need you to finish the last few for me. Please? My arms are killing me." Her face glowed with trust (or was that desperation?) as she offered him the comb and pomade, and he sighed. How could he refuse when she actually asked politely?

"Here," she said, "I'll move to the floor, that'll be easier. You can sit on the bed." First he got to put his hands in her hair, and now he was sitting on her bed? It was too much, really. He was positive something was going to go very wrong. If he messed up her hair, it would be eons before she forgave him.

She sat on the dusty wooden floor, and he carefully slipped in behind her, moving the green mosquito netting so he didn't poke a hole in it, letting his knees frame her shoulders. "I apologize that I don't have Viola's soft touch."

"Viola?"

"Yes, Viola. The beautician at Bluffton?" He picked up the next loc. "You don't know her name? That's terrible."

Rhodie shrugged. "'Young lady' usually works well enough."

"So elitist, though. You should learn people's names. You didn't know Petros's name last night, either."

Her shoulders shifted back, and he instantly regretted bringing up last night . . . Maybe it was like ripping off a bandage. Maybe he should just . . . do it. Get it over with.

"So about last night . . ."

"Yes?"

"I hope you didn't feel . . ."

"Yes?" Her tone of voice gave away nothing, and he cursed himself for not starting this conversation when he could actually see her face.

"Manipulated." He paused. "Given that it was a sad situation, I wasn't trying to take advantage, and I apologize if . . ."

"No need."

"No need? To apologize?"

"Correct."

"Oh. Okay. Well, good." She was quiet, and he kept his hands moving. "Did you know there's a waxy substance in your hair?"

She chuckled. "Believe it or not, I did. Believe it or not, it's wax."

"Shocking."

"I know."

They lapsed into silence, and he felt a growing discomfort stirring. *Say something, make small talk. Make big talk, make any talk.*

"Did you sleep well?" *Genius. That'll impress her.*

"In fact, I did. And you?"

He nodded. "I slept fine, thanks." *Lies!* his mind accused. *You tossed and turned the better part of eight hours, worrying that you'd hurt her somehow. LIES. And for what? She seems fine.*

She cleared her throat. "Shall we discuss the day's agenda?"

"Sure, I can multitask. Hardly anyone sees the back of your head anyway."

She ignored his joke. "At ten thirty I have a meeting with Dr. Maikel Martínez from Saint Teresa University. He's coming here to help educate my team about local flora and fauna. Then I will work in the lab from noon to five, then I will come back here to work until eight."

"Meals."

"Pardon?"

"You've neglected to put meals into your busy day, Dr. Broward."

"If there is time, I will take them."

"You may not need them, but I'm a growing boy."

"You're not a boy, you're a man."

"Just a joke, Highness. I don't wish my growling stomach to distract you from your work."

"And then at eight, you will accompany me on my run." He stopped rolling momentarily.

Does she remember that I'm off at eight? Surely she must. Then again, she doesn't remember Petros's name . . . He resumed rolling, trying to play it cool.

"That sounds good."

"Does it?" she asked softly.

"Naturally. Why wouldn't it? Are you implying that something's lacking in my physical fitness? I assure you that I'm in tip-top shape."

"I have no doubt." Rhodie resumed her reading, and when he finished rolling, he quietly excused himself to stand out in the hall, thankful that he'd already eaten.

CHAPTER TWENTY

THE HUMAN BODY HAS over five million sweat glands, she knew, most notably absent inside one's ears, on one's genitals, and on one's lips. As she bent to look into the electron microscope for the umpteenth time today, sweat rolled into her eyes again, stinging them, and she became unconvinced that it was only five million. Sweat was behind her knees, sliding down her back, glistening on the backs of her hands. Sweat wetted her hair. Sweat stained the sleeves of her plain white cotton blouse. And once again, she questioned how people could live in this climate without going insane.

A shadow fell across her lab notebook, and she pivoted. James held out a glass bottle of water with condensation running down it. She took it with a smile and downed most of it before setting it away from her notebook, lest her observations become smudged. He wasn't much better off, especially considering that his fatigues were much better suited to the climate in Orangiers.

"It's time to meet with that doctor," he said quietly.

She checked her phone: 10:28. "Oh. Thank you. I suppose I lost track of time . . ."

"That seems to happen often when you're working, *Dr. Broward.*"

Rhodie gave him a small smile and gathered her supplies. "Good thing I have you around, *Lieutenant.*"

James wouldn't crack a smile, but she knew the comment amused him. She never knew flirting was so . . . easy? It was with him, anyway. He held the door for her, and she spotted Dr. Martínez and gave him a wave. She knew his appearance from the university's website. He crossed the yard with his hand extended.

"Dr. Broward! Welcome to Trella, Your Highness."

When they met in the middle, he grasped her hand as if he wanted to shake it, but then turned it over, pressing a kiss to the back of it. James lifted his chin like he was about to chide the man, but Rhodie gave him a subtle head shake. She could allow for cultural differences; the man was just being friendly, and the rules against touching a royal didn't apply here. James's mouth snapped closed, but a muscle in his jaw was ticking like he was grinding his teeth.

"Thank you for having us, Dr. Martínez. We are thrilled to be able to learn from your expertise."

"You honor us with your presence, Highness." She had sent her standard email about how royal titles were unnecessary, she was sure of it. But if it made him feel better to recognize her lineage, what was it hurting?

"Shall we?" Her assistants had congregated behind her, and she indicated toward the tropical forest with one hand, inviting him to lead the way. Dr. Martínez held out his arm to escort her; with an audience, he left her no choice but to accept, however much the idea of contact with a stranger when she was so sweaty made her skin crawl. She did not embarrass him by showing outward disgust or hesitation, but James must have sensed it. She reached out to accept his offered arm when she heard James's voice behind her.

"I'm sorry, sir," James started, his voice respectful, "but Dr. Broward isn't to be touched unless she initiates it. Standard security protocol for royals."

"Oh, yes," the man said quickly, his face flushed. "I apologize, I do remember that now. It is our way here, we like to welcome our guests, make them feel at home, and we do that with touch, connection. I apologize."

"Are you going to punch him, too?" Joline muttered, and the rest of the assistants around her snickered as James reddened.

"I beg your pardon?" Rhodie said, pivoting to look at her, her gaze cool.

Joline glanced up at her briefly before casting her gaze down. "I apologize, Dr. Broward. It was just a joke. Poor taste. Sorry." Rhodie nodded slowly, and Dr. Martínez led them to the edge of the forest. Her assistants did most of the gathering, so she let them crowd closer to him while she hung back. She could still hear him. And anyway, Joline would likely write up a detailed report later; she had an excellent memory.

But what on earth had she meant by that comment? She glanced at James, who was standing off to the side, listening to the doctor while he scanned the area. She gave him a quick nod, and he came to her side.

"Yes?"

"What was the meaning of that comment earlier?"

"Which one?"

"You know which one, Lieutenant."

He cleared his throat quietly, pivoting to cast his glance around the camp. "There may have been an incident recently when I punched someone."

Shock rendered her momentarily speechless. "Here?"

"Yes."

"You *hit* someone? Under what circumstances?" Apparently, she wasn't controlling her volume as well as she'd thought she was, because three of her assistants turned to look at her before she waved them away.

"The circumstances are irrelevant."

"Well, I'm sure it was just a mistake."

"No, it wasn't." His voice was even, his gaze level. He had no remorse about this whatsoever? How could that be? James could lose his temper more easily than some, and he didn't mind sparring with Edward and his friends, but this?

She clasped her hands behind her back to keep from fidgeting. "Let's discuss this later."

"Yes, ma'am."

It was difficult to focus on the rest of the lecture. Every time she brought her mind back to the topic at hand, it wandered away again like the goats she'd seen around camp. What on earth had possessed him? It was another clear sign that he was dealing with some unresolved issues from his shooting . . . She cursed herself for selfishly allowing him to come along. She should've pushed harder to get his records released to her. She should've made sure. Guilt ate at her that being here was triggering him like that.

Rather than going back to the lab as she'd planned, Rhodie followed her assistants into the jungle to apply what they'd just learned. She turned to James.

"Would you fetch me a water, please?"

His eyes narrowed at the request, but he silently complied. He'd have her in his line of sight the whole time: the pump was near the center of camp. The moment he was out of range, Rhodie sidled up to Joline.

"About your comment earlier . . ."

"I'm sorry, Doctor; I shouldn't have said it."

"No, no, it's fine. I just have no idea what you're talking about. Might you be willing to fill me in?"

Joline's dark eyes widened. "Really?"

Rhodie nodded. "Truly." She had a good rapport with Joline. They often discussed politics and current events and saw eye-to-eye on many things.

"The other night, Lieutenant James gave the man who was guarding your tent a beating. I'm not sure why, I didn't hear the details . . ."

"How did I sleep through *that*?" Rhodie mused, tapping her chin.

"You're lucky," Joline chuckled. "I can't sleep worth a maid's hairpin here."

"Well, I'm sure he had a reason." She sighed. "Thank you, Jo."

"Of course, Dr. Broward." She pursed her lips. "I really do regret my comment. Lieutenant James seems like a good man; I shouldn't have disparaged him. I was just surprised, honestly."

So am I, she thought.

"Your water."

Rhodie and Joline both jumped. James held out a flask, his eyes flashing with silent discontent. Lord, he was quiet;

how long had he been standing there? As she tipped the water into her mouth, she resolved to find out more about this troubling situation—and soon.

CHAPTER TWENTY-ONE

HIS PRINCESS HAD WASTED no time. The minute she'd ordered him away from her, she was turning to her lead assistant, probably getting the skinny on that snarky comment she'd made. *Damn it.* There was no way for him to get her alone without it looking suspicious; she was booked all day. He stewed about it so hard and for so long, he didn't even notice that she'd skipped dinner again. He wasn't hungry anyway. When Petros showed up, he went quickly to change his clothes and came back to go running with her, hoping she hadn't changed her mind.

She was waiting on the tall wooden steps, dreads pulled back, scrolling on her phone.

"Ready?"

She nodded, and he let her set the pace down the dark beach; there was enough moonlight to see their way well enough, but he was still glad she stayed on the wetter, smoother sand. He was already going to crash and burn tonight metaphorically; he didn't need to do it physically as well.

When they were about a mile from camp, she said, "We need to talk about today."

"All right . . ." He was tense all over: his shoulders, his stomach, his back. He felt like a watch spring being wound. It was hard to even keep running.

"Why did you assault that man?"

"He fell asleep and left you unprotected. Anything could've happened to you. It was unacceptable."

"But was that a cause for such violent—"

"Yes." She jumped, and he knew he'd perhaps made his voice too insistent. "And I'd do it again. He was failing you. We all were. How can you not understand how much I . . ."

She slowed to a stop then, and he followed her, pacing a wide circle as his heart rate came down. Her eyes were bright, searching. "Why did you kiss me last night?"

He felt his cheeks flush, and his chin fell to his heaving chest. "I'm sorry, Rhodie . . . I shouldn't have—"

"No." She stalked over to him, and he felt her firm fingers on his jaw, forcing his gaze back up to hers. "Answer my question." In her eyes, he saw that she would not be pacified with platitudes. She would settle for nothing less than the truth. So he lied to her.

"I don't know." He tried to turn away, but she wouldn't let him, her hold unyielding.

"I don't believe you."

So much for that. Jester, what've you got for me? "I've heard so much about princesses and their magic lips and just wanted to see what all the fuss—"

"The truth, Arrondale James."

James swallowed hard. "Fine. I kissed you because I wanted to. Because I want to all the time." He tried to wipe the sweat from his palms on his shorts, but they wouldn't absorb it. "Now it's your turn to give me the truth. Why did you come to Briggin when I was shot?"

She blinked at him as her hand fell away, and he saw the flicker of fear in her eyes before it receded behind a calm, collected demeanor. That moment of fear: that's what had kept him from asking that question all these months. Driving her away was the last thing he wanted to do, and it would be so easy for her to retreat to Bluffton Castle and never text him back again as punishment for questioning her like a criminal.

"You were injured."

"There were plenty of doctors there."

"I don't know their loyalties. Perhaps they were aligned with Lincoln, perhaps they'd try to finish the job . . ."

"You'd have me believe that you came because you thought the other doctors were going to assassinate me?"

"No," she whispered, looking toward the ocean. "I wanted to see you. I wanted to make sure you were okay. I needed to."

"Why? What am I to you?" Before this went a single step farther, he needed to hear it.

"You're my brother's best friend. I care for him."

He stepped closer, resting a hand on her arm cautiously. "And me? Do you care for me, too?"

She dipped forward quickly, and her lips against his were a soft caress. His brain seized before it started screaming. *Kiss her back! Engage! Seize the moment!* He pushed the thoughts away as he leaned back, grinning ruefully, and ran a hand through his hair. Even in his addled, off-balance state, he could recognize when he was being played.

"That was a very nice kiss. But you didn't answer my question."

"I don't want to answer it." She smiled back at him sweetly, and he chuckled.

He took a few steps backwards as he said, "Then I hope you enjoyed that kiss, Princess, because it's your last one with me." Then he turned to start jogging down the beach again.

"Lieutenant," she called, frustration in her voice.

"Yes, Dr. Broward?" He turned around to jog backwards.

"I wasn't through with our conversation."

"Ah, but I was. I answered your question, and you ignored mine."

"Arron," she warned, picking up her speed.

"Rhodie," he gave her the same tone back, but he couldn't keep ahead of her running backwards, and she caught him by the shirt with both hands and pulled him close.

"Don't walk away from me," she whispered fiercely.

"I didn't. I ran," he replied, a little breathless. "Tell me what I am to you." He brought both his hands to her shoulders; Woz help him, he needed to touch her. He knew he was testing her limits when it came to self-disclosure, but he had to know. If she wouldn't say the words, there was no way this would work. He was tired of putting his heart out there; he felt like he was shouting into a canyon where his echo never came back to him, and his throat was tired and sore. "Tell me. Please tell me."

"Nothing," she whispered, and his chest felt like it had a crossbow bolt in it again. He stepped back, looking out at the ocean, but she shook him by his T-shirt, still fisted in her hands, until he looked back at her again. "That is, you *should* mean nothing to me, but . . ." She paused, and that pause was everything . . . She wasn't letting go. She wasn't done. "You do mean something. I don't know exactly what, but it's more than simple friendship. But you're all wrong, this is all wrong. I can't be tabloid fodder, not again. I'm not supposed to be involved in unsanctioned affairs." Her tone was resigned, defeated.

He couldn't help it; he laughed. "I'm sorry our mutual affection troubles you so, flower."

She scowled at him, and he grinned. James felt exultant; he was fairly sure he was glowing like a firefly. "Rhododendron, may I kiss you again?"

"Yes, that's why I chased you—"

He cut her off before she could finish her sentence. Her lips were just as sweet as the night before.

CHAPTER TWENTY-TWO

THEY SLID INTO A GOOD routine: During the day, they were all business. "Dr. Broward" and "Lieutenant James" were polite and professional. They did not touch each other except when absolutely necessary. They did not share long, lingering looks. In fact, most of the time, they ignored each other. They ate their nightly meal of rice and beans silently in parallel, like they'd been married for thirty years instead of dating for three weeks. If James was honest with himself, it was incredibly fun pretending like they weren't interested in each other. Especially because on their nightly run, it was an entirely different story.

As soon as they were out of sight of the camp, she stopped running and attacked him. She lapped into his mouth, tasting him, sucking at him, nibbling at his bottom lip as her hands slid under his T-shirt, and he tried to shake off the rapidly rising lust that was practically clouding his vision. It seemed to him that she was spending a lot of time on his chest today, massaging all around his pecs.

"Are you checking for breast cancer? Because I just had a mammogram last month."

"Take off your shirt," she ordered breathlessly, and he choked a little.

"Really?"

She smiled at him coyly, and with shaking hands, he crossed his arms and grabbed the edges to comply. Before he had it over his head, however, he saw her tapping at her phone, and the flashlight came on.

"Hey, pictures are extra, lady." He pulled his shirt back down.

"I said take it off."

James crossed his arms over the white tee, blushing. "I think I might like to know why first."

She closed the distance between them, touching his cheek as she whispered in his ear, "Because I can't wait any longer." Rhodie ran a hand over his chest, dragging her fingernails, and he shivered. "I want to see you."

"Why do you need the flashlight?" he whispered, though there was no one around.

"Because it's dark," she whispered back.

I'm still skeptical . . . "Not that dark."

"Fine." Without warning, she yanked the edge of his shirt up to his shoulders and held it there.

"Whoa! Hey, Rhodie!" He didn't push her away, but he did laugh and flex his abs instinctively, even as his hands went to his hips in consternation.

"I'll just be a moment."

"My incision is fine, Dr. Broward."

"It's not that."

"What the Jersey are you looking at, then?"

"Your third nipple. Which side is it on? Woz, you have a lot of freckles. I didn't realize you had them all over like this . . . You ought to wear a shirt when you're out in the sun, darling."

What? James couldn't believe what he was hearing. "How did you know about my third nipple?"

She looked up into his face. "Are you serious?"

"Yes!" He fought a scorching blush and failed; he could've ironed his uniforms with his face, it was so hot. "I've never told anyone about it! I only sunbathe in private!"

"You told *me* about it. In Briggin, when you were in the hospital."

He ran a hand through his hair, making it stand on end. "I must've been a bit high on all those painkillers. Woz, this is embarrassing."

"Why? It's just an anomaly."

"Oh, you wouldn't mind if I ripped your shirt off to examine your chest? I find that a bit hard to believe." He drew her forward by her elbows and hugged her. "It's one thing for you to examine me as a doctor; it's quite another for you to suddenly invade my personal space, especially when I've expressed reservations about it."

"I'm sorry," she said softly into his chest. "I guess I got a bit carried away." She turned off the flashlight and squeezed him back.

"I'll say."

He felt her fingers probing his chest again through his shirt. "Rhodie! Seriously?"

She took his face in her hands, and her eyes were wild. "I dream about it. I waste time imagining what it looks like, how it would feel under my fingers. I need to see it. It is driving me mad, Arron. Mad."

He scowled, but sighed. He couldn't take the pleading in her eyes. She must have sensed his defeat; she was practically bouncing with excitement.

"It's not that big of a deal," he said. "You're going to be terribly disappointed."

"I'll be the judge of that." She began to mess with her phone again, but he stopped her, shaking his head. He took her hand and guided her fingers under his shirt just below his left pec. "There."

"Just that?"

"Just that."

"It feels like a mole."

"It looks like one, too, if you don't look closely."

"I want to look closely. Why won't you let me?"

He kissed her quickly. "I've got to have some kind of mystery in our relationship. Mother told me no one will buy the cow if I give away the milk for free . . ." He tugged her forward down the beach, and she pouted as she broke into a run again. "You're not used to being denied, are you?"

"Not particularly. Though my brother doesn't seem to have any problem doing so."

"Why, what has he denied you recently?"

"I wish to move out of Bluffton."

"And he said no?"

She shrugged with one shoulder. "Technically, no."

"Because you didn't ask."

"Correct."

"You're such a chicken." He laughed.

She kicked sand at his ankles. "I resent that."

"So I feel. But he can't read your mind, love."

"My father wouldn't back my play."

"*Back your play?* Who *are* you? Where *am* I?"

She scoffed. "You're clearly not part of a political family."

But I'm going to be, when the duke dies. He mentally stamped a "Return to Sender" on the painful reminder.

"A fact I've presently never been more thankful for in my life. But I'm glad you're a chicken. Bluffton's the safest place for you."

"That's what my father said."

"He's not wrong, flower."

Though he doubted she was conscious of it, Rhodie sped up, and he had to put on a burst of speed to catch up.

"I'm not a flower. I'm not a commodity. I'm just a doctor who happens to have a king for a brother."

"Right. Just a genius, gorgeous physician who happens to have a king and queen for parents. Exceedingly average."

"What I know is that I'm a twenty-five-year-old woman who still lives at home. A home that happens to be an hour away from work. A home with very little privacy."

James snorted.

"What?"

"As someone who's lived with two sisters and my mother in a two-bedroom apartment, I can attest that you have more privacy than most people. You just don't realize it."

"Well, it isn't enough. I enjoy being alone without someone wandering in to invite me to a social event. Introversion benefits my intelligence and my disposition."

"That's an interesting hypothesis," he puffed. "What would your control be? How would you measure your intellectual output? Papers published? Successful experiments devised?"

"I am quite sure we could come up with a reasonable set of quantifiable indicators."

We. He loved that she was sharing her musings with him, loved that she assumed they'd work together to tackle a problem.

"Have you tried suggesting a roommate situation?"

"No. As I said, I enjoy being alone."

"But he might be more likely to agree to a situation in which you're not completely isolated. Say, living with a handsome soldier who has a second bedroom in his loft overlooking Grammarless Park."

She chuckled. "Nice try, Lieutenant."

"It was nice, wasn't it?"

The sparkle in her gaze told him that she didn't mind the suggestion. "Very nice. Very subtle."

"I do try." James was lost in thought after that, thinking about what it would be like to live with Rhodie as roommates. She'd probably never wash dishes, never pick up after herself. Come home late every night. Maybe he'd make dinner and leave her some in the fridge. She probably couldn't cook. There were more downsides than he usually imagined.

Then again, when he usually imagined them living together, they'd be married. So in that case, his imagination tended toward how many surfaces they could couple on or against without breaking anything. But his imagination also tended toward waking curled up next to her and slow dancing with her late at night after a glass of wine and reading together on the couch with her legs across his lap. And what their kids would look like. And whether she'd look like her mum when she was older, when her dreads gradually turned grey. And watching her career take off, standing next to her as she won awards for great scientific advancements. And being the only one allowed to monopolize her time at palace functions.

"James?"

"Hmm?"

"What do you think?"

"About what, love?"

Rhodie laughed the delicate laugh he loved. "Weren't you listening to me at all?"

"Sorry, no. My mind was otherwise occupied. It doesn't multitask, because I'm an extrovert who lives with too many people. I have less intellectual power available."

"Very funny, you." She paused. "What were you thinking about so hard?"

This question gave the man pause. He certainly joked about their future often enough, but he wasn't sure he was ready to just dive right into the conversation he wanted to have. They were too new. And deep down, he feared there was no future . . . not the way he wanted it.

"Tadpoles."

She pushed at his shoulder ineffectually. "You were not."

"Yes, tadpoles. What does it feel like when their tails fall off? Is it hard to go from basically a fish to basically a slimy rabbit? How do they feel about it all?"

"You're a strange man."

"Darling, you don't know the half of it." He wiped his forehead with his shoulder. "What were you trying to ask me when I was absorbed in my thinking about tadpoles?"

"I know it wasn't tadpoles. I was asking if you would consider speaking to Edward in support of my moving out of Bluffton."

"Sorry, darling. I don't get involved in family politics. Been friends with him too long for that."

Rhodie's phone plinked, and she pulled it out, her feet slowing to a stop.

"Who is it?"

"My brother."

"Burning the midnight kinging oil, is he?"

"Not that brother." Her eyes were wide.

"Andrew?"

She shook her head.

"Surely the nine-year-old isn't texting you . . . I mean, Simon's precocious, but—"

"It's Lincoln." Her chest was still heaving from their exercise. James was speechless. He took the phone from her. He stared at the screen.

Unknown number: Rho, it's your First Brother. Need your help. Call me.

James shook his head. "That could be anyone. That could be Heather, and it's a trap, and they're going to barter with your life. That could be a reporter, punking you. You're not answering that."

She snatched the phone back. "That *is* my brother, Arron. No one else calls me Rho. Hardly anyone knows that I call my siblings by their order of arrival. If he needs my help, I'll give it to him."

"You haven't seen the video of the night he came for Abbie. He's no innocent in all this. Don't think of him as some little lamb swept along by Heather's crook. That's not how it is." He cursed, leaning over, bracing his hands on his shaking legs.

"Nevertheless." She'd already decided to answer him. He could hear it in the timbre of her voice, pitched low, certain.

"We need to get off the beach." He put a hand on her lower back, urging her back toward the camp. "If you won't avoid this insanity, at least tell Edward. Let him know that you're in contact with him. He deserves to know."

"I'll consider it."

"If you don't tell him, I will. I can't keep something like this from him, Rhodie. I'm sorry, I just can't."

"You always did give away every secret."

"I can't even deny it. See? I couldn't keep that one, either."

She was quiet as they jogged along. "I would like to see it."

"What?"

"The video of the night he came for Abbie."

"No, you wouldn't. It would break your heart. He isn't the brother you remember, love."

"Nevertheless . . ."

Uh-oh, she was going full royal. That "nevertheless," that was the signal. *Fine, two can play at that game.*

"As your security, I can't let you engage with this person."

"What kind of assurances would you need?"

"Darling, there are not enough assurances in the known universe."

She huffed. How she could manage it while exercising, he'd never understand.

"So you want me to just ignore it?"

"Well, I'd prefer that you delete it, change your number, and forget that cell phones exist entirely, but I'll settle for ignoring it, yes."

"Fine." She wasn't meeting his gaze; she stared straight ahead, down the beach.

"You agree? You won't respond?"

"I won't respond."

"Okay. Thank you."

CHAPTER TWENTY-THREE

JAMES: Are you busy?

    Edward: Yes.

    Edward: What do you need?

    James: Lincoln contacted Rhodie last night.

    Edward: How?

    James: Sent her a text message.

He thought for a moment. It was unfair to just throw it in there, but maybe he could use one thing he didn't want to tell Edward to distract from the other.

    James: Also, I kissed your sister.

    James: I have continued to kiss her.

    James: She is okay with it.

    James: No, that's not—she likes it.

    James: Wait, you don't want to hear that, either, do you?

    James: I PROCURED CONSENT BEFORE PRO-CEEDING.

    James: CONSENT IS BEING GIVEN.

    James: I AM GENTLEMAN-ISH.

    James: Edward, say something.

    Edward: Lieutenant James, this is Scrope. His Majesty is asking if he can give you a call in a few minutes?

    James: Yes. Thank you, Scrope.

It was hard not to be embarrassed that his friend's assistant had just read his rather personal admission, but it couldn't be helped now. James answered immediately when the phone rang half an hour later.

"Sorry, I was finishing up with some delegates from the World Conference on Hunger."

"That's fine, I'm just searching for my ritual sacrifice dagger . . . Oh good, found it. That should save some trouble on your end."

Edward laughed. "You're a fool. Why do you think I sent you with her?"

"To . . . protect her?"

"Yes, and?"

James blew out a long breath. "I've no idea, mate."

"You both like each other. You've known each other a long time, you make each other laugh. You're reasonably good-looking . . ."

"Compared to a post, you mean?"

"And you're both genius-level smart."

"No, I just have a good memory."

"James, I saw your IQ score. 181 is nothing to sneeze at."

James stilled his pacing. "How?"

"In school. You left it on your desk, and I'm an entitled royal who doesn't mind snooping. And apparently, I haven't been explicit enough with either of you, but your 'will-they-won't-they' vibe is getting quite old, and I'd much prefer you just explore your relationship. In a healthy way."

His mind sputtered indignantly. He'd worked so hard to protect the secret of his intelligence, to hide what his mind could do, and here Edward had known all along? And more than that, he'd thrust him together with his sister as a form of blessing?

"That's—you can't—I didn't—" The sputtering was in his mouth now. It was not an improvement to the situation.

"That's a lot of sentences you're starting. Think you might finish one anytime soon?"

James regained his emotional balance. "I don't think so, no. Goodbye."

"Wait, we still have to talk about Lincoln!"

"Oh, that."

"Yes, that. Did she respond to the message?"

"She told me she wouldn't, but . . . I'm not sure I believe her. She was very convinced that it was Lincoln based on his verbiage, and she very much wanted to reply."

"Well, I can check on our account and see what messages have been sent. She's part of our family plan. Maybe even block the number or attempt to trace it."

"Good, please do that. She's got a soft spot for him still."

"That's because she hasn't seen the video."

"She asked to, last night."

"No. There's no need for her to see her brother's attempted kidnapping of her sister-in-law in stark black and white like that."

"That's what I said, as well." He paused. "How's . . . everything?"

Edward paused. He seemed to know that James was trying to ask about Abbie. "Everything is . . . okay. Not great. Soldiering on."

"Right." James wished he were physically with Edward. In moments like this a brotherly shoulder nudge or a sympathetic smile came more naturally than putting his emotions into words.

"Keep me informed, please, of any new developments."

"Yes, I will. Bye."

"Bye."

HE STEPPED BACK INTO the lab. Rhodie was having a staff meeting.

"We have some good data coming in so far, but please make sure that you're standardizing your tabulations. We all remember the Great Unit Disaster of 515, don't we?"

The women nodded somberly.

"And remember to use significant figures, all, because without them, decimal numbers would be pointless." They groaned at this, chatting with each other, jostling each other's shoulders. It was obvious to him that the assistants had bonded from being in the same quarters. Meanwhile, Rhodie stood apart from them, up front. His heart ached for her a little; she was always the expert, always the leader. It looked lonely.

Well, she did have her book club, but having never attended, he wasn't sure precisely what their dynamic was. He'd like to meet the group someday.

Rhodie dismissed the assistants, and they each went back to their stations. She went back to her own work, not even sparing him a glance. He pulled out his phone.

Arron: That was a terrible joke. Significant figures deserve better.

Feeling the buzz, she pulled out her phone and read the message. She smiled. That was all he wanted, really. He wondered if it could be added to his job description: *Royal protection and security. Military operations. Making Rhodie smile.*

He always loved watching her, but he particularly loved it in the lab. This was where she was in her element; it was so obvious, from the way she fixed the autoclave when it broke to how she organized her many notebooks. From the way she muttered to herself as she touched the end of her pen to her lips, as if she wanted to chew on it, but knew she shouldn't. On days when it left a mark, he kissed it off later without telling her.

His phone buzzed, and he pulled it out, hoping it was from her, telling him off.

> **Unknown number:** James, it's Lincoln. Please tell Rhodie to answer my messages. I need to speak with her. Please.

He's sent more? Anger balled up in his chest; this was so much worse than finding Tracy asleep outside her tent. This was a real, verified threat, and he knew exactly how to get to them. Without a word, he texted the information to Edward's secretary, then blocked the number. Lincoln could go to Jersey for all he cared. There was no way he was putting his princess in touch with him. Not for all the rice and beans in Trella.

CHAPTER TWENTY-FOUR

THEY'D BEEN ON MISSION for two months. Rain rammed into the roof of the lodge, louder where they were on the top floor. The air was so saturated, James could smell the water, musky and fresh at once, and the plants opening to welcome it, letting it wash over them. He and Rhodie sat across from each other, the bedroom door open a crack for appearance's sake. Just two old friends playing chess, not two lovers who wished they were making out on the beach. But this was good, too; they didn't have a lot of time to just sit and talk, even though they spent most of the day together.

"Chess isn't like real life," Rhodie said, interrupting his thoughts.

"How so?"

"Each piece has a defined role. There's no ambiguity. No gray areas."

"I'm not sure I agree with that," he said, shaking his head. "People make tactical decisions all the time. They have different strengths and weaknesses, even within their defined roles. That's like real life."

She took his rook with her bishop. "Certainly, they do. But consider if the relationships on the chessboard were real. Wouldn't any king worth his salt seek to defend his queen, rather than sending her out to fight on his behalf, powerful though she may be?"

"Perhaps he trusts the queen to know her own heart. Perhaps he trusts that she wants to fight for him, too, knowing that he can't defend her from all of life's pains and problems."

"Perhaps."

"I know I have an inordinate amount of strong women in my life, but I've not often found that they need me all that much when it comes to fighting their battles. They seem to do just fine on their own." He moved a pawn forward two spaces.

"Mmm."

"Or perhaps she's rubbish in the sack, and he's just as glad to be rid of her."

Rhodie laughed silently, shaking her head. She was about to move her bishop when he spoke again.

"May I ask you a question?"

"Whatever I say, it wouldn't stop you, would it?"

He put his hand over hers, and she looked up. Was that . . . insecurity?

"You may want to hear the question first."

"Very well."

"Why don't you have a marriage contract?"

Her gaze dropped to the board, and she pulled away from James's touch instinctively, tucking her hands under her thighs as her mother had taught her to do when she really wanted to cross her arms across her chest defensively.

"They tried."

"Why didn't it work? What happened?"

"It includes facts of a medical nature. I know you're squeamish."

He grinned at that. "You know me well . . . but in this case, I shall persevere in the face of visceral details. Though I can't imagine anything about you being all that disgusting."

"As you may remember, I was quite a scrawny little thing."

"Thin and lanky. Beautifully so."

"Not everyone thought so." She moved the bishop she'd originally intended, breaching his defenses. "And at age twelve, I hadn't yet begun menstruating."

"So? Is that odd?"

She shook her head, her loose dreads swaying. "Not at all. But you must understand that these people are trying to arrange breeding stock, essentially. If you can't guarantee fertility, regular cycles, the classic signs of childbearing readiness such as wide hips . . . they just pass on to the next."

She'd so envied that about Abbie, who'd blossomed into her curves at just the right time. She'd been happy for her brother, but at the same time, two years older, still waiting for it happen to her, she'd cried a few jealous tears as well. It seemed so stupid now, given that all Abbie's "rightness" still hadn't added up to a child.

"Your parents told everyone they were just waiting for the right arrangement for you. Being picky."

Rhodie smiled. It covered a breaking heart well, she'd discovered.

"They were very concerned that it would damage my reputation needlessly. They still thought a contract would happen for me . . . but I didn't start my cycles until I was fifteen, and they were still somewhat irregular, and by that time, I was considered too old."

He snorted. "Royals. Too old for marriage at fifteen? Absolute nonsense." He took her bishop with his queen. "You'd make any man a wonderful wife."

"Betrayed by my body, I suppose."

His face hardened, and even though she knew his anger wasn't directed toward her, it made her want to squirm. "Growing in your own time isn't a betrayal, love. It was wrong for them to subject you to such rigorous expectations at such a young age, especially when it was entirely outside your control."

"Well," she said, moving to pin his queen with her knight, "I did try to compensate. Being the perfect princess in every way. But alas, it wasn't enough."

"Rhodie." He waited until she looked up at him. "You are enough."

"Oh," she said, waving a careless hand, "of course. I know."

"No." His voice rumbled in his chest. "I don't think you do." He sighed. "But I can't help but be glad."

"Glad? Glad I was rejected by my peers?"

James glanced over his shoulder toward the open door. "First of all, you have no peers. Secondly, yes, I'm glad," he whispered. "I'm glad for their stupid standards and rules, if only because their loss is my gain." He picked up his queen and stared at it, lightly tossing it back and forth between his hands. "They let a real queen slip through their fingers." He put the piece back on the board, next to his king once more.

"You're the only one who thinks so," she said, focusing harder on the board to try to keep her tears at bay. She brought in her bishop to reinforce the knight's position.

"Trust me, woman, I'm not. You're a treasure. A jewel. Gold, in every way that matters."

"You've always said so," she whispered. "I thought you were teasing me. I thought . . . I told myself you couldn't be serious."

James slid his foot forward to rest next to hers. "Serious as a heart attack."

Petros cleared his throat in the hall, and they shared a long look before continuing the game in relative silence. Rhodie was coming to know his expressions better, and this one was as full of longing as she'd ever seen him. Were they on the beach, she was quite certain there would be no distance between them. She took his queen and, within five moves, won the game.

CHAPTER TWENTY-FIVE

JAMES WAS WAITING FOR Rhodie outside the latrine. She'd been in there for quite some time, and he was starting to get antsy about it. He replayed their chessboard conversation over and over from that night. *That's where it comes from. The "don't touch me" feelings, the coldness. She hates her body. She thinks she's damaged goods. I made it worse with my flippant comments about her beauty. And I haven't the slightest idea how to change her mind. Not as the knight or as the jester or any other member of her court. A wound so old, so internalized . . . I don't know if it can be healed.*

He shifted his weight and debated knocking or going to get Joline to investigate. His phone rang, and it was a blessed distraction.

"Did my gift arrive?" Edward asked without the usual greetings.

James swatted at a mosquito. "You've sent me a gift? I haven't seen it, no. I hope the rats haven't gotten to it . . ."

"Not for you, mate. For Rhodie. It's her birthday come Saturday."

"That sneak. She's said nothing," James said.

"Of course she hasn't. It's Rhodie. She hates a fuss."

"Even on her birthday? But that's a day to be celebrated and sung to by one and all!"

"You're going to go overboard, aren't you?"

"You know me so well. How's Abbie?"

"She's, uh . . ." Edward gave a deep sigh. "I don't know, mate."

"She hasn't run off again?"

"No, no, nothing like that. She's just not herself. She's dropped all her classes. She . . . she cries a lot. I've tried to get her out of the house, tried to encourage her to do something, anything, besides sit around and watch TV, but she is very firmly disinclined to listen to me. You know how she is."

"Yes, I do." *My princess is the same way.* "Give her time. She'll come around."

"I'm sure you're right."

The stall door banged shut behind Rhodie, who was already making her way back to the lab, still rubbing the hand sanitizer into her skin.

"I've got to go, Edward. Let me know if I can do anything to help."

"Yes, I will. Bye."

"Everything all right at home?" she asked without looking at him.

"Yes, ma'am."

Plans were already forming in his mind as she got back to work. There was no way he was letting her birthday slip by unnoticed.

RHODIE CAME OUT OF her room for dinner and found James standing there in shiny black dress shoes, gray trousers, and a lavender dress shirt open at the collar. His hands were in his pockets and his sleeves were rolled to his elbows. She loved his forearms and was momentarily distracted by the sight of them . . . *So strong.*

Her suspicions had been high already that he knew it was her birthday. He'd been acting weird all day, fussing over her even more than usual, whispering to people when he thought she wasn't paying attention.

"Why are you dressed like that?"

"I've got something special planned for dinner tonight. He held up a black blindfold. "Silk, see? It won't even muss your hair."

Rhodie brushed by him down the stairs. "No."

"Please? I promise, no tricks. No jokes. You'll like it."

"No."

He chased her across the yard, then pulled her toward the trees where they'd gone hiking for the fungi, into the shadow of the canopy. He laced his fingers as if praying, shaking them in front of his chest, his voice low so as not to be overheard. "Please, please, please, I went to so much work for this. I hate work. If it's all for naught, it'll bring me to tears."

Her eyes narrowed. "What kind of work?"

He held out the blindfold, grinning. Rhodie crossed her arms over her stomach.

"I will examine your efforts, but I make no promises. And I'm not wearing that. I shall simply close my eyes."

He scowled good-naturedly. "Don't you trust me?"

"No, not at all. So I suppose *you* will have to trust *me* instead."

"Very well," he said, taking both her hands. "But if you open them before the time, I shall be very put out."

"A pouty lieutenant. Woz preserve us."

He gently tugged her forward, and she shuffled her boots along the path. "How far are we going, anyway?"

"Yeah, that might've been my one miscalculation," he chuckled, still coaxing her along the path. "Why are you taking such tiny steps?"

"I don't particularly relish the idea of falling down. That might put a damper on my birthday."

She felt the heat of him as he pulled her closer, putting her hands on his shoulders and his hands on her hips.

"I'm not going to let that happen," he whispered.

"Clearly, you do not realize how clumsy I am," she whispered back, and he laughed. "How are you even watching where we're going if you're walking backwards? Do I hear fire?"

"Very perceptive, Dr. Broward. What else do you sense?"

"I hear . . . people talking." Her eyes popped open and he slapped a hand over them. "This better not be a surprise party, Lieutenant, I shall not be amused."

James laughed. "How stupid do you think I am? No, don't answer that. What do you smell?"

"Your cologne . . . it reminds me of the beach . . . and time spent there together . . ."

"You shameless flirt." She heard the huskiness in his voice and knew he was thinking about it, too. She smiled.

"What else?"

"Food . . . seafood."

"Yes, and?"

"And mosquito candles?"

He laughed. "That's right. It wouldn't do to get brain bender fever on your birthday." He let his hand drop from her eyes, and she gasped. In a small grove of coconut trees, there was now a table set for two with a white linen tablecloth, crystal candlesticks with tall white tapers, and a centerpiece of orchids. Balls of soft light floated around the edge of the clearing by magic, bobbing on an unseen tide. More orchids had been attached to the trees, wreathing the clearing in every shade of violet. James took her hand and led her to the table, where he pulled out a carved wooden chair for her to sit on.

That's when she noticed the people whose voices she'd heard: an older woman, her black hair streaked with white, and a young girl of about thirteen.

"Good evening," she said in Trellan as she sat down, and they responded softly, curtsying.

"Oh, right, yes. This is our cook, Auri, and her daughter, Heaven. Heaven has been kind enough to translate for me as I did the planning . . ."

"Lieutenant said to make a sexy meal, so Mama did her best." Heaven grinned.

Rhodie's eyes cut to James in time to watch his face explode into a furious blush. "*Romantic*, Heaven. Romantic and sexy are not the same."

She shrugged, the smile never leaving her face. "The dictionary, it was not so clear, Lieutenant. It is good food, traditional Trellan food. You will like it."

"What have we got, then?" He took the cover off a ceramic pot using the striped towel that rested on top. "It smells amazing."

"That is creamy crab and coconut soup." She pointed to another plate with a mesh cover to keep off the flies. "This is fried plantain cups with avocado and shrimp stuffing." Heaven pointed to the one next to it, then quietly turned to her mother to ask a question in Trellan. "And this is cheese-filled cassava balls." Rhodie was already salivating, and she opened up her napkin with a satisfying snap.

"I've heard enough."

Heaven ignored her. "And this is stewed conch—not tough, not cooked too long. Conch is good for lovemaking."

James massaged his temples. "Again, I said *romantic*, not sexy. No aphrodisiacs necessary. We're not even married."

"Mama says that doesn't matter. Maybe you'll get married now."

Rhodie's abs hurt from holding her laughter in, but she didn't want to start an international incident over a culinary misunderstanding.

"And this is pigeon peas with coconut and white rice."

The quiet dismay on Arron's face was not making the laughter easier to hold in.

"I said no rice and beans! We're sick to death of rice and beans!"

Heaven lifted her chin. "These are better. Peas are not beans." The girl and her mother had another conversation, this one less quiet and a little more heated.

"And as a gift, Mama brought spiced rum. She says have a shot now."

It didn't seem they could refuse, so James poured them each a shallow shot, and Rhodie clinked his glass before she took a sip. It was strong; very strong, and she tried to breathe slowly against the scorching trail it left down her esophagus.

Auri said something to her daughter, and she giggled. "I don't know if I say this right, but Mama says this will help the man make children. It has something from the manhood of the sea turtle . . ."

James stood up quickly and offered them each a handshake. "Okay, great, well, thank you so much, off you go. Have a lovely evening." There was a low conversation Rhodie couldn't precisely hear, but it appeared he'd waited to pay the second half upon delivery, and this was done quietly as mother and daughter left the clearing.

He sat back down hard, and she let her laughter tumble out.

"Your face," she said, wiping her eyes. "I will never forget your face when you realized she'd cooked us an aphrodisiac meal instead of the romantic birthday dinner you had planned . . . I didn't know that shade of red was possible for white people."

"I live to amuse you, Princess." He stood back up and began to serve her from the pots and dishes, filling her plate. "Is there anything you don't want?"

"Well, I don't think I'll have any more sea turtle semen rum . . ."

He laughed then, too. "Oh, you didn't want more of that? Shame. I hear it does wonders for the skin as well."

"You'll have to get Auri back to the camp next week so I can find out more about that for research purposes. Perhaps this is a miracle cure for erectile dysfunction, and I can become the fixer of floppy penises everywhere."

"You're killing me right now," he said, his face flushing again. James handed her back her plate. "Happy birthday, Rhodie."

"Thank you. As I should've said already, this is a lovely surprise."

He stabbed at his own food. "I did say no rice and beans. I was quite clear about it; I even learned how to say it in Trellan, so I know I was understood." He sighed, and she giggled. She took a spoonful of the soup: it was salty, but sweet from the coconut milk, and the crab must've been caught that morning. Next she tried the plantain cups. Though they'd had pressed plantains quite often, the addition of the creamy avocado filling elevated the dish, and Rhodie was caught up in the surreal feeling of the moment. The elegance of the food shouldn't have surprised her, but it did. James regaled her with tales of his own past birthdays, and she told him about the time she'd been so sure she was getting a horse that she'd had the grooms put hay in a stall with the name she's already picked out posted on the door: Butterfly.

"But there was no Butterfly the horse?"

She shook her head. "Sadly, no. Not that there weren't horses for me to ride. But I was just sure that at five years old, I'd outgrown ponies and was ready for a horse of my own to ride whenever I liked. Mum and Dad were subjected to a week of dramatics after that."

"They didn't give in and just get you one?"

"Oh, no!" The thought alone horrified her. "That would've just encouraged me. Oh, no. The Browards don't negotiate with terrorists, even tiny terrorists of their own making."

"Tiny terrorists," he laughed. "I'm going to use that. That is so . . . accurate."

"Surely your mother wouldn't have given in to a fit over a present?"

He swallowed a sip of water, and she noted with relief that he hadn't gone back to the rum. "My mother barely had money for a cake, let alone other presents. We knew that fits would do us no good. Didn't stop us from throwing them, of course, but she just laughed at us."

"You've moved up in the world."

He cocked his head at her.

"Your place by the river," she clarified, "that's a step up, then."

"Oh, that. Well, it turned out on my twenty-first birthday that I had a trust waiting for me from my absent father, who turned out to be neither dead nor a deadbeat, as we'd long imagined."

"You'd had no idea?"

James shook his head. "No idea at all. Mum wouldn't even give me his name. She says I'm better off not knowing." He swallowed his food. "She said not to look a gift horse in the mouth."

"And here, that's all I wanted at age five," she quipped, and James shook his head, groaning.

"I hope your jokes will improve now that you're over a quarter of a century." He stood up, brushing off his hands on his trousers. "There's one last thing, and then we go down to the mess hall for dessert."

"I don't eat dessert."

"I did remind them of that," he said, pulling out his phone, scrolling through its screens. "But they insisted. Something about everyone else in the world liking cake and mission morale, blah, blah, blah. Don't worry, I'll feed your piece to the snake, if you like." Orchestral music poured out of his phone in a sweeping melody, and she looked at him in wonder.

"'The Enchanted Evening Waltz' by Radinoffsky. I love this."

"How lucky. Who could've guessed?" he asked, offering his hand to her, drawing her toward an open area away from the table. "I mean, it's not as if I had Simonson hack your phone to find out what your most played song was."

"Did you really?" She laughed before she caught the nervous look on his face.

"Before we start, I must apologize in advance to your toes. Dancing is not my strong suit. It wasn't a favored activity by the kids down at the docks."

She moved his hand to her lower back and his other hand out to the side. He looked down.

"Don't look at your feet," she said softly. "Look at me. What was a favored activity?"

"Trying to bean seagulls with glass bottles."

"Mmm, it's a good thing they weren't flying over the bay." He stared at her blankly as she stepped backward into a box step. "Because then they'd be bagels . . ."

He groaned as he tried to follow her lead into a slow waltz, but stumbled. "Distract me with terrible puns and you will only have yourself to blame when you're injured by my ineptitude."

"Left forward, right out, step together. Right back, left out, step together," she directed. He tried to look at his feet again, and she brought their foreheads together. "Lieutenant?"

"Mmm?"

"Don't quit your day job."

He laughed. "I've no plans to. I'm sorry, I wish Edward were here to dance with you."

"Truthfully . . ."

He finally looked up, his hazel eyes warmer than the tropical night.

"Truthfully, I'd rather be here with you." She swallowed hard. "Thank you for making me feel special on a day when I was missing my friends and family."

"You're welcome, darling."

Darling. A shiver went down her spine, and the rollercoaster drop feeling that accompanied his kisses started in her stomach even before she felt him leaning forward. Glancing around to ensure they were alone, he pressed a sweet kiss to her lips, then pulled away quickly. "I'll give you more later."

She blinked. "Pardon?"

"I wasn't speaking to you, I was speaking to your lips. They're lonely for me."

"Are they?"

"Yes, I can tell. Unfortunately, your colleagues admire and respect you and want to honor you, so we should probably return to camp."

"Their adoration is so inconvenient."

"Isn't it? I've always thought so."

CHAPTER TWENTY-SIX

RHODIE STARED AT JAMES across the chessboard. He seemed distracted tonight, but he'd taken far more pieces than he usually did. It was competitive, of course, but she always won. *I always win* . . . Her mind turned this fact over, and suddenly, it made no sense. James wasn't stupid, and he didn't seem that tired. Yet he never won a single match. The scientific part of her brain went into overdrive. *Surely he isn't trying to throw the game* . . . There was only one way to find out. Well, technically, there was more than one way, but light deception in the name of the greater good was her preferred method.

Rhodie moved her knight forward into the path of his bishop. "Your turn." James was staring off into space in the direction of her desk, and his attention suddenly snapped back to the board. She watched him assess the board, his hazel eyes calculating. Ignoring her blatant baiting, he moved a pawn out two spaces from the home row and went back to his staring.

She moved her bishop next to his queen. Surely that would entice him. She cleared her throat, and James looked at her, then at the board. Rather than taking her piece, he retreated. She could see no reason for him to do so; he could've safely taken her bishop, then retreated on his next turn. Her curiosity was rabid now. She'd try one more time to cast her pieces into danger, then she'd confront him. This was nonsense.

After some internal debate, Rhodie moved her queen. She put it directly in the diagonal path of his recently mobilized pawn. It would cost him nothing to take it. "James," she said softly. He snapped out of whatever he was stewing about and turned back to the board. That little wrinkle appeared above the bridge of his nose, that sign that he was thinking hard about something, and she knew he'd finally figured it out.

"What are you doing?" he asked.

She leaned forward, placing her elbows onto her knees. "I'm trying to lose, but I'm guessing it's not possible. I think I'm going to have to settle for a stalemate."

His eyes narrowed. "Why would you try to lose?"

"Why would *you*?"

There it was, that beautiful blush that told her he knew he'd been caught. "I wasn't."

"Really?" She pulled out her phone. "Do you know how to calculate the statistical likelihood of me winning every game of the fourteen we've played? Because I do."

"Unlikely, is it? Well, my princess is a genius, after all. I don't think it's all that surprising that you've won so often, especially pitted against a donkey like me."

She felt her ire grow as he clung stubbornly to his deception. "I don't want pity wins," she said, trying to keep her temper under control by keeping her voice low. "You play to win, or I'm not playing."

"Play to win? What else would I play to, my strengths? A crowd?"

"Stop joking for once!" she snapped. "Woz! How stupid do you think I am? Did you really think I wouldn't figure it out?"

His look hardened, and he stood up. "I don't have to listen to this. I'm going to bed."

"Sit down."

James crossed to the door, and for a split second, she thought he was actually going to leave. But when he closed the door, her stomach unclenched.

"Look," he growled, "if I play to win, you'll never beat me, and then you'll stop playing. I don't want that. I like playing with you." She could see how tight his shoulders were from across the room. James was a lot of things, but when it came to his own abilities, she'd never heard him laud himself. He wasn't arrogant, yet he said it so matter-of-factly.

"How do you know?"

"How do I know?" he bit out. "Because that's what happened in school. I could pound any opponent, but my own teammates refused to play with me. They said it was pointless, said I didn't need any practice. Sam and Edward were the only ones willing to keep trying to win." He leaned forward, his tone turning sarcastic and sniping. "So I guess I don't know for sure, but if we're talking about statistical likelihood, I feel like the chances are pretty good."

Rhodie stared at him, warring between feeling insulted and feeling sorry for him. The kinder emotion won out, even if he was being a jerk about it. She nodded slowly, then started putting her rooks back in the corners, her knights just inside, her bishops next, until every piece was back where it had started. She looked up at him again when she was finished, and he just looked perplexed.

"What?" she asked. "Even if I lose, I still get to stare into your eyes and stealthily admire your physique."

He sat down hard, still watching her warily. "You're not angry?"

"Oh, yes, I am angry. But at least I understand why you did it now. You can make it up to me later. Don't worry, it'll be a light recompense."

A microscopic smile played at his lips. James reached out and moved the pawn in front of his king forward two spaces. She moved out a knight, and he brought out a bishop from behind the neat row of pawns. Rhodie moved the pawn in front of her queen, thinking to mobilize her powerful pieces early, and James flashed a lightning smile before sobering again. *Uh-oh.* He moved a knight toward the middle of the board, pinning hers in the corner. She moved out another pawn, the one in front of her bishop, and he moved his bishop forward.

"Check."

She stared at the board: he'd taken advantage of the narrow tunnel of access to her king that she'd practically laid out for him. Why hadn't she seen that? He was too far away to take with a pawn; even if she could take his bishop, it was supported by that knight, and she'd lose the piece.

She stared at him. "I think . . . I think it's actually checkmate." Her ego stinging, Rhodie moved her pieces back to start. She hadn't actually believed him. *That was what, four, five moves? That was just embarrassing.*

"Rhodie. It's just a game." His voice was gentle, his expression apologetic. Of course he could tell she was unhappy.

"A game you're very good at, apparently," she replied coolly.

"See?" He threw his hands up. "Now you're upset. I should've gone to bed. You should've let me go, you shouldn't have made me play to win. We were still having fun."

She glared at him. "I'm angry with *myself* for leaving you such an obvious opening, not angry with *you* for winning. You did exactly what I would've done in your shoes."

"Not wearing shoes," he muttered, shifting his bare foot to cover hers under the table, and she smiled.

"In your place, then. Again."

"Again?" He blinked, withdrawing his foot.

"Yes." She nodded insistently. "Again. And I'll try to last longer than four moves this time."

"If it makes you feel better," he said, resetting his half of the board, "I once took Edward in three."

"It does not," she said crisply, and he chuckled. He was reaching out his hand to start when she grabbed it. "Oh, but I forgot to mention the stakes."

"Stakes?" he asked, confused. "Didn't we just establish that I'm better than you?"

"And as such," she said, rubbing her thumb over the back of his hand, "I should get to choose the stakes."

"Very well. What are they?"

"Loser makes out with the winner."

James withdrew his hand slowly from her grasp, grinning wickedly, and rolled up this sleeves. "In that case, Princess, pucker up."

She made it ten moves before he won again, then sat in his lap and made out with him until he had to go back to his tent. As soon as he was gone, she ordered an e-book on chess strategy and read it until she fell asleep.

CHAPTER TWENTY-SEVEN

IT WAS THEIR EVENING run, near sunset.

"What's that?"

"Hmm?" James acted like he hadn't heard her, when she knew for a fact that he had. That feigned innocence was thick in his tone. "What's what, flower?"

"That large pile of debris down the beach?"

"Probably a shipwreck or something that washed up." His choice of words, without a joke, was too practiced.

Rhodie grinned inwardly. *I can be sneaky, too, Arron.* "Oh," she said, lacing her tone with sadness, "I don't wish to see that. Let's turn around and go back. We can go the other way tonight, or into the woods."

"First of all, you seriously overestimate my bravery if you think I'm going into those nightmare-infested woods in the pitch dark. There could be snakes. There could be rats. There could be giant spiders, of which I recall you're not much of a fan." Though it was unladylike, Rhodie narrowed her eyes; he was totally stalling. He went on, "There could be monkeys, there could be skinks."

"Skinks? What's a skink?"

"You know. Those giant lizardy things. If you catch the tail, it comes off and they keep running. The men have been trying to rid them from the camp for weeks; they hide under the house. They're freakishly quick."

By now, they were coming up fast on the pile, and she realized he'd successfully baited her with new scientific information. *Damn my curiosity.* She slowed to a stop, but to her surprise, he kept jogging straight over to the pile and pulled something out of his pocket. A match flared briefly in the dark, and he touched it to the base of the stack before him. As the kindling caught, she could see that there was more: several logs had been pulled over as seating, and a black backpack hidden behind a coconut tree.

"Why, Lieutenant, is this a date?"

In the firelight, his blush looked even redder than usual. "If anyone asks, we happened upon this scenario and didn't want the wine and marshmallows to go to waste."

"That seems perfectly plausible to me." She perched herself on the log, and James sat down next to her, close enough that their hips and knees were touching. "You're seated quite close . . ."

"Not half as close as I'd like to be," he muttered, and she stared into the fire to hide her amusement.

"Marshmallows? Your sweet tooth knows no bounds."

"Those are for me, since I'm still technically working. The wine's for you. But you can toast my marshmallow for me, if you want," he said, leaning closer. "Just don't set it on fire."

"Coals are best for marshmallows, not flames."

He blinked at her as he passed her the bottle. "That's right. How'd you know that?"

"I'm not completely helpless in the real world, you know."

He laughed, popping a plain marshmallow in his mouth and talking over it. "Yes, of course. I'd forgotten, toasting marshmallows is a real-world skill that your tutors would've covered."

She looked at the bottle of white wine in her hand for the first time. "Didn't you bring glasses?"

"Nope. Couldn't swing it. Drink from the bottle, love."

"I hardly think so . . ."

"Rhodie Broward, ladies and gentlemen. Humble enough to wash beakers, but too fancy to sip alcohol from the bottle." He lifted a finger to stroke her cheek. "So uppity."

She leaned into him, putting her lips a breath away from a kiss. "So cheeky."

"Royal pain."

"Ruffian."

"Beautiful," he said as he caressed her neck.

"Brave," she countered breathlessly.

He gave a low chuckle. "Only when there's no snakes involved."

"Be quiet and kiss me already."

"Yes, ma'am."

Rhodie hooked a finger into the collar of his sweaty shirt and tugged him nearer to close the distance between them. He tasted like spun sugar, and she let out a small sigh. Here, with the nighttime noisemakers tuning their instruments to play for them all night, here was where she wanted to be. Rhodie felt herself heating up, and it had little to do with the exercise she'd just done, the now-roaring fire next to them, or the alcohol she had yet to consume. It had everything to do with this thoughtful man and the privacy he'd carved out for them. Based on the singular way he poured himself into their kisses, she was fairly sure it was for his benefit, too. They kissed under the stars until the fire began to fade, the wine and sugar forgotten in favor of the feel of each other's lips, a sweeter pleasure by far. The sweat on her skin had dried, but her damp workout clothes had held it in, and she shivered as the twilight breeze moved down the beach. James pulled back, rubbing her arms with a touch meant to warm her.

"Damn, I meant to bring a blanket."

"You mean, you didn't have it covered?"

He snorted, then slid down to the sand with his back to the log. "Come sit. I'll hold you." Rhodie stoked the fire as she went to sit between his bent legs, letting his chest serve as her back's cushion. He wrapped her in his arms tightly, pressing a kiss to her bare shoulder.

An unwelcome thought made her shoulders tense . . . *Did he pull this off alone? He was with me almost all day. If he needed help, do they know we're together?* She'd assumed he knew that their relationship was a secret, based on how he treated her when other people were about.

She opened her mouth to ask him, but his fingers . . . his fingers were causing a slight problem with logical thought at the moment. He drew them up her forearm between her radial and ulnar arteries, pausing to caress the inside of her elbow before brushing them back down to her wrist. Up and down, up and down he swept the tips of his fingers over her skin, his pace steady, unhurried, his touch soft. It made no sense; yes, it was affectionate, but it was nowhere near her sexual reproductive organs. It shouldn't be affecting her this way.

"Why does that feel so good?" she whispered, turning to nuzzle his cheek.

He smirked. "Always wants to know why, this one. I love you."

Rhodie inhaled sharply. Caught in a whirlpool of sensations, her mind scrambled for dry ground, something to explain away what he'd said. *He couldn't mean that, it's too soon, he's just joking.*

He paused his stroking for a heartbeat, cleared his throat, then continued his sweep toward her wrist. "Love *that*. I love that, about you, is what I meant to say."

It could be true, she thought, even as her heart thrashed around in her chest like a beached whale. Rhodie shifted uncomfortably on the sand. Her instincts were telling her to get up, make an excuse, get them moving back to camp. But her traitorous body sank deeper into James's, and she nestled her head against his shoulder.

"Now do the other arm," she commanded.

"Why?"

"For science, naturally."

"I knew your insatiable curiosity would work to my benefit someday." He squeezed her with his knees as he switched sides, and she felt the gratitude in his embrace for ignoring his mistake.

Mistake. Was it a mistake? How silly. Of course it was. Love, she reminded herself, *is just oxytocin and hormones poorly disguised. Helpful in forming family bonds that keep children alive. An evolutionary advantage.* There were any number of holes in this theory, but Rhodie didn't dwell on them. After all, if she started thinking about how much she wanted to spend the rest of her life counting Arron's freckles and sitting across a chessboard from him and letting him try to make her laugh out loud, the whole thing would fall apart.

"Well?" he asked.

"I beg your pardon?"

He brought his lips close to her ear. "Does it feel as good on this side?"

It did. It really did.

"I haven't collected enough data yet. Continue."

"I think you're going to fall asleep on me if we stay out here much longer. I don't want to have to carry you back to camp." His voice was so soothing when he spoke to her like that.

"Mmm." She closed her eyes anyway, listening to the crackle of the fire, the steady breath of the ocean, the song of cicadas.

"Rhodie. Stay awake, love."

"I'm awake," she said through a yawn.

He chuckled low in her ear, and she felt his chest vibrating. *And that's another reason why we can't be in love . . . He almost died in the line of duty. I'd make a terrible widow.*

He started to move away, but she caught his arm. "Wait, I promised my sisters . . ."

"Pardon?"

She pulled out her phone. "Smile, Arron." She took a selfie of them together, his chin resting on her shoulder, both of their skin bathed in the dying firelight. She squinted at it. "It appears this camera cannot expose both of us correctly."

James shifted to his right and speared a marshmallow on a stick, handing it to her. "Here. Something to keep you occupied so you don't fall asleep."

"I'd rather *you* keep me occupied . . ."

"Don't tempt me, flower."

Rhodie's face heated, and she took the stick. She sat up, giving him some space, and he shifted to sit next to her instead, spearing another marshmallow for himself. Staring into the coals emboldened her to ask.

"How many, then?"

"Marshmallows? I brought a good-sized bag, but I know you don't care for sweets . . ."

"No, not marshmallows. How many . . . women." She cleared her throat. "How many women have you . . . kept occupied?"

He rotated his stick. "Well, I stopped counting after the first hundred . . ."

Rhodie elbowed him, and feeling ignored, her marshmallow erupted into flames. She cursed softly as she smothered it in the sand, and she could feel him shaking next to her as he tried not to laugh. She held out her hand primly for another one, which he supplied straight-faced. "All that good real-world tutoring, all for naught . . ." She narrowed her eyes at him, and he grinned. He pulled his off the stick and popped it straight into his mouth, gasping at how hot it was.

"You're not going to tell me?" She pouted.

"Does it matter?"

"Yes!"

"Why?"

"Because," she said. "It just does." He reached over her and grabbed the wine.

"Sure you don't want to pop this first? Might ease the sting . . ."

"I never know when you're joking, Arrondale James."

He tucked the bottle back into the backpack. "Well, if you want the truth, I've snogged plenty of women, but only bedded three."

"What were their names?"

"Oh, I don't think you need their names . . . I assume you've got trained assassins at your command. I'd hate for them to meet an untimely death."

"Circumstances, then."

"Very well. The first was my prom date. It was the first time for both of us, and she found the experience . . . unsatisfying. We did it in the back of her father's wagon. Unfortunately, he did not realize we were there, and he came to collect it in order to take his sick mother to the doctor, planning to come back for us . . ."

Rhodie's hand flew to her mouth, her shoulders shaking uncontrollably.

"Just let it out, love."

She let her hand fall and roared her laughter into the night sky, her eyes filling with tears.

"Needless to say, he was a bit surprised to see us when Grandmama tried to get into the back. So that was memorable, and I wasn't allowed to see her again."

"Naturally," Rhodie said, wiping her eyes, still giggling.

"Lady number two I picked up in a bar while celebrating my graduation from university. That was the same weekend I found out about my trust fund, and I can't say I handled it very well."

Rhodie slid her hand into his, interlocking their fingers, drawing circles with her middle finger around his kneecap with her other hand. "How so?"

James shrugged. "I never wanted anything from my father, but it was painful to know that nothing had kept him from me except apathy. Well, correction: he cared enough to share his wealth, which was apparently considerable. But not enough to claim me. The money just made me feel dirty."

"I know what you mean."

He looked over at her, his eyes vulnerable. "You do?"

"Certainly. It's difficult to see my colleagues taking on considerable debt in order to get an education I purchased outright. Difficult to see students whom I know won't be able to achieve their potential, simply because they're poor. There's nothing worse than a genius who can't explore her limits, can't contribute to society as she'd like to."

"Oh, I don't know. I'm sitting next to a genius right now, and while the world is open to her, she holds back out of guilt and fear of showing off. That's pretty sad as well."

She sniffed. "You vastly overestimate my potential."

"I don't think so."

"And number three?"

"Ah, yes, number three. Number three is how I discovered that some women get very swoony over a medal on a man's chest. Swoony is fine, but it felt . . . hollow. I was a conquest to her."

"I'm sorry."

"So am I, actually." He kissed her temple. "I'd never have touched them if I'd known I actually had a shot with you, darling. Though I'm sure you'll throw me over now that you know my sordid sexual history . . . not quite the wealth of experience I've touted, I know."

"I knew you were joking, anyway."

He was quiet for a beat. "Is it safe to assume you haven't any history?"

She nodded, staring into the fire. "Too well guarded, I suppose. A bird in a cage." She felt a nervous buzzing overtake her chest. "I know we have not yet discussed progressing in our shared intimacy . . ."

"Rhodie," James groaned. "Stop."

"What?"

"You have this way when you're nervous. You won't use contractions and you sound like you're trying to win a contest for most multisyllabic words."

She made her lips into a flat line. "Fine. You want forthrightness? Directness? I'm not yet ready to take that step in our relationship. I feel that should remain between a husband and wife, and I'm not sure where things between us are leading."

He kissed the back of her hand. "Thank you for sharing that. It comes as no surprise, and I shan't push you for more. As for where things are heading between us? Toward ruin, assuredly, but I'm having a marvelous time along the way."

The comment surprised her. *Does he not want to marry me?* The way he talked, she'd assumed that was his intention.

She scowled at him as he began to pack things up. "What sort of ruin?"

"Mine, mostly, when you put me out to pasture. Just don't send me to the glue factory, darling. I'm sure I'm still good for something."

Rhodie got to her feet, brushing the sand from the backs of her legs. "Stop joking for a moment."

He ignored her request. "You need a thoroughbred, not a mule. Eventually, you're going to quit messing around with me and go find the right kind of horse."

"Stop it, Arron. You're not a mule."

"Perhaps. But I'm not a thoroughbred, either, darling," he said, putting the backpack on his shoulders, "and you know it." He smiled at her as though completely unconcerned, which just ratcheted her anger up higher. "Walk back or run?"

"Run," she muttered, anxious to burn off some of these tight feelings in her chest, so packed in she feared she would burst.

I would, she wanted to say, their feet falling into a steady rhythm. *I would marry you, if things keep going this way. But I know you're going to figure out soon that it's not me who's too good for you . . . It's the other way around.*

They ran back in silence, but James's steps slowed as they neared the camp.

"One more thing. I know things between us are unequal, if you will, in the sense that I technically work for your brother. And if there should come a time when things go poorly between us . . ."

Rhodie felt her heart softening. "James . . ."

He held up a hand for silence. "If you tire of me, just tell me. I'll request a transfer myself. Please don't feel that you have to go through channels or through Edward. We're both adults. We can handle a bit of direct communication from time to time."

"Very well, I agree." She laid a hand on his stubbled cheek. "Not too often, though. Like all good Orangiersians, directness gives me hives."

"My poor darling," he said, straight-faced. "Show me where it hurts and I'll kiss it all better . . ."

"Maybe tomorrow," she murmured, all too aware of the possibility of being seen.

CHAPTER TWENTY-EIGHT

JAMES WAS HUNGRY. RHODIE had forgotten to take lunch again, or chosen not to—he never knew which. He'd asked a passing private to grab him a sandwich before he passed out, and he assumed that the man walking straight up to him was the one he'd sent. But this man wasn't in uniform. He wore a hat low over his eyes, and his skin was the same color as Rhodie's, but he was tall, taller than James.

"Arron," the man said, his voice so low it was barely heard over the passing wagons. *That voice. I know that voice.* He peered under the hat; Lincoln's eyes met his, full of fear, full of hope. James stared into the face he'd searched for, slogged through jungles and marshes for, the face he'd been shot for. The face of the person he'd been shot by, if indirectly. Lincoln was still like a brother, and it was a brother looking into his eyes now, begging him silently for help, and at the same time, commanding him to save him.

"Are you trying to start a riot?" He'd always intended to take the man alive; he wasn't one of the many who wanted to see Lincoln dead for how he'd ripped apart their country, how he'd betrayed his nation by attempting a coup. But there were plenty here in their ranks who felt that way. James wanted to grab him by the arm and lead him somewhere less public, but he couldn't leave Rhodie behind. *Rhodie.* She'd want to see him immediately.

"Get inside," he growled. James did grab him by the arm then, his heart pounding out of his chest, sweat pouring down his temples. *Where can I hide him? How can I get him and Rhodie out of here? If they think she's conspiring with him, she may be in danger from the mob as well. If I handcuff him, he'll have no way to defend himself if they go after him . . . but if I don't, it'll seem like I wasn't doing my duty.* Desperate, James unbuttoned his uniform shirt and threw it over Lincoln's head to make him less recognizable, then bound his hands loosely with one of his shoelaces. He led him into the lab. *These doors lock. I can lock us in here until I figure out what to do with him.*

"I apologize," he said to Rhodie, trying to sound collected when he felt as scattered as a thousand-piece jigsaw puzzle. "Colonel Weathers says he needs the whole contingent in the mess hall immediately. There's a magical confluence gathering around this building, and they need to make sure it's not dangerous. Shouldn't take long."

"What kind of confluence?" she asked, not looking up from whatever she was piping into an agar plate. At her voice, he felt relief.

"He didn't say, Dr. Broward."

"Well, we're not even close to done for the day . . ."

"You can return to your experiments shortly. I promise."

"Who's that?" Could she tell the man in James's grasp was Lincoln, even from across the room, with his dreads cut off and his face covered? Her voice was so sharp, he felt cut by it.

"Local guy. He was caught stealing something, I'm dealing with it. Could you move along, please?" Well, parts of that were true. He bore deep into her gaze, trying to imbue

into his stare all the urgency he could without actually showing how much he was panicking.

"Very well." She sounded suspicious, but she was complying. "But he'd better not cause any problems with my
equipment. And if he does, I'm holding you directly responsible." His thoughts were stuttering like an old TV in a thun-
derstorm, the transmission broken and jumpy. *She's, she's
complying. It's okay, okay. He'll be behind a locked door in just
a minute, in just a minute.* Grumbling, her assistants filed
out, grabbing purses and backpacks, muttering about magical encroachment and how Trella's Veil was really a poor sub-
stitute for their own system.

"Is the back door locked?" James asked as Rhodie went
by, raising his voice to be heard by all of them. "I don't want
anyone tampering with your equipment or belongings . . ."

"No, it's not," she said, digging the keys out of her bag.
Everyone else had filed out. "Where's your other shoelace?
Why are you half-dressed?"

James took the keys from her and locked the front door.

"I thought you said we had to leave. Really, darling, what
on earth . . ."

Lincoln shook his head to relieve himself of the shirt,
and James saw her take a breath to scream. He lunged forward and put a hand over her mouth. "Don't. At this point,
we'll be lucky to get him out of here alive, and we can't have
you alerting everyone just yet." Her eyes were wide, shining,
and he wanted to pull her into his neck and hold her until she calmed down, but it wasn't the right thing to do. He
needed to get Lincoln settled first, find out his intentions.

Without removing his hand from Rhodie's mouth, he turned to Lincoln. "Why are you here? What do you want?"

"I'm surrendering." He pushed up the brim of his hat with his bound hands to see them better. "I can't live with Heather anymore. I can't live with what she's intending to do."

"You were part of it." James turned and put Rhodie behind him, silently berating himself for locking them into a room with someone who'd tried to kidnap Abbie. "I saw the video. You tried to take her . . ."

He nodded, pinching his bottom lip. "I did. But I wouldn't have hurt Abbie. She's my sister-in-law; she's my family."

"Why should we believe you? You've lost every scrap of credibility you ever possessed with me."

"I let you tie me up. I came without weapons. I came alone."

"That's worth something . . . but it's not enough," James said. "If I take you in now, I can't guarantee your safety."

"I realize that. But I want to end this."

"Why not go to Edward?"

"You were closer. And there are fewer people here who want to kill me."

"In sheer numbers, maybe. Not as a percentage. How did you know where we were?"

"Heather tracks all their phones."

He could feel Rhodie behind him, patting her pockets for her phone, and Lincoln's gaze slid to her.

"Rho . . ."

"No." James was in his face before he'd even realized he'd moved. "Don't talk to her. You lost that privilege. You have no idea what you've put your family through."

"Arron . . ." Rhodie was tugging him back, her voice rough with emotion, and he pivoted to her, still not willing to turn his back to the man.

Lincoln huffed a laugh. "Her intelligence said that you were together, but not *together*. Though I guess it shouldn't surprise me."

"Shut your mouth," James growled, and he felt Rhodie turning his chin toward her with a gentle hand.

"What's the plan here?"

James wiped the sweat off his forehead with his shoulder. "One of us has to go get Weathers and let him know what's happening, preferably avoiding an angry mob in the process, at least until we get a few reliable people with weapons in here to protect him." He gestured to the phone in her hand. "And let's not use the Heather tracking device, shall we?"

"She can't listen to your calls," Lincoln put in. "Why would I have asked Rhodie to call me otherwise?"

"Why didn't you call her yourself, then?" James threw out his arms. "Why text her? And how do we know you're not baiting us into using the phone, to give her some kind of signal?"

Lincoln tilted his head. "What kind of signal?"

"How should I know? You're the traitor, not me."

"Trust me, it's better that she doesn't know where I am. You don't want her storming your castle."

"She'd come here? She'd come after you?"

He nodded. "She doesn't exactly know that I left . . . I sort of slipped out while she was traveling. She'll be back soon, though."

"Was she holding you prisoner?" Rhodie asked, and James could hear the hope in her voice.

Lincoln's gaze met hers briefly, then he shook his head. "I'm so sorry, Rho. I'm sorry for everything I've put you through."

It was like watching cement harden on a time-lapse video: one minute, Rhodie was soft, understanding; but the minute she determined his culpability, she was completely closed off.

"Love? You did it for love?" She spit out the words.

He nodded miserably, and she strolled closer to him. "We loved you, too, you know. We still do." The shame on his face in response to Rhodie's declaration made James sick to his stomach. She turned to him. "I'll stay here with him. You go get Weathers."

James shook his head. "I can't leave you alone with him. I'd call Petros, but he's asleep."

"I think he'd understand you waking him for this . . ."

"Yes. Right. All right," he said, pulling out his phone. By the time he'd dressed properly, having secured Lincoln's wrists with a length of copper tubing supplied by Rhodie, Petros was knocking at the door.

CHAPTER TWENTY-NINE

"YOU SHOULD'VE CALLED me sooner, James," Petros growled, his gaze locked on Lincoln with an intensity that unsettled Rhodie.

"I'll file that away for future captures of traitorous royals." He glanced at her; she'd gone back to her work. She couldn't have her emotions rioting when there might be actual riots happening outside. He said something quietly to his friend, and Petros gave him a single nod.

"Lock the door behind me."

"Yes. Now go."

Rhodie worked in silence. She could feel Lincoln watching her, and when she could stand it no longer, she lifted her head. "What?" she snapped. "What do you want to say? This is your chance, while my keeper is gone." The acid in the words surprised her; did she resent James's protection? She wished she had the brain space to think about it.

"First of all, I am sorry. I'm very sorry. I was wrapped up in Heather, and I let her make me forget all the other things that were important to me."

"I don't accept your apology. You had chances to make things right; no one forced you to fight a war, to kill your own countrymen. You did that. You're lucky Edward is against the death penalty."

His chin trembled and his eyes filled with tears. "He's not going to execute me?"

Her dreads swayed as she shook her head, returning her gaze to her work. "He's expressed the intention to simply imprison you. And honestly, I don't think he wants to do that, but your faction is giving him a terrible time politically." She glanced up to note his reaction to this statement and found him with his hands covering his face, his shoulders shaking. Rhodie started across the room, but Petros put out a hand before she could touch him.

"No, Highness."

Lincoln didn't look like he was putting her on; he looked broken. *Love broke him.* She wanted to reject the thought, but she couldn't find anything to replace it with. And yet, she felt a strange comfort in watching him sob. Being unloved romantically had made her feel damaged her all her adult life . . . and yet, here was a man who was loved, and yet he was still so unhappy. *Maybe it isn't love itself that's the problem. Maybe it's about who we let love us and who we love in return. Whose voice matters. Whose opinions.* Rhodie felt the yoke of public opinion across her shoulders, and she knew she'd let it steer her for too long. But James . . . her heart melted at the thought of him. His love was nothing like Heather's or the public's; he'd never come between her and her family, he'd never try to manipulate her with it. It wasn't fickle, subject to fashions and appearance. James's love was something else. A deep resolve settled over her; she would say yes to this kind of love. She would hold on to it with both hands.

"Lincoln," she started, but she didn't know what to say.

"I want to explain what I did," he choked out. "But I can't. There's no explaining it. She said she loved me and I believed her. But looking back, how could she have? How could she have if she put me through all this?" He wiped his eyes one at a time. "I'm h-happy for you, Rho," he hiccupped. "I'm happy you found someone despite everything that h-happened with your con-contract. I'm happy for you. And after all the misery I've caused, I'm glad I got to see you happy one more time."

Disregarding Petros, she stepped forward and grabbed his hand, gripping his fingers too tightly. "You will see me again. I'll come visit you. I promise."

A pounding at the door startled them both. "Dr. Broward? What's going on?" It was Joline. Rhodie moved to the door and put her hand on it.

"We've just hit a bit of a snag here, Jo. I promise I will get you back in here as soon as possible."

"Could you please put my hyaluronic acid solution back in the fridge?"

"And my tissue samples?" came another voice.

"And my sandwich?" came a third.

Rhodie chuckled despite the situation. "Yes, I will. Thank you for your patience. I'm on it." But her answer was lost to the chorus of angry voices and bodies shuffling outside the locked door, and then Petros was unlocking the door.

CHAPTER THIRTY

JAMES'S MIND RACED as Petros locked the door behind him. It was killing him to leave Rhodie and Lincoln in the lab; he had no idea what he might try to say or do. He kicked himself for still wanting to trust the man after everything that had happened. He tried to squeeze between the crowd of research assistants and lab techs outside the building, but they were having none of it.

"Where's Dr. Broward?"

"When can we get back to our experiments? I left my samples out, and if they thaw . . ."

He held his hands up. "Just a few more minutes, everyone. Have patience . . ."

"And there was no meeting in the mess hall, by the way!" Joline called after him.

"Go back and wait there. Someone will be there in a moment to explain." James tried to appear unaffected by the upset crowd as he crossed the yard, but inside, he was already thinking of ways to get rid of them while they removed Lincoln from the building. It would be easier to defend the lodge against his irate countrymen. He took the stairs two at a time and hurried down the corridor to Weathers's room and pounded on the door. James could hear voices inside, which paused at the sound of his knock, then resumed their conversation.

"Sir! This is urgent, sir," James called through the door, and the conversation paused again.

Through the door came a muffled "Just a moment, General," then the door cracked open. Seeing who it was, Weathers glared. "I'm on a conference call, Lieutenant."

"This is more important, sir. I promise. On my mother's biscuits."

His mouth a flat, dissatisfied line, the man backed out of the way and let James in. "Now, Lieutenant—"

"I've captured Lincoln. He's here, he's locked in the lab."

Weathers went completely still.

"Did I hear that right?" barked a voice through the computer. "Lincoln's been captured?"

James stared at the computer. The voice sounded familiar, but he couldn't be sure . . .

"Somebody start talking! Hello? Weathers!"

"Just, just a moment, sir. Lieutenant, you're saying the traitor is here? Is he secure?"

He nodded. "Petros is with him. And Rhodie. He's surrendered himself."

Weathers's eyes widened. "You left the princess *alone* with him?"

"He was tied up. I didn't want things to become violent. I wanted her help in keeping everything calm."

The colonel sat down hard in his desk chair. "General, I'm gonna call you back."

"Keep me informed."

The colonel turned to him. "You know him best, you've spoken to him. Why's he here?"

"He says he wants to turn himself in. He's been cooperative so far, and he had no weapons."

"We should, though, if only for crowd control."

James nodded. "I thought we could bring him into the lodge, easier to protect him that way. He has to stand trial. We can't allow mob justice, especially on foreign soil."

"Agreed." Weathers flipped open a footlocker at the end of his perfectly made bed. "You want a crossbow?"

"Yes."

The older man handed him a weapon before taking two for himself, a sword and a dagger. "You know the men's politics better than I do. Who do you think can be trusted to stay on mission and not let personal feelings get in the way?"

"Petros. Sanchex. Troy. Chance."

"Six should be enough. Two go in front and clear the way, two flank the prisoner, two bring up the rear. Go get 'em."

Within twenty minutes, they were armed and assembled at the doors to the lab. The timid portion of the crowd (most of the scientists) had dispersed, while the drama seekers had gravitated closer.

"Back up," Weathers barked, and the crowd quickly obeyed.

James knocked on the door. "Petros, it's me. We're ready." The door opened slowly. Chance had been spooling up a defensive spell, just big enough for Lincoln, and as their prisoner stepped out, it fell over him like a cloak, shielding his face from onlookers. It looked almost like silk, James thought as he took Lincoln by the arm and followed Weathers and Sanchex, who cleared the way.

Murmurs of "Who is that?" and "What's going on?" overlapped as they hurried through the crowd, and they'd made it to the stairs of the lodge when James suddenly realized that in their panic, they hadn't left a guard for Rhodie.

"Sir! We forgot Rhodie!" In his head, he'd meant to bring her with them to the lodge, but in their haste and confusion, she'd been left behind. Without waiting for Weathers to respond, he spun and charged back toward the lab, but the sudden movement disrupted Chance's haphazard spell, and someone got a good look at him.

"It's *Lincoln*!" a man shouted, and chaos erupted. James fought back the now-angry onlookers, lifting the crossbow to his shoulder.

"Get back!" he yelled as his contingent powered up the lodge steps, the illusion of control shattered. The moment the lodge doors slammed shut, he was shoving his way through the crowd to the lab, which had been forgotten. James pounded on the back door.

"Rhodie, it's me! Let me in!"

The key turned in the lock, and she yanked him inside.

"What's going on out there? Is he all right? I heard shouting..."

"He's fine; we got him inside. He's fine, I promise." He bent and put his hands on his knees, trying to catch his breath. "Are you all right? I'm so sorry, love, I meant to bring you with us, but then Petros came out with just him and I didn't think about the fact that you were here alone and ..."

"I'm fine, Arron. I'm just fine." He hugged her so hard he cracked her back, and they both laughed shakily. "You did it. You brought him in."

"Yeah." Not just his laugh was shaky now; his whole body had decided that this level of stress was not containable to one human body, and it reacted by attempting to vibrate it out of his system. Rhodie felt it, and she pulled back.

"You want some water? Come here, sit down."

She brought him a glass of water from the large blue jug in the corner, and he gulped it down. But he didn't get as much time to recover as he needed before his phone was ringing.

"James? You all right?" It was Petros; they were concerned when he didn't make it into the building.

"I'm fine. What's happening? He's secure?" He put the call on speakerphone.

"Yes, but there's something else happening. Something worse."

"What? What's going on?"

"Is there a radio in the lab?"

"No, I prefer quiet," Rhodie replied.

Weathers took the phone. "Both of you get up here, now. Come in the back."

James began quickly gathering up Rhodie's things. Unsure when they'd be able to leave the lodge again, she put away the materials that were going to go bad, and he noticed her hands were shaking.

"Hey." He put a hand on her arm. "It's going to be okay, all right? I won't let them hurt you. I promise."

She nodded, then they moved quickly out the back. The central yard that had just minutes before held a hundred angry Orangiersians was completely abandoned. James felt a shiver work its way down his spine; it was downright creepy.

"Come on," he whispered. They ran in sync; it was easy to match her stride from all those nighttime beach runs.

They pounded on the back door and Chance lifted the magic seal he'd placed on the door before letting them in.

"What's going on, what is it?"

Chance swallowed hard. "There's been an attack on Bluffton Castle."

"What?" Rhodie's voice sounded faint, and he turned to see her stumble into one of the kitchen chairs.

"Here," he said, motioning them forward. He led them into the living room where fifteen people were gathered around a small screen. A grainy video showed smoke pouring out of the west wing of the building, near the entrance. Lincoln stood with them, his hands still bound, tears streaming down his face.

His gaze fixed on the screen, he asked, "Do you know what the expression 'Jersey hath no fury like a woman scorned' means?"

"I believe so."

Lincoln shook his head. "Not like you're about to." He rubbed his temples. "This is my fault. I should've gone to Edward, then she wouldn't have attacked them. If I'd just . . ." His voice trailed off, and they all just stared as Rhodie's house burned.

CHAPTER THIRTY-ONE

AS IT TURNED OUT, THE attack on Bluffton wasn't the worst part: they'd had no communication in or out of Orangiers since the video was posted. Someone in Heather's camp had taken the footage with a drone, uploaded it from somewhere in Op'Ho'Lonia . . . or maybe routed through a dummy IP address. There was no way to know.

The strangest part to Rhodie was how camp life just . . . pivoted. In the hours since the attack, work was being done: the chefs cooked, the soldiers trained, her research assistants tabulated and interviewed . . . but everyone had a radio on. Those who didn't have the physical machine were streaming it on their phones, listening with one ear, even as they walked through camp. Distracted, they bumped into one another, mumbling excuses—"Didn't see you there, should look where I'm going, apologies"—when they all knew it was the crisis that caused the collision. They whispered. Young women cried, young men tried to comfort them. A number of secret relationships suddenly became public, the couples apparently deciding that whatever the consequences, life was too short to hide what you really wanted.

Rhodie was in the mess hall. She wasn't eating, but she was there.

"Have you heard anything?" a blonde woman asked a brunette at a nearby table.

"I heard it was a bomb at the palace . . ." They cast a glance askance at Rhodie, who pretended not to hear, despite being desperate for them to keep talking.

"I heard that the Grand Duchess is taken hostage and being held for ransom by Heather." *That can't be true.*

"I heard a tidal wave knocked out the Veil network completely. And the king and his family were evacuated to La Bonisla."

There's no evacuation contingency plan that includes La Bonisla . . . Hearth House maybe or Fort Pierce. But not the islands.

"Dr. Broward." James stood over her, frowning. "I've been calling to you, didn't you hear?"

"No, I apologize, my mind was elsewhere."

"The colonel would like to brief you in ten minutes."

She swallowed hard, though her throat was dry. "Me?"

He nodded curtly. "You are the ranking royal in camp. Until we can get a hold of them, you are, in a sense, in charge. He wants to keep you informed."

She nodded faintly. "And you'll be there?"

"Of course. If you want me." For once, he kept the suggestion entirely out of his voice. He looked at her with sympathy. "Are you done here? It wouldn't do to be late." She nodded, but didn't move. He started to gather her books.

"Aren't you worried about them?"

He stopped. "Of course," he said gently. "Of course I am, but if I stop to really think about it, I'll be fairly undone. And something tells me you need a useful James at your side at the moment, so I'm going to worry later when no one needs me. I'm just deferring my worries, Doctor." The look in his eyes said he wanted to touch, to comfort, to soothe, but didn't dare in public. His truth wasn't ready to be lived aloud, apparently, and even though she'd been the one to keep them a secret, Rhodie was a little bit sorry.

She nodded stiffly, collecting herself physically and emotionally as they packed her satchel. They crossed the camp without seeing it, ignoring the stares and whispers that followed them like a swarm of bees. He opened the door of the cabin for her, but she didn't walk through it. Couldn't walk through it, not yet. Walking through that door was accepting a new chapter in her life, a new role that would define her like no other.

"Rutha used to tell me how lucky I was."

"Your nanny?"

Rhodie nodded. "She said I was lucky I was born a girl because it affords me the luxury of being royal without the responsibility." She stared into the cabin. "I guess she was wrong."

James stepped back, letting the door swing shut without going through it. He led her by the elbow around the side of the building, pulling them into the shadows, away from the prying eyes. "You can do this, Rhodie," he said, his voice low, his eyes ablaze with aggravation. "You're as capable as Edward. They just want to keep you in the loop. No one's going to pressure you to make decisions without advisors. And if you need my opinions, I'm not using them at the moment, so you're entirely welcome to them." His body language was incongruous with his words; the tenderness of them against his stiffly crossed arms, high shoulders, hands jammed into his armpits. Her heart softened as she realized that he was trying to hold himself away. *Both hands. I'm taking his love with both hands.*

"How badly do you want to kiss me right now?" she whispered.

"So badly," he whispered back. "I can think of nothing else. I need it. I need you."

"Then do it," she said, letting her satchel drop to the ground.

"Don't say that," he grumped, straightening his uniform. "Someone would see."

"Queens consort with whoever they want." She pulled him forward by his collar and he kissed her then; she felt the tension drain out of him, felt his muscles unwind.

"You're not queen yet, flower," he whispered, his face twisted like he'd taken a fist to the gut, raking his fingers through his hair. "And if that responsibility is thrust upon you, then this"—he gestured between them—"will be over. We both know it, so let's not pretend."

He's right, she thought, as she turned to enter the cabin. *My whole life will be taken from me, and handed back in pieces. I'll have to marry someone else, likely someone whose family rejected me a decade ago. I won't have the benefit of my family to guide me . . . All their love and support will just be . . . gone.* She couldn't cry just then: she felt like she couldn't even find her soul, she was so lost. Rhodie felt like she was sleepwalking as she entered the cabin, and every person rose out of deference. She motioned for everyone to sit, and she took the chair an aide pulled out for her at the head of the table. James took up a position along the wall where she could keep him in her peripheral vision. She turned her head to give him the longest glance she dared give, and he winked at her.

"Right," she said. "Colonel Weathers, what's the situation?"

"Your Highness, we haven't been able to establish contact with Bluffton; communications are still down countrywide. We did, however, receive a message from the Op'Ho'Lonian Ambassador to Orangiers, Mr. Manuel Martinex. He was boarding a blimp to Op when the attack hit. From the air, he could see that at least two units of Black Feathers had taken up a defensive position around Bluffton already. He did not see any fire, explosions, or other damage to the castle beyond what happened in the west wing."

"Do we have any idea when we might reestablish contact with them?"

He shook his head, and she saw James's shoulders slump. "During a regular outage, it should've taken the Veil Technicians no more than a few hours to have things back up and running. If it was a coordinated attack affecting multiple power stations, it may take longer. Days, even."

She gave them a curt nod. "In the meantime, what actions do you recommend we take?"

He slid a piece of paper across the rough table to her. "We've prepared a statement for you to read at a nearby radio station, condemning the attack and asking the nations to hold Kiriien accountable for Heather's actions."

"Do we know for certain that she is involved? Perhaps some opportunistic nation . . ."

Weathers nodded to someone over her shoulder, and she turned to see them bring Lincoln into the room.

"Hi, Rho."

"Lincoln." Her voice was cool; she couldn't afford to show weakness at the moment. But her distant demeanor snapped the minute she noticed the puffiness around his right eye. She pinned every man at the table with a lengthy stare one by one. "Who?"

"Your Highness?"

Who. Did. This?

"Your Highness, there was a scuffle when the prisoner was first captured . . ."

"Yes, I know, I heard it." She stood and probed his injury gently, and he winced. "This, however, happened more recently than that."

Weathers's throat moved as he swallowed. "We apologize, Your Highness; one of the guards got out of hand when the prisoner was being interrogated. It won't happen again."

"See that it doesn't. Traitor or not, he is still a member of the royal family."

"Yes, ma'am." Weathers turned to Lincoln. "Tell her what you told us."

"Heather had contingency plans for everything; I'm sure my disappearance has her panicking. If she thinks I'm in Orangiers, she may have crashed the Veil in order for her magic to take precedence, in order to look for me."

"Thank you."

The guards led Lincoln back out, but she didn't miss the turbulence on James's face at the sight of him. Rhodie sat back down, quietly crossing her ankles under her chair.

"When is my radio address scheduled?"

"Tomorrow morning at 0800."

"For consistency's sake, I will take Lieutenant James and Corporal Petros with me as my personal guard, as they are familiar with my needs."

"Yes, Highness."

"Was there anything else?"

"Yes, ma'am. You should be prepared to leave as soon as we get word from the palace; they may need you to come immediately if . . ." He cleared his throat. "If the situation is worse than we've feared."

You mean, if my family is gone? She couldn't believe that yet. The ambassador said everything looked fine. She would believe that. She would use her iron will and make it true, even if it was only in her own mind.

"Your Majesty," Colonel O'Grady said, leaning forward, "please know that we are here to serve you. You needn't feel alone in all this. We are suffering with you as we wait for news."

Rhodie stood, and they all stood with her this time, saluting, frozen until she woodenly returned the gesture. "Thank you, Colonel. Thank you, gentlemen."

James was at her elbow, opening the door for her before she could signal him that she wished to leave. She stumbled out onto the muddy yard, her legs carrying her, but her mind disengaged.

"Arron," she whispered, "he called me Majesty."

"Hang on, flower," he murmured back. "Let's get up to your room."

"Faster," she said, tears threatening to fall.

"I know," he said. "Me too."

They powered into the house and up the stairs, ignoring more stares and whispers. James slammed the door to her room behind them just before she crumpled to the floor.

"He called me Majesty," she cried. "He thinks they're all dead. He thinks I'm his queen."

"We don't know that yet," James said, joining her on the floor, rubbing her back. "He's trying to show you his support. But we don't believe that, do we?"

She shook her head violently.

"There is still hope. We don't have enough evidence for any other conclusion."

"Hope is entirely logical." Rhodie believed the words, but her body had been taxed beyond what it could accept. She lay down on the wooden floor, one arm under her head, feeling her body curl into the fetal position. It was all she could do.

"Come on, love. Let's get you into your bed."

"Only if you get in with me," she said, sniffling.

"I can't, flower. I'll get fired," he said, brushing the locs back from her face.

"By whom?" she asked. "You work for me now." She didn't protest as James got to his feet and lifted her under her arms and legs, carried her across the room, and bent to remove her shoes before he tucked her in under the quilt and straightened the mosquito net.

"You told me that closeness was impolite," he said, conjuring a smile, and she knew he was forcing it.

"Please, James." She touched his face gently and could tell his resolve was weakening.

"I'll come back," he said, kissing the inside of her wrist. "When I'm off duty, I promise I'll come back. Petros won't say anything." He looked around. "Do you want a book or something? A scarf for your hair?"

She shook her head.

"I'll bring dinner when I come."

"I'm not hungry." She rolled away from him.

"I'll bring dinner," he repeated firmly, "so you don't have to go downstairs." The door shutting behind him was the last thing she heard before she fell asleep.

IT WAS DARK WHEN JAMES finally came back. If he knocked, she didn't hear it. She sat up when he set the tray of rice and beans down on her desk.

"What time is it?"

"Dinnertime. You can have a kiss for every bite." There was something oddly thickened about his voice; he was speaking more slowly than usual. James sat down in her desk chair and lit the lamp before he unlaced his boots . . . she was surprised he was keeping his distance. He took off his outer uniform shirt, revealing the white T-shirt underneath, and she wondered simultaneously how he managed two layers in the heat and if this is how it would feel to be married to him, getting to come home to those biceps every night. But as soon as he was done, he stumbled over to the bed, lifting the mosquito net and crawling onto the covers.

As he nestled into her neck and dragged his body on top of hers, she caught a whiff of his breath. "Have you been drinking?"

He nodded. "Just a little bit."

"You were drinking on duty?"

"Just needed to take the edge off," he mumbled, pressing light kisses along her neck, moving down toward her collarbone, his hand on her hip over the quilt. "Woz, you feel so good." It did feel good, and that pissed her off. If he'd been sober, maybe he could've comforted her. But now?

She shook her head. "Arron, you can't . . ."

He lifted his face. "I can't what?"

"With all that has happened today, I cannot see how having an intoxicated man in my bed is going to benefit me right now."

He grinned. "Oh, you'll see what the benefits are soon enough."

She pushed him away gently and sat up. "I think perhaps I will have that dinner."

"Suit yourself." He flopped back down onto the bed, and she was forced to clamber over him.

"I don't remember you drinking this much in the past."

"I didn't have this many problems in the past."

"Well, it's unbecoming."

He rolled and propped his head up on his hand. "Unbecoming of what? An officer? A boyfriend? A paramour? A duke?" His throat bobbed as he swallowed hard. "A friend of the king?"

"All of the above. And if you're going to throw up, I'd prefer you do so in a toilet." *No,* she thought, *this isn't what I'm trying to say. This is coming out all wrong.* His next words confirmed that her concern wasn't coming across.

"First of all, I'm sorry I repulse you so. And secondary, secondly, secondarily," he said, "I would never do that to your floor. I have the utmost respect for you and your space."

"You do not repulse me, I am simply pointing out that your behavior is unusual for you." She paused, unsure how to proceed. "When you did your mandatory counseling, did they talk to you about PTSD?"

He snorted. "I don't have PTSD. And I told you that already in no uncertain terms, but you keep asking and asking and asking about it, so you clearly don't agree."

"You needn't be insulted. I'm trying to say that I'm concerned about you."

"I needn't be, but I be." He got to his feet, swaying. "I'll leave you to your repast, then, if you actually plan to eat it. Sometimes I'm concerned you've forgotten how. If you do eat, it will be your past repast, and I look forward to that." James put his shirt back on and slipped his feet into his boots, tucking the laces inside, when there was a knock at the door. "Come in," he called, though he had no right.

"Your Highness, we've had contact with them. Everyone's all right."

Relief burned through her so quickly, her skin tingled. "Thank Woz. May I speak with them?"

"Yes, Highness; I'll take you down to the communications office now, it's a satellite connection."

"Excellent, Corporal. Thank you." She turned to James. "I'll see you in the morning, Lieutenant."

"Yes, of course," he mumbled as she swept out of the room.

DISMISSED. JUST LIKE that. Crisis over, don't need him anymore. James stared into his drink, watching the bubbles rise. *I should just tell her about my father. Tell her about the dukedom. And then I'll never know if she actually loves me or if I'm just convenient. Maybe I'm just convenient now . . . I notice she's not anxious for anyone to know about us. Maybe there is no us. Maybe I've just concocted all this in my head, and I'm having some sort of very long dream. I'll probably wake up in my bed back in the loft in a few hours, ready to face the day with gusto . . . or maybe I'll wake up back in camp, still drunk as a skunk.*

"Well, look who we have here."

Speaking of skunks . . . James didn't look up. "What do you want, Tracy?"

"Drowning your troubles again? Or should I say *still*?"

"Go find somewhere else to sharpen your wit, Private, it's not cutting."

Tracy muttered something under his breath, but James caught one word of it: "Disgrace."

"Oh," he said, rising, "and I suppose a coddled rich boy like you is doing the uniform proud? Woz, I hate you. You're the worst kind of imposter."

"Feeling's mutual, Drunko."

"How am I an imposter?"

"Parading around here like it's not your connections that got you where you are. The only reason you got that medal is your friendship with the king!"

James's fist met the man's cheekbone before he'd even finished speaking. Once wasn't enough: he grabbed the man's collar with his left hand and pulled back to punch him again when a blinding pain erupted in his right eye. He let go and cursed, opting to put his knee in the man's stomach instead.

"Take it outside," the Op'Ho'Lonian bartender called, calmly drying a pint glass. "Whatever you break, you'll pay for."

Tracy hadn't been unprepared this time. Two of his friends hauled James outside by his arms, and he found himself caught in the middle as they circled him like sharks.

"How does it feel," Tracy taunted, "being on the other end of an unfair fight?"

"It wasn't a fight, you idiot," James spat. "You neglected your duty. You put her in danger. You got less than you deserved."

With his inebriated attention fully on Tracy, he never saw the kidney punch coming. He groaned and spun to face the other two men. He recognized them as two of Tracy's cronies, Darken and Wright.

"Camp's buzzing with rumors about your late-night runs together," Tracy said behind him. "You haven't gone and fallen in *love* with her, have you?"

Temper fueled his fist as James lashed out and managed to land a solid right cross on Wright, who backed away, holding his gushing nose. James pivoted and backed up until his attackers were both in front of him. *One down . . .*

"What kind of future do you think you could possibly have with someone like her?" Tracy laughed. "A woman like that? I'd tell you she's out of your league, Drunko, but you're not even playing the same game."

I know, he wanted to cry. *I've always known. I made a play for her anyway. It won't last. It can't.* James felt the weight of all that had happened in the last few days crushing him, pulverizing him, and with their laughter ringing in his ears, something inside him snapped. Later, he would not remember clapping their heads together like coconut shells, breaking Tracy's cheekbone with his knee. They knew military combat, but James scrapped like a street kid: he was throwing elbows and going for their eyes. He pulled hair and stomped on the bridge of Tracy's foot. He poured his grief over almost losing Edward and his family into a maelstrom of pain for his attackers. By the time someone from the camp arrived, all they found was three broken men—four if you counted James, who was mostly broken on the inside.

"Self-defense," he mumbled as Granger tied his hands behind his back and loaded him into the wagon with his groaning, cursing coworkers.

"That's not what the bartender said, Lieutenant. He said you started it. Said you threw the first punch." That had been shrewd of Tracy, inciting him in front of the bartender, gaining witnesses so that he'd be blameless. He might have even paid the man off. Something told him he'd probably have plenty of time to think about it.

CHAPTER THIRTY-TWO

THE NEXT MORNING, RHODIE paced her room, waiting for James's knock; he would go with her this morning to do the radio address. Since Bluffton didn't have reliable communications back up yet, they still wanted her to be the one to make it.

She had to admit . . . it hadn't been a bad thing to have the night to herself. There was so much to think about. The last few weeks had been all new. And Lincoln was captured; that alone would take some time to process. But now she had so much to tell James: her family were all fine, every last one of them. They'd been evacuated to Harbor House, their fortress farther up the coast, immediately after the Veil fell. She'd cried openly, talking to each precious one of them, relieved just to hear their voices.

But his knock didn't come. Six, six thirty . . . She finally opened her door to see if he just hadn't announced himself. Petros looked at her expectantly.

"Where's your daytime counterpart?" she asked.

Petros shrugged. "Got in some sort of trouble last night, I hear. He's in the brig with Tracy and his goons."

She stepped into the hallway. "Let's go." Rhodie walked as calmly as possible down the hall to the military mission commander's office and knocked softly.

"Come," he barked, and she opened the door.

"Colonel, I apologize for intruding on your time at this early hour."

The older man stood up, took off his reading glasses, and gestured to the seat across from him. She sat and he followed her lead.

"What's on your mind, Your Highness?"

"My security has been arrested."

He nodded. "Your security sent three men to the medic last night. Bartender says he started it. I'm tired of this shit, frankly."

"Lieutenant James has struggled as of late," she agreed, ignoring his use of coarse language, given all they'd been through in the last few days.

The colonel's face hardened. "That's an understatement." He gestured to the stack of papers on his desk. "As soon as I finish filling out these forms, he's out of the military. I don't care if he captured the traitor or not; he's damn reckless. We'll assign you another guard."

She pressed her shoulders back and sat up straighter, if only to remind him to whom he was speaking. "Sir, my friendship with James goes back many years, and I can promise you that this is out of character for him. While I'm not a psychiatrist, I believe part of it goes back to PTSD from when he was shot. I know you're a man of staunch integrity, unswayed by promises of royal favors; that isn't what's happening here." She paused.

He was watching her carefully.

"But as a friend and a medical professional, I beg you for leniency. Please don't dishonorably discharge him. He's wounded in ways you can't see; he needs a supportive community around him. Yes, he's always had a temper, but not like this. He's been under an incredible amount of stress with the Lincoln situation, and I believe he's being triggered by the environment here. If you could find a way to keep him on, I believe that small mercy would not prove you a fool."

"I can't let his behavior go unanswered, Doctor."

She reached out to touch his desk. "I know. I know, Colonel. And I would never undermine your authority over your soldiers. But I also know that this man matters to you. If you discharge him now . . ."

"What?"

"I don't know. But I know it would be a crushing blow. Unlike so many, he didn't join the service out of need. And once he's in his right mind again, I know he'll be an asset."

The colonel sat back, breaking their connection, and folded his arms across his large belly. His deep sigh gave Rhodie hope.

"I'll send him back to Orangiers, then, with the prisoner. I can't have him disrupting the rest of the mission."

"Of course," she said quickly. "And if you can, I'd rather he didn't know I was involved."

He nodded. "I'll try to keep you out of it, Doctor."

She rose and shook his hand. "Thank you for your time."

There was no time to go see James when she was already running late. She grimaced as Petros followed her to the wagons. James's friend Chance climbed into the back with her so that Petros could get some sleep. He gave her a flat smile, as if silently apologizing for not being the person she wanted. She practiced the script they'd given her on the way, but reading in the moving vehicle nauseated her.

The squat radio station building sat on the edge of the town, which made it easier for her to get inside relatively unnoticed. The radio hosts and producers were polite and deferent, and she enunciated the script she'd been given crisply and cleanly. They shook her hand when she was finished like she'd done them a favor instead of the other way around.

"They want a meeting with you," Chance said, looking at his phone, as they bumped back to camp.

"Who's they?" she asked, annoyed that she'd have to delay checking on James.

"The colonels. They've had more information from Orangiers."

"Very well." She stopped by her room briefly to change, surprised she had no messages from James of any kind. Had they taken his phone away when they arrested him? Was he still being held? It was in her mind to march back into Weathers's office and ask, but he was probably already in the briefing she was required to attend.

They'd already started when she slipped in, nodding her apology for being late. Mostly, they wanted to adjust their plans for the rest of the mission, take her and the rest of the group to a location farther from the border with Attaamy, where Lincoln had reported Heather had several safe houses. It made sense, but she really didn't need to be sitting here listening to them detail the pros and cons of the different locations they'd found. She had to stop her knee from bouncing no fewer than five times, and subtly check her phone under the table.

The cabin doors banged open. Everyone jumped. Rhodie stared. James looked livid.

"Staff Sergeant, you don't have authorization to be in here."

Rhodie's breath caught in her throat. Staff sergeant? *Weathers stripped him of his commission. He's not even an officer anymore; he's ruining his life . . .*

"I need to speak with Rhodie," he bit out. The sharp grumbles of the military officers rippled through the room at his informality. Colonel Weathers looked at her, and she shook her head slightly. This wasn't the time and place; she gave James a meaningful look, as if to say "What are you doing?" Was he trying to expose their relationship in front of everyone? The guards at the door moved toward him, and he charged away from them, deeper into the room.

"One minute. Please." She held up a hand, and the guards paused, their hands already on his arms.

"Speak your piece."

"Privately, please." The discomfort in the room was growing faster than E. coli in week-old ground beef.

"Staff Sergeant," she said calmly, "you are infringing on our time. I'll come speak with you privately after my meeting here has concluded."

"One thing," he whispered. "I only ever asked you for one solitary thing. And you couldn't even give me that."

"What on earth are you talking about?"

"I thought we'd agreed not let it come to this, but you had to go over my head. You couldn't just be honest with me." Yelling, she could've handled. Yelling was what she expected given his past behavior. Whispering was something else entirely.

"I'm done," he said, shrugging off the guards. "Sorry to interrupt. It won't happen again."

So much for keeping me out of it, she thought, as he stormed from the room. *Thanks a lot, Colonel.*

CHAPTER THIRTY-THREE

THE MEETING CONTINUED after a few seconds of awkward throat clearing and paper shuffling. *You had to go over my head.* Did he think *she'd* sent him home? No, how could he?

They finished the briefing, and Rhodie went to the lab. Stacks of samples, poorly labeled, wilting in the heat, sat on her metal workstation. She pulled back her dreads to get to work. "Sergeant Graeham, could you please let James know I would like to see him?"

Chance shifted uncomfortably. "He's already left, ma'am."

"What do you mean, left?" she asked, sorting through half-begun reaction sequences that littered the counter.

"He's been assigned to take the prisoner back to Orangiers. He left an hour ago." Good thing she was a cold-hearted princess; if a heart of ice shattered, would it melt or stay broken forever? Worse, evaporate entirely? Being unfamiliar with the physics of love, she decided she'd wait until later to examine the pieces. Mindful of how suspicious it looked, Rhodie whipped out her phone.

Rhodie: Where are you?

Rhodie: Arron, answer me.

Arron: I'm on my way home.

Rhodie: How could you leave without saying goodbye?

Rhodie: Arron?

Arron: I didn't choose this, you did. So we're over. I'm done.

Rhodie: I don't know what you think happened, but I am not responsible for your transfer.

Arron: So you didn't tell Weathers I have PTSD?

She sucked in a sharp breath. *The guard. Petros.* He must have overhead part of their conversation and taken it out of context. She hadn't betrayed him; she'd *saved* him. This was just a silly misunderstanding. She couldn't exactly deny it, however.

Rhodie: Yes, I did. You've been acting out of character. It's a logical explanation.

Arron: Except I told you repeatedly I DON'T HAVE PTSD.

Arron: You pulled your princess strings, and now you don't have to deal with me and my embarrassing problems.

Arron: It shouldn't surprise me, given that you won't deal with your own issues, either.

Rhodie: That is NOT how it was.

Rhodie: All this drinking, the anger. It's not like you. I just wanted to help.

Long minutes ticked by with no response, so she tried a different tack.

Rhodie: He was going to discharge you, I had to do something.

Arron: Funny, Petros didn't mention anything about that.

Rhodie: What on earth does he have to do with anything? Why would you believe him over me?

Arron: I told you, if you wanted me out of your life, all you had to do was ask. You went to Weathers, you asked him to transfer me: true or false?

Rhodie: Technically true, but that's not the whole story.

Arron: You wanted a goodbye? This is it, Dr. Broward. Have a nice life.

With trembling hands, she scrolled down to find his number as she barreled out the back door, where she might have a little more privacy. It rang and rang. No answer. She called again. Rang and rang, rang and rang.

No answer.

SHE CALLED HIM EVERY day, but never got through. Based on the empty circle next to her messages, her texts weren't being delivered, either. They moved the camp ten miles down the road to a military compound with better security. The opportunity for exploration was nearly nonexistent. They stayed another two weeks, and then packed up and made the long sail home. With her on board, they flew the king's standard, and she felt it was mocking her with every flap and flutter.

You retreated to your safe place, it seemed to say, *you went over his head. Princess. That's all you are. All you can be. A broken thing that no one wanted before, and no one wants now. You're a symbol, a one-dimensional object. Flat.* She spent a lot of time at the railing, watching the ship cut a V in the calm water, feeling cut herself. She ate when she remembered. She slept poorly.

Even though she'd urged them not to, her entire family was waiting for her on the docks, which were sagging under the weight of all the security they'd brought with them. The grief of nearly losing them paired with the grief of actually losing Arron had her crying while she was still on the gang-plank, forcing herself to walk when she wanted to fly down it with no regard whatsoever to its slick surface in particular or gravity in general. Rhodie stopped three feet away from them, all lined up. Her dad looked up and down the line.

"We've committed the classic blunder, it seems."

Edward grimaced. "We definitely should've discussed who gets the first hug."

"I think Mum should get it," Andrew mumbled, and the others made noises of agreement.

"I think we all should," Lily said, her voice predictably watery. She'd always been teary; Rhodie would've been offended if she hadn't been crying now. The queen mother tugged her family forward, and they encircled her in a gigantic group hug. Rhodie breathed in the scent of them, closed her eyes to relish the tight press of their arms around her torso. Simon complained that he was being squished, and they all laughed, letting the embrace break apart. Apparently, not having had enough of her, they each lined up for individual hugs. Her mum got in line twice. She was kissed and patted and side-hugged and squeezed; it felt wonderful.

"I'm so glad you're all okay," she said, making eye contact with each one of them. "I was so worried about you."

"We were worried for you, too," Dahlia said, wiping her own wet face. "We were trying desperately to warn you, but we couldn't get through. It was horrible." The others nodded and grunted their agreement.

"Apologies, all," Edward said, "but the Black Feathers would like us to move this reunion up to Bluffton. Something about having every member of the royal family out in public with no cover is making them nervous, if you can believe."

They all chuckled lightly and started back up toward the carriages. Abbie linked arms with Rhodie quietly as they walked, letting them drift to the back of the group.

"How are you, Abbie? Feeling better?"

She shrugged one shoulder. She'd hardly said a word. "Still really tired."

Rhodie patted her hand in what she hoped was a supportive way. "These things take time to recover from. You should continue to take your prenatal vitamins . . ."

"I don't think it's that kind of tired," Abbie murmured. "But I am, anyway." She cleared her throat. "How are things with James? Parker tells me there's a romance afoot . . ."

"I don't think we . . . that is to say, it's not . . . we're not together anymore." It was the most diplomatic way she could think of to say "He dumped me like week-old caviar." She turned her face away, but Abbie understood.

"Oh, Rhodie, I'm so sorry."

"Don't be. We never had a chance." She forced a smile, but it felt as fake as a three-dollar bill. She wanted to say more, to offer insight into how different they were, how ill-suited, but it turned her stomach to even think it. "I'm sorry for your loss as well. I hope Edward passed on my condolences."

Abbie nodded. "He did indeed." She paused. "I hope this isn't painful for you, but do you happen to know if James went up to see his mom when he got back? The guys have had no success in getting through to him."

Her heart stopped. "What? He hasn't come by?"

"Not at all," Abbie said, and Rhodie could see in her eyes that she shared her mounting concerns about what that might mean. "I'll put Edward onto tracking him down today and let you know what I find out . . ."

"Thank you," Rhodie said softly. "Please do."

CHAPTER THIRTY-FOUR

"HER ROYAL HIGHNESS—" Petros started.

"No." James closed the door. He'd kept everyone away for weeks; ignoring their texts and calls was easy now that his cell phone battery had died. The charger was in one of the open suitcases scattered on the living room floor, somewhere. But he couldn't be bothered to look for it when he was so busy feeling sorry for himself. And email? He'd thrown his laptop off the balcony. Simple. His housekeeper, Marcia, was the only one with an extra key, and he'd fired her when he came home. He didn't want to see anyone, even someone who was there to help.

The same polite knock came once again. He opened the door.

"Her Royal Highness—"

"I swear to Woz, Petros, I will break your whole face." James went to shut the door again, only to find Petros's giant boot in the way.

"*HerRoyalHighnessQueenLilywouldliketocomeup*. Will you permit it?"

"Lily?"

Petros nodded, slowly, giving him a stern look that seemed to convey some urgency.

He felt himself bristle that someone he trusted was no longer part of Rhodie's detail. "Why are you guarding Lily? Who's guarding Rhodie?"

Petros shrugged, and he knew the sneaky bastard was holding out on him.

"Yes, of course." He left the door open as two security came in and began to sweep the premises . . . and James realized in horror that it needed sweeping of another kind as well. The kitchen and living room were in utter chaos. With one arm, he dumped all the dishes and trash on the coffee table into a laundry basket, which was unfortunately already overflowing with dirty clothes. He shoved said basket into the bedroom and slammed the door. Frantic, he looked around to see what more he could do, but there was no time. He could hear them on the stairs. James quickly wiped the crumbs off his shirt and finger combed his hair, noting how long it'd gotten. *My ex-girlfriend's mother. My best friend's mother. But which one is she now? Regardless, she was my queen. She deserves my respect.*

Then she stood in the doorway, smiling at him genuinely. He hurried forward to greet her. "Please, Your Highness, come in. How lovely to see you."

"Arron." Though her visit itself was a surprise, he was in for an even greater one when she stepped inside, took his head in her hands, and bent it down to kiss his forehead like a son. Without waiting for a response, as if she knew she'd stunned him, Lily breezed into the living room and moved a sweatshirt to sit on his couch. James felt like crying, but he didn't know why. Looking into her face was painful, yes—it reminded him so much of Rhodie's—but that wasn't it. It was the tenderness in that gesture. The kindness in it. It had undone him. It took so little these days, so little was holding him together—chewing gum and baling wire, as his own mum would say.

"Come sit with me."

He moved to obey, sitting across from her on the coffee table. She smiled at him again. "How are you, Arron?" She hadn't called him by his first name in years, always by his rank. Of course she would know that his rank had changed. Of course she would realize that would be painful for him.

"I'm fine, Highness. How are you?"

"You don't look fine. You look like Jersey." She turned to Petros. "Young man, be a dear and put on some water for tea." She turned back to him, clearly waiting for a response of some sort. He hadn't looked in a mirror for a while, but she was probably right. He rubbed his unshaved chin; apparently, he'd started a beard without meaning to. It was probably spotty and unattractive, and he suddenly felt self-conscious.

"Did Rhodie send you to check on me?"

"No, Edward did. Since you've stopped taking calls from everyone, they figured I'd handle it best if you were dead." A whisper of a smile crossed her face, and he realized she was joking.

"You're the one I'd want to hear it from, if I were them."

"Of course I am. That's as it should be." She reached out and laid her hand over his. "I am here for you, Arron. So are Edward, Francis, Sam, Ignatius, all of us."

He looked away so she couldn't see the thought that flickered across his heart: *Not her, though. Not the one I wanted the most.*

"I know you're hurting right now. But please don't do anything foolish. Please let us help. We love you. The world is a better place with you in it." She squeezed his hand, then withdrew hers. "Also, call your mum. She's losing her mind with worry, and that takes a toll on women our age." Lily turned. "I'll take that tea now, Petros."

"Yes, ma'am."

"I'm going to invite you to a party next week, Arron, and you're going to come. There will be no alcohol served." He felt his face contorting as he tried to think of how to ask what he needed to know most. Lily pretended not to notice. "The party is on Friday. You will shower, shave, and get a haircut beforehand." She gestured toward his face. "This—whatever this is—is not working for you, dear. Do we understand each other?"

"Yes, ma'am," James echoed. He did laugh then, and when the tears came with it, he wiped them on his shoulders. *How can I go there, when she might be . . .*

"In case it interests you, my daughter will be working and will not be able to attend."

"How is she, Your Highness? Rhodie? Is she . . ."

She shook her head, smiling. "My dear daughter is still very much a closed book. But I do know that her phone number hasn't changed, if you wish to contact her . . ." Lily cleared her throat meaningfully. "Francis also asked me to communicate that he can find you an appropriate date if you—"

"No." He stiffened when he realized that he'd interrupted her, and he tried to soften it. "No, thank you, ma'am. I don't think I'm quite ready for that yet."

She nodded. "Very well. Make sure your tuxedo fits." She settled back into the sofa, sipping her tea. "Now. What are we playing?"

"Ma'am?"

She gestured vaguely toward the screen. "I assume you have more than one controller?"

"Oh." He jumped to his feet, weaving his way through the piles of clothing and open suitcases on the floor. "Yes, let me just . . ."

"Is it *Dragonfire's Revenge*? Oh, I haven't played this in an age." He straightened up to give her a perplexed look. "What, dear? You don't suppose that Edward got his skills from his father, do you?"

Lily proved repeatedly that he hadn't.

Before she left, she put her hands on his shoulders. "You have a medal for valor, Arron. And if you hadn't earned it on the battlefield, you'd deserve it for how you've loved my daughter all these years: Bravely. Wholeheartedly. Perhaps not with your eyes as open as they should've been"—she cocked an eyebrow—"but genuinely. It takes courage to let your heart get broken, and even more to put it back together afterward. But you will."

"Not by Friday," he joked, and her answering smile was kind.

"It doesn't have to happen by Friday. Come be with people who care about you. Start there. The rest will happen with time." She put a hand into her coat pocket and drew out a business card, which she set on the coffee table: *"Dr. Gordon Waffle, Clinical Psychiatrist. Discretion guaranteed,"* it read. It was the same doctor the military had recommended. As soon as his phone had charged, he took a picture of it this time, knowing what a cesspool his home had become, then called him to arrange an appointment . . . and then immediately called Marcia to grovel in case Lily came back again.

But he saved the hardest call for last. James sat on the couch, his leg bouncing uncontrollably, his chest tight. His mother's phone rang only once before she answered it.

"Arrondale Percival James, you're speaking to a ghost. I'm dead with worry. Honestly, you can't do these things. You know I can't come check on you, I can't leave work, they don't have enough people to cover the clients we have—"

He grasped for patience as his temper threatened to take over. "Mum, I haven't been—"

"What? You mean to tell me that in six days, you haven't had the slightest moment to call and tell me that you're all right?"

"Me?" he cried, outraged. "Uh, speaking of calling to tell things, you kept your affair with the Duke of Greenmeadow Downs a secret from me *my whole life*! And now he's trying to hand me this enormous thing that I'm as prepared for as I am to do brain surgery! Whereas if you'd *told me*—"

"You listen to me, son," she snapped. "You don't know what he was like back then. I was alone and scared and I made the best decision I could. I hoped and prayed that he'd never call upon you to take this up, but he has." Her sharpness was fading the longer she went on. "And I'm not sorry, because I know that your good heart and big brain will do the world good, and putting more resources behind them can't hurt any, love."

James paced the kitchen, the only space clear enough to do so, still fuming.

"Arron? Still there?"

"Yes," he bit out.

"I'm sorry if I hurt you."

"You did," he said, then he hung up.

CHAPTER THIRTY-FIVE

RHODIE TRUDGED THROUGH the halls of Bluffton a little after eight, yawning. She'd been scheduled to attend a conference tonight until nine, but it was a relief to be done earlier. Her suit was rumpled from the auditorium seats, and she knew her hair looked like Jersey; she needed to wash it tomorrow for sure. The week had sort of gotten away from her . . . again. Lying awake all night, replaying her and James's last conversation, had led to some rough mornings. Staring at photos of him on her phone made her lunch hour disappear quickly, and explaining why they couldn't play the classical radio station in the lab was exhausting—the last time she'd heard the Radinoffsky waltz, she'd had to excuse herself and hurry to the bathroom to break down in tears.

Oh, good, her mother appeared to be having some kind of party. That would excuse her from submitting to questions about where she'd been and why she hadn't called to let them know she wouldn't be at dinner. She did need to speak to her about the charity auction for the veteran support group, though . . . She paused at the doorway to the ballroom, debating internally.

"Can I help you?" Tezza Simonson stepped toward her, blocking the entrance with her body.

"No, I'm just looking for my mother. I need to speak with her briefly." Rhodie moved to enter and was surprised to find Tezza move with her.

"You're not allowed in the ballroom right now, ma'am."

Well. Perhaps she's not such a nice person after all.

"I beg your pardon?"

"You're not allowed inside. I apologize."

Rhodie drew up to her full height. "This is my house, and I'll go where I please. Now step aside."

Tezza stayed statue-still, her voice low. "I'm sorry, Dr. Broward. I have my orders."

Rhodie huffed. "You'll regret this."

"May I text your mother and ask her to come speak with you?"

"No, you may not. Of all the ridiculous, unreasonable . . ." She caught a flash of red hair inside the ballroom, and her irate speech died on her tongue. *Oh.*

James looked great. Perfect, really. He'd always filled out a tux nicely. He held a glass of water as he laughed with Saint and Edward. He was obviously doing fine. Better than she was, clearly. He wasn't brokenhearted without her after all. *Well, good. That's . . . good. This is what I wanted,* she reminded herself. *I wanted him happy and whole. He'll be fine without me. I just wish I could say the same. I think . . . I think I need help. Professional help.*

He turned toward the food table and saw her. She gave him an anemic wave. All the color drained out of his face, and he turned and whispered something to Edward, whose gaze went to her immediately. James handed his drink to Saint and moved toward the rear exit. *Where is he going? Why would he leave? Is he still so angry with me that he can't stand the sight of me?*

Rhodie bit her lip and turned away from the door before Edward could come over to scold her for chasing James away.

THE NEXT DAY BEING Saturday, Rhodie decided not to go into work until the afternoon. This proved to be a mistake, as her family assumed that her presence signaled her availability to spend time with them. After already discussing historical controversies with Andrew and playing a board game with Simon, she looked up to see her mother in the doorway to her sitting room. Her mother was prone to summoning: you'd get a message to report to her sitting room, and you'd drop what you were doing and go. It was a power move, but Rhodie had never minded it. Still, it was nice that her mother had come to her quarters for once.

"May I come in?"

"Of course."

Her mother strode in and sat down in the tall wing-backed armchair across from her.

"I feel I owe you an explanation regarding your denied entrance last night . . ."

"Oh, don't be silly. I wasn't invited. That simple."

Her mother pursed her lips. "Please just listen for once, Rhodie."

Startled, Rhodie stared at her mother.

"I'm sorry if you were hurt by Tezza denying you entrance. I had asked her to do so, since I hadn't had the opportunity to explain to you the purpose of the event."

Rhodie folded her hands over her closed book. "And what was that?"

"James is struggling. Edward and I wished to help him begin to move on after your breakup, and it was imperative that you not interfere."

Rhodie lifted her chin. "I beg your pardon, but why would I interfere?"

"I don't know, darling, why would you? Why did you interfere with his work in Trella?"

Rhodie looked toward the window. "This will come off as flippant, Mother, but you don't know anything about Trella."

She nodded. "That's probably true, dear. But it's not for lack of trying." Rhodie took a breath to respond, but Lily held up a quelling hand. "Please let me tell you a story, and then I'll be happy to listen to you tell me how wrong I am."

Rhodie sat back, perplexed. After a moment, she gestured for her mother to go on.

"Do you remember Dr. Teegan?"

Rhodie nodded. "The palace physician who delivered us."

"He didn't deliver Simon."

Rhodie nodded again. "I assumed that had something to do with his birth being complicated due to his trisomy 21."

"No. It did not." She cleared her throat. "When we found out about Simon's trisomy 21 during the amniocentesis, it came as a huge shock, as you can imagine. Not only was I older, pregnant with an unplanned child, but the child would have problems. Huge problems that would upend our lives, disrupt them. With that in mind, Dr. Teegan advised me to abort Simon."

Rhodie stared at her mother, trying to make sense of the words. "Are you serious, Mother?"

"Yes, Rhododendron. He said he wouldn't deliver him, wouldn't be part of such a disgrace, such a foolish decision." Lily leaned forward, her eyes fierce. "But choosing to love my precious, precious son has never been a mistake. Did it make me different? Yes. Was it what people expected from me? No. Our decision drew criticism from many other sources beyond medical professionals, but when it came down to it, your father and I knew that we would rather shoulder that than go on knowing we'd ended something wonderful in our lives." Lily put her hand to her chest. "I know that someone like Arron James is not how you imagined your future . . . Frankly, he's not who I imagined for a life partner for you, either. But having known him for many years, I want to emphasize the goodness of the man and how well I believe you could do in a marriage together. Don't disqualify him based on his upbringing."

"I haven't, Mother. He dumped me. I made a mistake, I . . ." This was where her personal disclosures usually ended, before the sordid details. She swallowed. "I had him transferred. I thought he had PTSD. I have since learned that that's not the case, but . . . I didn't listen to him. I was so sure I was right. I was just certain he was in denial."

Lily shook her head, her lips pursed. "Thank you for sharing that. We're just alike, you and I. I know how easy it is to retreat to a professional persona rather than deal with a personal problem. I'm ashamed to inform you that you likely picked up that habit from me. It won't come easy to you to right a wrong . . ."

Rhodie felt her nose tingling, warning of tears on the way, and her mother covered her hand with hers.

"But I assure you that it's worth it. Do you want him? Need him?"

Eyes fluttered closed, she shrugged, unable to make her voice work.

"Well, you should decide before time runs out. And if you do find a way to even the score, you may find something as unexpectedly precious and beautiful as I did. Let the critics be damned for once—they've always been wrong about you, anyway."

Rhodie looked up at her mum, feeling helpless. It was as if she'd just taken a hammer to all her insecurities at once. "Even the score? How?"

Her mother shrugged. "He suffered your rejection quite publicly. Perhaps start there."

Rhodie straightened her spine. "Let him reject me? In front of others? What if I damage my reputation beyond repair? Would you have me live my whole life alone, if he won't have me?"

Lily leaned over to look her in the eye. "Deep down, even if Edward finds you someone else to marry, won't you be alone, anyway?" Her mother pressed a kiss to her forehead, then walked out without waiting for an answer.

Rhodie stared into the fire, the flickering flames warming the drafty room. Fire had looked romantic and otherworldly when she was curled up with Arron, his teasing whispered into her ear, his arms around her. His toes digging into the sand with hers, his heart beating in time with hers. All she saw now was combustion, a chemical reaction. Surely that lens and those feelings weren't limited to her interactions with one person . . . but she couldn't imagine opening her heart to someone new right now. Maybe ever.

CHAPTER THIRTY-SIX

RHODIE FIDGETED WITH the braided edge of the couch in the girls' wing. Her sisters were all out; her mother had promised to keep them busy in order to prevent distraction or uncomfortable questions. Arron's parting shot about her not facing her issues had been rattling around in her head for weeks, and it was time to do something about it.

Dr. Waffle sat across from her, his legs crossed, a tablet on his lap. "How would you like to be addressed?" he asked, his eyes trained on the tablet.

"Dr. Broward is fine."

He looked up with a smile. "Great. I'm Gordon."

She nodded. "Thank you for coming to me, I realize that's not your normal arrangement . . ."

He waved away her comment. "Your mother and I always met here as well. And in case you're wondering, no, I can't tell you what she and I spoke about, just as I won't tell her what you and I speak about. If we see each other in public or at a palace event, I'll simply pretend I don't know you. I'll ignore you unless you initiate an interaction. How does that sound?"

"That sounds fine."

"So how can I help you, Dr. Broward?" His eyes were crinkly at the corners, like her father's, and his too-large, slightly rumpled clothes gave him the air of a forgetful professor she'd once had. It was hard not to like him.

She touched that braid again, running her fingers over the fringe. "I suppose . . . I suppose I have some concerns about my mental health."

"Then you're talking to the right person. What kind of concerns?"

She swallowed hard. *Why is it so difficult to say it out loud?* "I hate my body."

"I see. Since when?"

"Since I was twelve."

"You sound pretty sure about that."

"Yes."

"Was there an incident or an event at that time . . . ?" He was tapping on his tablet, and he noticed her staring at it. "Are you concerned about the tablet? This isn't connected to the internet, so it can't be hacked, just so you know."

She nodded faintly. "No, that's fine. I . . . I didn't get a marriage contract when I was twelve because all my suitors said I was too skinny. They said since I hadn't started menstruating, I wasn't going to be able to have children."

He sat back for a moment against the high back of the pale-blue chair. "Wow. That's heavy." He cocked his head, his thumb stroking the upholstery absentmindedly. "How did that feel?"

She shrugged one shoulder. "Confusing, mostly. I looked exactly the same as my mother at the same age, from a body shape standpoint." *And yet, she had no trouble getting a highly coveted contract, even though she wasn't even royal.* Rhodie was startled by how much she found she resented that, now that she thought about it. It had felt more like a puzzle at the time, a riddle: *What's like a princess, but not good enough for a prince? A Rhodie.*

"What were you thinking about just now?"

"How unfair it was that my mother had no trouble getting a contract."

He nodded. "I agree. Our culture puts a lot of emphasis on physical attributes, doesn't it? And the standards are especially high for royals." He shifted in the chair, settling back into it. "Did you want a marriage contract?"

"You know as well as I do that it wasn't optional."

Gordon grinned down at his tablet. "I didn't ask if it was optional. I asked if you wanted one."

No one had ever asked her that before. Not her book club friends, nor her siblings, nor her parents. Not even the press.

"I was the eldest girl," she said softly, straightening her posture as if someone were scrutinizing it. "I was letting them down. I was supposed to be a catch, and instead, I was a castoff."

"But did *you* want one? Were *you* disappointed?"

Guilt rose like bile in her throat. "No," she whispered. "I never did. I wanted to be a doctor, not a queen. And I got what I wanted, even though I shouldn't have."

"Well, that's a loaded statement we'll need to unpack, and I'd like to get back to your resentment with your mum and dad in a moment, but first, can you expand on what you hate about your body? You mentioned your shape . . ."

She waved a hand. "Well, my shape is more acceptable now."

"You hate your eye color?"

"Well, no, not that."

"And your hair?"

"No, I love my hair." She touched it self-consciously. She'd finally restored her dreads to their normal state after her trip, and they looked great. She was thankful that they were the royal tradition.

"What then? You hate the way you walk? You have constant diarrhea, what?"

She sneered without meaning to. "Dr. Waffle..."

"Gordon."

"Gordon, it's nothing like that."

He set the tablet on the table next to him and took off his glasses. "Have you ever stopped to think about all the things your body is doing for you?"

"I am an expert on the human body, sir."

"In theory, perhaps. But not in practice." He paused, giving her an assessing look. "Do you like to be touched?"

"No," she said, more forcefully than she meant to, and Gordon cringed.

"That sounded too forward, didn't it? I apologize. Here's what I meant: eating disorders like yours are often about control. Being touched by other people can make you feel out of control, unpleasantly so, prompting arousal or emotion that feels too vulnerable." He'd said it out loud: *eating disorders like yours*. He'd just said it, opened his mouth, and said this thing she'd been denying all her adult life, like it was so obvious.

"I have an eating disorder," she repeated.

"Seems that way," said Gordon, straightening his glasses. "Doesn't it?"

"But I never . . ."

"You never what?"

"People like me aren't supposed to have eating disorders."

"I think we've already established that bodies and brains do what they like, despite cultural pressure."

Rhodie sighed. "I did have a boyfriend, once. I liked his touch, innocent as it was."

"I take it he's not in the picture now."

She shook her head.

"What did you like about his touch?"

"He made me feel . . ." *Why does that feel so good? Always wants to know why, this one. I love you.* She pushed the painful memory away quickly, lest he ask her what she was thinking about again. "He made me feel cherished. Beautiful."

"Do you consider your body beautiful?"

"I suppose so, yes."

"So let's see if I'm understanding the situation," he said slowly. "You consider your body beautiful, you like the way it looks, it's functioning well, you're in good health, and you hate it. Is that right?" There was nothing accusatory in his tone, and yet the words burned like hydrochloric acid. Yautia's words over their truce breakfast of eggs and fruit came back to her: *Using something and trusting it are two different things.* She pressed her lips into a flat line.

"You're oversimplifying it. It didn't do what I needed it to do. It isn't . . . trustworthy. It cost me something important." That sounded stupid now that she'd said it, and yet her heart beat harder to hear it outside her own head, as if drumming its approval that she'd finally spoken the truth.

"So what would need to happen for you to forgive your body?"

"Forgive it? Has it sinned against me?"

He shrugged. "You tell me."

Rhodie stood up and paced to the fireplace, her arms across her chest. She wanted him to leave. She subtly checked the time on the antique clock on the mantel: still thirty-seven minutes left. *Damn it.*

"Okay. So you hate your body. How does that affect your mental health?"

"I feel like I have to monitor it constantly. It's hard to eat sometimes, because it's misbehaving."

"Misbehaving how?"

"I don't want my shape to change; once I hit puberty, it filled out acceptably. I want it to remain like this. It resists that."

He nodded slowly, putting his glasses back on, picking up the tablet again.

"Do you punish it?"

She wanted to lie. It was on the tip of her tongue . . . but it didn't matter. She could see that her silence had given her away.

"Yes. Sometimes, I guess. With exercise. By withholding food."

"Because you don't trust it to tell you what it needs," he said. It wasn't a question. "Do you cut yourself? Pinch yourself, give yourself bruises?"

"No!" Her voice was low with horror at the thought.

"Because it would leave a mark, or because you don't like the idea of pain?"

"Neither. It would be unbecoming a royal."

Gordon typed something with one finger on the tablet. "Do you weigh yourself every day?"

She nodded, staring into the fire.

"How many times?"

"Just twice. Morning and evening."

"What would happen if you couldn't weigh yourself?"

Rhodie scowled. "Couldn't?"

"Yes, couldn't. You break both your legs, your scale had an accident, whatever."

She snorted. "You forget to whom you're speaking, Gordon. If my scale breaks, the staff brings me another one."

"Outer space, then. You're the first scientist to break away from gravity. Can't weigh yourself. What would happen, how would you feel?" She lost her train of thought for a moment, imagining being a space explorer.

"Nervous."

"Would that be very different from now?"

Rhodie felt her shoulders drop. "No," she whispered. She turned to face the man, and he just grinned at her as if they were passing a pleasant teatime together.

"You shouldn't smile as you disassemble my world piece by piece."

Gordon chuckled. "I like to think that we're putting it back together as well."

They kept talking, the two of them. He asked so many questions about her feelings. Things she hadn't thought about for a long time. Things she was afraid to say out loud, afraid they'd somehow change things for the worse. It reminded her of a poster she'd had as a child, of a famous optical illusion: some people saw a bear eating berries, while some people saw the profile of a woman wearing a fur hat. Meeting with Gordon was like seeing the woman for the first time. A whole new way of looking at the same life, the same history.

He slapped his knee. "Let's set a goal for this week. What would you like to aim for? What's making you feel trapped in this body-hatred thing you've got happening?"

She considered this for a moment, staring at the flames again. She thought back to her conversation with Edward over lunch, ages ago now, when he'd asked for her favorite dessert.

"I don't eat dessert. It has no nutritional value. But I see that other people enjoy it, and I would like to learn to enjoy it. I would like to have a favorite dessert."

His bushy eyebrows bounced above his glasses. "An admirable goal. Of course, to find out your favorite, you'll probably have to try some different kinds."

"My brother often invites me to eat dessert with him. He has a terrible sweet tooth . . ." She glanced at him sidelong. "Don't spread that information around."

Gordon's grin was huge. "The *Barrowdon Bugle* won't hear it from me."

"I could try a bite when he next orders it. I don't think he'd mind."

"Good. And let's try to just weigh yourself once a day. That should be more than enough, don't you think?"

Rhodie swayed, momentarily off balance. She chewed on the inside of her lips for a minute until Dr. Waffle gently prompted, "Dr. Broward? Can you do that for me?"

"Yes."

And that night as she took off her clothes, all she had to do was put the scale in her closet, shoved all the way to the back, in order to stay off it. All she had to do was put her arms around her middle and hold herself and cry. All she had to do was whisper into the darkness, "You're forgiven, body. You're forgiven. You failed me, but I forgive you."

CHAPTER THIRTY-SEVEN

IT SHOULD'VE BEEN THE perfect day at the beach. Several weeks after her first meeting with Dr. Waffle, Rhodie lay in the shade of a striped umbrella next to her mother, who had finally ceased nagging everyone about sunscreen.

"Especially you, Abelia," Lily called across the beach. Well, almost ceased.

Abbie and Parker were racing each other to the surf, Simon trailing after, Ignatius hurrying to catch up before he went into the ocean alone. The twins were sunbathing in floppy straw hats, trading magazines occasionally. Andrew was complaining that there was nothing to do, and his mother wordlessly passed him a book. He sneered at it, then got to his feet, looking out to the white sailboats that stood out like buttons on a sailing uniform against the azure sky. He walked off down the beach.

The weather was gorgeous, and Rhodie lay her head on her arms and watched a flock of seagulls in the distance swirling like petals from a cherry tree in spring, finally settling on the water like foam. After deciding the water was too cold for him, Simon was back, determined to build an awesome castle. She convinced him to build it downwind of the ladies.

"Looks like someone has a visitor," Ignatius said, nodding toward the shell-strewn path they'd come down.

A bobbing red-haired head, strong build. Military uniform.

Rhodie sat up. Her heart reacted like a faithful dog whose owner had just turned into the driveway. "I can go see," she said, trying to keep her voice even. She popped up and hurried across the sand without her sandals. *Ouch.* The sand was scorching. Halfway to him, her feet burning, she realized she'd also left behind her wrap . . . *Why did I let Gordon talk me into a bikini?* It was navy with white polka dots, very vintage, and it coordinated perfectly with her gold-rimmed aviator sunglasses.

She broke into a run; she couldn't take the pain in her feet, but she sure as Jersey wasn't going back to the blanket for her sandals. James's eyes were wide by the time she got to him. When she came to a stop, she kicked the top sand away to stand on the cooler, wetter sand below. *Stay open,* she told herself. *Don't go cold, don't put on a mask. Let him see how much you've missed him.*

"Hi." She smiled as widely as she could. "Hi, Arron." Rather than warming him up, this seemed to shut him down.

"Hello."

Maybe I should go back to running in a bikini. "How have you been?"

"Fine." He cleared his throat. "I'm sorry to bother—they needed Edward to sign for receipt of this diplomatic packet, and they couldn't find him, and I was having lunch with Saint, so I said I'd . . ." His voice trailed off as he gestured to the packet. He thrust it toward her, but she didn't take it. "Could you please just give this to him, Dr. Broward?"

"It's Rhodie."

He lifted his gaze to hers, and he looked desperately sad. "I'm not going to call you that."

"Why?" She shuffled closer, trying to keep her injured feet below the top layer of the burning sand. "You used to call me that."

"Before you dumped me," he snapped.

Now we're getting somewhere.

"I didn't dump you, Arron."

He snorted. "No, you just betrayed me and asked for me to be transferred off your detail. Petros told me everything."

"Considering Petros wasn't even in the room with us, isn't it possible he got the details wrong?"

He folded his arms across his chest. "That's your defense? Really?"

"Would you please have dinner with me? Let me explain?"

"I don't think so." He shoved the envelope into Rhodie's chest. "I'll wait here."

She suddenly realized why he wasn't coming onto the beach; it was for family only. He needed permission. He couldn't complete his mission without her help . . . She grinned.

"Well, this is quite a predicament."

"What is?" he asked, shaking his head.

"Well, you need this packet signed, and I seem to have forgotten my sandals over on my towel. The sand is very hot. See?" She put a hand on his shoulder, feeling him stiffen, and leaned over to catch her ankle and show him just how pink the bottom of her foot was. His eyes bounced between her somewhat exposed chest, her injured feet, and her face, like he wasn't sure what the safest place to look was.

"So what are you saying? You can't take it to him?"

"Well"—she tapped her chin thoughtfully—"I *could*, but due to the pain and suffering involved, there's some light recompense required." She flashed him a Cheshire grin. "Please have dinner with me."

"You could just grant me permission to enter the area."

She nodded slowly. "I could, yes, but even if I do, Edward's in the water, and you can't go in dressed like this . . . And I'd still be stuck here."

She could see him clenching his jaw. Maybe she was taking this too far.

"I have a solution," he said. Before she knew what was happening, he'd scooped her up in his arms and begun walking with purpose toward the ocean. He held her against his chest, his arms under her knees and shoulder blades, and she looped her arms immediately around his neck. Her parents stared at them as they passed.

She was afraid to say anything at first, but holding the words in burned like acid. "Arron?"

"What?" he grunted.

"Why are you carrying me?"

"So you won't hurt your feet." He said it as if it were the most logical thing in the world. "Have you gained weight?" James muttered.

"Yes. About five pounds." *Because I eat crème brûlée on Sundays. Because I only weigh myself once a day now . . . usually.* She swallowed hard. There was one more reason that she didn't want to think or speak, but her mind called up her mother's words about evening the score. "I'm seeing a psychiatrist." He took his eyes off the sand for a brief moment and lifted her a little higher into his arms.

"So am I."

"Do you talk about PTSD?"

He shook his head, staring straight ahead at the ocean. "As I told you, I don't have PTSD; he assessed me on our first visit. We talk about how the love of my life broke my heart."

"She didn't mean to," Rhodie whispered. "She made a mistake."

"Nevertheless."

Edward had apparently seen them coming, because he was plowing through the waves toward them.

"You there, strange redheaded man carrying my sister," he called out with faux irritation. "What're you doing on my beach?"

"Rhodie said I could."

Technically not true . . . but he called me Rhodie.

She held out the paperwork to her brother, and he looked around for a towel to dry his hands. He rubbed a hand over his head as he looked around, spraying them with water. Rhodie turned more toward James, protecting the paperwork between them.

"Second Brother, watch where you're flicking, please, you'll get Arron in trouble."

"My apologies," he said, smirking. "Are you going to provide an explanation about . . ." He gestured to the two of them.

"No," Rhodie replied, as James said, "She hurt her feet."

Over her brother's shoulder, she could see Abbie, open-mouthed, giving her two very overt thumbs up. She subtly tried to shake her head and prayed that James wouldn't notice. Thankfully, at that moment, he put her down on the wet sand and turned so that Edward could use his back as a makeshift table to sign on.

"Thanks, mate. You want to stay? More than welcome."

"No, I can't. I have to get back." James glanced at Rhodie, then turned to go.

"First Boyfriend?"

James froze, but didn't turn. Edward gave her a gentle push toward him, and she walked on shaking legs over to where he was standing, the shaking having nothing to do with all the blood rushing around her body every which way.

"Arron," she whispered, too aware of their audience, "I miss you. I miss you so much. Can't we at least be friends again?"

He spun to face her. "We were never friends," he whispered back. "I worshipped you, and you let me. Then, like all legendary interactions between gods and mortals, you turned on me when I least expected it."

Rhodie kept her voice low, but firm. "Being a mere human with no immortal friends, I can't say for certain what they do . . . but I can tell you for certain that you and I were friends."

He lifted his chin. "Prove it."

"I can. I will. I will prove that we were friends—*are* friends." *How? How the Jersey are you going to prove that?* her mind impolitely inquired. No matter. She'd figure it out. There was no deadline.

"Fine. I'm free Friday night."

"Friday?" She barely got the word out before her throat began to close up, like an allergic reaction to that much stress coursing through her body.

His eyes narrowed. "Friday's not good for you?"

"No," she said quickly, "Friday is good, Friday is fine. Friday's fantastic. Thank you."

"Don't get excited," he said, turning to head back to the steep pathway. "It's just dinner."

The moment he was out of sight, Rhodie sprinted for her phone.

"Dear, is there something you need to—"

"Not now, Mum. Emergency. Relationship emergency crisis."

Rhodie: I have to prove to Arron that we're friends. How do I do that?

Rhodie: Deadline Friday.

Bridgette: You're jacked.

Carlie: Not helpful, love.

Bridgette: It's true, though.

Mariona: Does he need a ride to the airfield? Or help moving?

Carlie: Those are two marks of real friendship.

Rhodie: I don't know if he needs anything, I didn't ask.

Carlie: Ask Edward, he'd know.

Rhodie: Right, of course.

Bridgette: Are you freaking out right now?

Bridgette: I think she's freaking out.

Mariona: Of course she is, she's in love!

Carlie: It'll be okay, Rhodie.

The conversation was quickly devolving into pointless platitudes and sympathies. She needed action. Rhodie dropped her phone and hurried back to the water, again cursing the bounciness of her body in the bikini. *Never again.* She waded into the ocean until she was chest-deep.

"Edward. I need to speak with you regarding two things."

He laughed. "Fine, go ahead."

"First of all, please don't take this the wrong way, either of you, but I dislike it when you two are physically intimate in public parts of the castle. I'd appreciate it if you kept your amorous activities confined to your residence."

Abbie had turned a shade of red that reminded Rhodie of the alcohol in a thermometer, but Edward just laughed.

"Very well, I apologize for making you uncomfortable. Thank you for making me aware of the issue."

"For the record, we were just kissing," Abbie whispered. "Now please excuse me while I swim away without being followed, which is completely normal."

Rhodie put a staying hand on her arm. "Secondly, I have to prove to Arron that we're friends. Do you know of any area in which he might require assistance?"

He and Abbie shared a look.

"You're not going to like it, hon," Abbie said. "Seriously."

Rhodie shook her head. "I'll do whatever. I don't mind. Just tell me."

Edward sighed. "He needs help doing inventory at work; he's been assigned to manage one of the military's main supply depots. He told me that he's shorthanded."

"Is that something I can volunteer for?"

"Not a normal civilian, no. But you have a high enough security clearance that I think I can swing it. I'll pull some strings if you want." He paused. "But Rhodie, it's hard, dirty work. There's a reason why no one wants do it."

"I'll do it. Monday morning."

"They start at 5:00 a.m."

She sneered. "I think I know why no one's volunteered . . . but I can do it. I'll work there for a few hours and then go to work."

Edward bobbed in the water. "Is James going to be all right with this? I don't want to piss him off further. He's barely speaking to me as it is."

"I think he will," she said, looking toward the hill he was still climbing. "He's the one who threw down the gauntlet."

CHAPTER THIRTY-EIGHT

THEY HADN'T YET LIT her fireplace when Rhodie rose at 4:15, and she shivered her way into the bathroom. *Perhaps I'll gain a bit more weight, just to have more insulation on my bones . . .* The thought made her chuckle as she hurried to brush, wash, and dress. Her night guard seemed surprised to see her emerge, ready for her day, at 4:45. The castle was dark and quiet, and it took no time at all to arrive at the depot. She'd decided to wear sensible clothes: flats, stylish jeans, and a loose blouse.

James scowled when he saw her. "What are you doing here?"

She smiled sweetly. "Volunteering, friend. Edward said you were shorthanded. I thought my two hands would be welcome."

James shook his head, scowling. "You're going to ruin those clothes. Go home and change. Or better still, just go home."

"Good morning to you, too, Staff Sergeant, and yes, I'm very anxious to get to work. I am at your complete disposal." She laid an affectionate hand on his arm, and he glared at her. She removed it hastily.

"How would you like to be addressed here?" he asked.

"By you?"

"No, by your coworkers."

"Dr. Broward is fine."

James muttered something under his breath as he turned toward the woman standing at his elbow. "Could you please go get Dr. Broward some coveralls? Size small."

A group was slowly forming around them, and Rhodie heard her name whispered.

"Good morning, all."

"Good morning, Staff Sergeant," the rest of the group chorused bleakly.

"As you may have noticed, we have a new member of the group with us today. Her Highness Princess Rhododendron has offered to help us with our inventory, knowing that we were short-staffed. She would like to be addressed as Dr. Broward, and she'll be with us as she's able. Please make her feel welcome, but treat her as you would any other soldier. She's not to receive special treatment in any way. I won't tolerate favoritism, is that clear?"

"Yes, Staff Sergeant," they replied in unison.

"Let's get to work."

The female soldier came back with the coveralls and handed them to Rhodie with a shy smile.

"Thank you. What's your name?"

"Private Garrett, Your Highness."

"Please, call me Dr. Broward. Where do we start?"

"Staff Sergeant says you're assigned to food."

She blinked. "Food?"

Garrett nodded. "We need to keep track of all the preserved goods and such, check their expiration dates. It's not the best duty, I'm afraid."

He was trying to scare her off. *Not so fast, mister.* "Very well, please lead the way." They picked up where Garrett had left off yesterday with preserved fruit. Half an hour in, Rhodie picked up a jar of peaches to check the expiration date on the bottom and a cockroach scurried out from behind another jar. She screamed and dropped the peaches, shattering the jar on the concrete. Garrett laughed.

"Scared of a wee bug, Princess?"

Rhodie rolled her lips, trying not to smile. "I apologize, it just startled me."

"I'll go get a mop," Garrett said.

"No." James was at the end of the row, arms crossed over his chest, no doubt summoned by her scream and the sound of breaking glass. "She'll get it herself. I'll show her where."

Rhodie moved to where he stood and stopped. He was looking at her strangely.

"You don't have to walk a step behind me here. You're the ranking official," she said softly.

"Why are you here?"

She linked her fingers behind her back so she wouldn't mimic his stance. "Edward said you needed help. Friends help each other. We're friends."

He rolled his eyes. "This isn't going to work."

"Why, because I broke a jar? I'll gladly pay for it."

"No, not the work, the work is fine. This isn't going to change my mind about us, Dr. Broward." If his words were any colder, she could freeze tissue samples with them.

Rhodie said nothing. Since that first kiss on the beach, she'd learned how much she could express just by staring into someone's eyes, and based on his expression, she knew all her love and longing and sadness and regret was coming through just fine.

"Could you please show me where the mop is? I don't want someone to slip and fall in the mess."

Without another word, he led her to a broom closet near the office and turned on the light for her before abruptly slamming his office door. By the time she left at ten, her feet were sore from standing on concrete, her nose was full of black snot from all the dust she'd breathed in, and her hands were filthy. Not wanting to be late for her classes, she carefully removed the coveralls and left them folded outside his office. The door was shut, and James was patiently explaining to someone why they couldn't have more than seventy-five rolls of toilet paper at a time. She waved at him through the window, and he pivoted toward the opposite wall, giving her his back. Well, it was only Monday.

Goodbye, you stubborn man. I'll see you tomorrow. I love you.

CHAPTER THIRTY-NINE

"SO YOU KNOW THE SERGEANT?"

Rhodie nodded. "Very well. I have known him since childhood."

"Is he always so serious?" the private asked.

She burst out laughing and Garrett jumped. "James? Serious? Hardly. No, he's one of the funniest people I've ever known."

Garrett was looking at her out of the corner of her eye. They were still cataloguing food: today, it was working in tandem to weigh bags of beans, rice, wheat, flour, sugar . . . large bags. It was backbreaking. Lying in bed that morning, she'd considered ringing for the palace masseur, but decided that was a bit too royal. She'd tough it out . . . assuming she could still move tomorrow.

They lifted the heavy bag together, and Rhodie's grip slipped on the slick bag, breaking her index fingernail.

"Damn." Rhodie slapped a hand over her mouth, and Garrett laughed. "I very deeply apologize. I've never cursed in front of one of my citizens before."

"Yeah, best be careful they don't kick you out of the club, Princess. You're acting more and more common lately. Hard work calls for hard language, don't you think?"

"That would explain a lot about my brother and his friends. They all work extremely hard. Work hard, play hard."

"That's right," Garrett grinned. "But you're only getting half the deal."

"I beg your pardon?"

"You should come out with us. We go out drinking on Fridays at the Rusty Nail."

"Well, I don't particularly care for the infectious implications of the name, but I will consider it. I tend to put a damper on outings due to my security's presence and over-protective nature." She paused. "Does the sergeant come too?"

"He's been invited but hasn't shown yet. Bet he would if you were going . . . ," Garrett quipped, recording the weight of the bag and its identification number on the tablet.

"Cheeky," Rhodie muttered as they removed the bag together, but she gave her a shy smile. The morning went quickly. Since she had no classes to teach, she decided to stay the whole day, only running quickly to the lab at lunchtime to start her TA on a few lab processes before coming back.

"Did you forget something?" James asked as she walked in.

"No. I'm back to work," she said, rewrapping her hair in a scarf to keep the dust off.

He shook his head, and she felt his eyes on her as she turned to go find Garrett.

"Your partner had to leave."

"Oh? What a shame. She's a lovely girl." Rhodie turned to her new security. "Come on, Trosen, you can help me lift everything onto the scale. We'll give her a surprise when she gets back. I bet we can get the rest of the bags done."

James crossed his arms. "He's not authorized to help you, Dr. Broward."

Rhodie sighed, closing her eyes. Her body already ached. This was not going to make it better. "Fine, Sergeant." She strode back down the rows and rows of shelving until she reached the dry goods. She stood, arms crossed, looking at the bags. The ones on the shelf, she could hold, weigh with her own body weight, then subtract her weight. Simple. But the ones already on the ground . . . there was no way she could lift them by herself. A soft cooing had her looking up to the rafters for doves, and she smiled. She strode back to the front of the building and tapped a tall young man on the shoulder. He was laughing with a group of his fellow soldiers, but they all sobered quickly upon seeing her.

"I apologize for intruding on your levity. Might you render me a bit of assistance?"

"Certainly, Doctor. What can I do?"

"I need a long length of rope, a ladder, a pair of work gloves and a pulley, if you have one."

He shook his head, thoughtful. "I'm not sure we have the pulley, but if anyone does, we do. Give me a moment."

"I'll wait for you here. I never ate lunch, anyway." Rhodie pulled out her food and watched James through his window, working on his computer. It was a nice view, and it made the eating easier. About ten minutes later, the young man came back.

"Here you are, Princess. Everything you asked for."

"Thank you, soldier. What's your name?"

"Corporal Jacobs, ma'am."

"Thank you, Jacobs." She hauled the rope, gloves, and pulley down to her work area, ignoring curious glances and whispers. When she went back for the ladder, she found

James frowning at her from the doorway of his office, and she tossed him a grin over her shoulder.

"Dr. Broward."

"Yes, Staff Sergeant?"

"You know you're supposed to be weighing dry goods, right?"

"Yes, sir. That's just what I'm doing." She threaded the ladder over her shoulder and moved slowly down the aisle. She didn't want to have to buy any more peaches or any other jarred goods. She heard footsteps following her, and when she put the ladder down, she saw they belonged to James.

"Do you know how to use that?"

She laughed lightly. "A ladder? Why yes, I believe the feet go on the ground and the pointy part goes in the air . . . but then again, I'm just a silly princess." She was attracting a crowd, and surprisingly, James didn't tell them to get back to work. Perhaps he was hoping she would embarrass herself . . . It was indeed more likely than not.

It was convertible between A-shaped and extension style, so she laid the ladder out as long as it would go and locked the legs in place. Then she scooted the feet against the shelf so that she could lift it rung by rung, walking up under it until it was straight up in the air.

"Ma'am," Jacobs started, "might I—"

"No, Corporal, you may not," James answered. "Let's see what our princess can do."

Inwardly, she cringed. No wonder his subordinates thought he was a jackass; once again, her presence was impeding his career. *No matter. That's on him, not me. That's his broken heart speaking.*

She pivoted the ladder so that it was against the rafters, then threaded the rope through the pulley and proceeded to carry it up the ladder to the very top. After her first day, she'd decided to wear her running shoes; they offered only slightly more comfort than her flats against the concrete, but they protected her feet better. She hooked the pulley onto the rafter and climbed back down, trying not to think about how many men were looking at her backside. Then she tied one loose end of the rope to a bag of rice with a slipknot and donned the work gloves before taking up the other end of the rope. Hauling the rope straight down, she slowly lifted the bag into the air and over to the scale, her muscles shaking to keep it hovering. When the bag touched the scale, the group applauded, and she took a bow.

"You see, Sergeant? Nothing is impossible for a woman of science."

"All right, everyone, your royalty has proven her worth. Back to work." James was still watching her as she recorded the weight, lifted the bag again (only the two inches required to slide the scale out), and set it down, untying the rope.

"Party tricks will get you nowhere, Doctor."

"Tricks?" She shrugged. "If you want to speak about deceptions, we can. You accepted my help with the intent to embarrass and punish me. You tasked me with something you thought impossible. As usual, I find I enjoy proving you wrong." She paused and lowered her voice. "Just as I will prove you wrong about our friendship."

James stalked toward her then, and she backed up, bumping into the shelving behind her.

"You won't." He didn't stop until their noses were almost touching. In her peripheral vision, she could see Trosen take a step toward them, and she subtly waved him away, never taking her eyes off James's face.

"I will. We're friends. I wouldn't still be here if we weren't." She pushed against James's chest, and he took a step back to keep his balance. "More than that, I'm in love with you, and I thought you were in love with me, too. I was in error in how I tried to help you, but that doesn't change the fact that my motive was a deep affection for you." She backed him slowly across the row, one step at a time, until he was the one with his back to the shelving. "You've not been yourself, Arron. Not since Trella, even before. Standing in that river, losing your balance, you told me to let you fall. Shame on you for knowing me so little; I would never let you fall. Not then, not now." She leaned even closer to him, her nose nuzzling his cheek.

"Rhodie," he murmured, his voice cracking. "Please just . . . stop."

"Stop what?" she whispered back.

"People break up. People . . . drift apart. It happens. You'll move on, you'll find someone else."

She didn't know what to say. Pleading would be pathetic, and she'd already tried it on the beach with very limited success. "That's what you want?"

He nodded, his gaze not meeting hers. "It is. I'm sorry."

She stepped away from him, brushing off her hands. "Would you prefer I finish this first, or . . . ?"

"No, Garrett can finish it. Just . . . just go. Please go."

"Very well." It wasn't. It wasn't well at all. In fact, she felt sick, scalded inside, her emotions so raw they couldn't even be touched. She had no idea what kind of balm would ever heal it.

"And dinner on Friday?"

"Friday's off. Everything's off, Rhodie," he grunted.

"I see," she said, taking a long pause to gather her wild thoughts. "I really have to thank you, though. I know I set out to prove something to you, but I've ended up proving something to myself as well. I'm not as useless for normal endeavors as I once imagined."

He stared at his shoes, then turned and walked toward the back of the warehouse, in the opposite direction she was going.

She drifted home, not really seeing where she was going. The current of her life carried her forward, back to Bluffton, to her quarters. But her hand groped for her phone when she got there.

Rhodie: Are you awake?

Edward: Yes.

Rhodie: May I come to your quarters?

Edward: Of course.

Tezza and Sam were at the entry, and he opened the door for her. "Thank you, Sam."

"Ma'am?" Tezza said softly. "I want to apologize for the other night."

"No need. You were just following orders."

Her shoulders dropped, and she gave a curt nod in agreement. Rhodie put a hand on her arm. "In actuality, I appreciate how you were trying to protect Arron. You're a good friend."

"Thank you, ma'am."

Rhodie went into the residence and shut the door. Edward sat on their long white sectional, the news playing at a low volume in the background, his computer open and his bare feet on the coffee table. She looked around.

"Where's Abbie?"

He gestured behind him toward the bedroom door, which was closed. He shut his computer. "Your expression is grave, Your Highness."

"Rhodie." She sat down and let her posture crumple into the comfortable couch so that her head rested against the back of it. "Edward, what am I going to do?"

"About James?"

She nodded. "He fired me. My grand gesture didn't work. He doesn't want to see me. He says it's over." She turned her head just enough to see him. "Is it? Is it over?"

"Let me tell you a story . . ."

She threw up her hands. "Oh Lord, what is it with Browards and telling a story?"

He chuckled softly. "Fine, no story then. I don't think he's over you, if that's what you're asking." He lifted his hips and pulled his phone out of his back pocket. She thought he was responding to someone until he turned the screen so she could see it.

James: Rhodie get home okay?

Edward: I assume so. Why?

James: She was very upset when she left here.

Edward: Why, what happened?

James: I said things. Stupid things. Upsetting things.

James: Will you check? Please?
Edward: She got home a few minutes ago.
James: Thank you.

"If you want my professional opinion as one of his oldest friends? He's just too hurt to try again right now. He may yet come around. He's at least as stubborn as you are, and that's saying something."

She sighed and turned her head back to watch the TV. "I liked being in love. I don't think I could marry politically now. He's ruined me." He squeezed her hand briefly, and she remembered who she was talking to. "Of course, I would if you needed me to . . ."

"No, no. None of that. Stop with the duty talk. I've no plans to ask that of you."

They were quiet for a long time.

"I don't know what to do now."

"Have you thought about taking a sabbatical?"

"Work is all I have left. Black is white, up is down, Arron loves me but won't be with me, my niece is gone, but work is always there for me." She heard herself saying the words, but couldn't stop them in time. She covered her mouth with both hands, horrified. "I'm so sorry. I shouldn't have said that."

"No, it's all right." He scooted closer to her and gave her a one-armed hug. "What about a vacation, then? Get some sun, take your girlfriends." She shook her head. Hot tears were forming behind her eyes. "It's all right, Rhodie. It'll be all right. You'll figure it out. Just give it time."

All of her recent communication with her body had come back to bite her in the backside. She was *crying*. In front of the *king*, no less. Rhodie reached for a sense of shame . . . but she couldn't find it. *Maybe those counseling sessions are working after all . . .*

"I want to move out of Bluffton."

His eyebrows snapped together in a deep V. "Even after what happened with Heather?"

She nodded. "Yes. I want to be closer to work."

"You've got more than work left, Dr. Broward. You've got us. You've got your friends, your intellectual pursuits. Don't reduce your life to that."

"Is that a no?"

He pressed his lips into a flat line. "No, it's not a no. But I want to think about it. I would want to see your proposed residence and their security measures."

She nodded, wiping her eyes. "I will get through this."

"You certainly will. And knowing you, it will be with panache."

Rhodie laughed softly. "Thank you, Second Brother."

"You're welcome, Rhodie."

CHAPTER FORTY

JAMES WAS TYPING UP reports in his office. Everyone else had gone home; meanwhile he was picking at his Imaharan food, rewarding himself with cold dumplings every time he finished a page. A quiet knock at his open door made him look up. A man with hair as white as snow stood in the doorway, holding a black cane with an ornate silver handle. He had a neat reddish beard with white woven in and wore a tan three-piece suit, probably silk, and his hazel tie matched his eyes like it'd been dyed that way. His eyes—he'd seen them somewhere before. *In the mirror.*

"Father?" He breathed the word softly, and the man nodded.

"May I come in?"

He shot to his feet, his mother's training regarding politeness with one's social betters taking over. "Yes, of course, Your Grace. Please, make yourself comfortable." Before he shut the door, James peeked out his office door to check if anyone might've seen, but there were only two burly men dressed in black who he assumed were his father's security.

"I apologize for showing up like this. I was in town for a meeting, and I thought I'd make the most of the visit. Your cleaning lady said you were here."

"You're forgiven." This man, this strange man, who bore such a familiar resemblance to him, would of course assume that he was forgiven for stopping by without calling. But the phrase meant much more than that at this point. "What can I do for you?"

"We had a meeting. You didn't show." James felt surprise at the casual way the duke spoke. Maybe there was hope for them after all . . . except for that pesky cancer. He swallowed.

"No, sir, I didn't."

The duke nodded slowly. He leaned back, hanging his cane on the edge of the desk. "I won't waste your time. Tell me your concerns about accepting the dukedom."

James felt sweat break out along his forehead. "I just don't think it's for me, sir."

"Because?"

"Because I hate snooty people."

His father chuckled. "You're friends with the king, aren't you?"

"Yes, but he's actually not terribly snooty once you get to know him."

"I see." He looked at the obligatory workplace safety posters on his office walls. "Well, one advantage of being a powerful duke is that you can choose your own friends."

"I do that now."

"So you do." His father stroked his beard, then chuckled. "I really didn't think it would be this difficult to get you to accept. Most people who're handed a fortune are excited about it."

"I never wanted a fortune," he snapped. "I wanted a father."

The man's chin trembled. "I wanted that for you, too, son. I'm sorry. But I had to respect your mother's wishes. She wouldn't marry me, didn't love me."

James's eyes widened. "You proposed to her?"

The duke nodded. "But I'd made a mistake in how I started things with Aideen, and she wouldn't forgive me." He leaned forward. "Would you come to the house? Just for dinner? You can bring someone with you if you want, if you're uncomfortable coming alone." Either Sam or Saint would go with him, he was sure . . . but his stomach twisted when he realized that the only person he really wanted was the pretty black-haired princess he'd pushed away.

The duke went on, "I won't pressure you. I just wanted to make the most of the time I have left. Say the word, and I'll leave you alone. But I really would like to spend time with you, whether you want your birthright or not."

James couldn't help but stare at him. A memory flashed into his head—sparklers and sunshine and the taste of sugar in his mouth.

"Did you . . . did you come to my birthday one year?"

The man smiled. "I did indeed. We had cheap white cake with strawberry filling, you and your sisters screamed yourselves hoarse, and I loved every minute of it."

"Why?"

"Because I got to be your father for a day. I got to see you in action. Your mother just sent still photos."

He felt his mouth drop open. "She sent you photos of me?"

"Of course. I wanted to see that you were being taken care of. If she wasn't going to let me know you, it was the least she could do."

James stared hard at him. So much of what he'd hated about the man had just been negated. What did he really have to lose? Some time, a long carriage ride, maybe. He was an adult; if it was unbearable, he'd just leave.

"Very well. But I demand cheap white cake with strawberry filling, and if I scream myself hoarse, you can't say a word about it."

The duke barked out a laugh, a single tear falling on his cheek. "You're Aideen's boy, all right. Lord love me, you're Aideen's through and through." He held out a hand, and James shook it firmly.

TWENTY MINUTES AFTER his father left, he was still staring off into space, deep in thought, when another knock at his door startled him.

It was Petros. They hadn't really spoken since he'd shown up with Lily at his apartment, and James nodded toward a chair. "Hey."

"Hey." Petros ran a hand through his hair, and James recognized it as a gesture of embarrassment. "You weren't home, your cleaning lady, she said . . ."

James waved a hand at him; he didn't want to do this part again. Yes, he was working too much. *Thanks for the tip, everyone.*

"How've you been?"

"Not good." Petros sighed, his knee shaking the desk as it bounced. "There's something on my mind. Something I didn't tell you," he mumbled, "about the morning you were sent home."

"What?"

"I knew you two were getting closer, you and the princess, but I didn't realize it was . . . serious. You never came to her room at night except to play chess, you left the door open, I didn't think . . ." He sighed. "I jacked this up."

James leaned forward, his heart in his throat. If it was about Rhodie, he wanted to know right now. "Skip to the end of this apology."

Petros nodded curtly. "She said you had PTSD, that part was true. But she begged them not to dishonorably discharge you. Weathers had the paperwork all filled out, he was going to can you . . . She saved you. Saved your job."

James replayed that text conversation in his mind, the one where he'd said goodbye as coldly and gruffly as possible, now realizing that his actions came on the heels of her using her influence to help him, risking outing their relationship . . . He felt like the biggest heel alive. *And by extension, she saved my possible dukedom. I can't imagine Father would've wanted a disgraced ex-military officer for his heir.*

James's mouth fell open for the second time that night. This was turning into quite the evening of revelations. "Why didn't you tell me this earlier?"

"I don't know. I knew you had a secret, something you weren't telling us. Never used to be like that with you, me, and Chance. I knew you were still pissed that I lost my temper with Lincoln. I wanted to get back on your good side. I wanted things to go back to the way they were. I'm sorry."

James pinched the bridge of his nose. "Next time, could you please come clean before I push my groveling ex-girlfriend away for good?"

Petros winced. "Too late, huh?"

"Maybe."

CHAPTER FORTY-ONE

ON FRIDAY MORNING, Rhodie felt a depression steal over her. She was supposed to be having dinner with Arron tonight. She was supposed to get to explain. Now her plans were dead in the water. She felt just as lost as she had all week, but it was compounded by the fact that she had to keep starting over on her reports, because she couldn't focus. Spinning her wheels at work was new; usually work was the one thing she could always do well.

By eight, she needed to blow off some steam. Her phone pinged with a text.

Garrett: I got your number from the staff sergeant. I'm sorry we didn't get to say goodbye. Thanks again for all your help.

Rhodie: I quite enjoyed it, Private. Thank you for your wonderful instruction.

Garrett: Offer still stands for that bar hop. We're starting at the Rusty Nail.

After changing out of her work clothes, she marched out of her suite, determined. Rhodie caught a glimpse of her mother, entertaining in the sitting room.

Mum: Where are you going?

Rhodie: I believe it's called the Rusty Nail.

Mum: Stop by my suite on your way out, please.

When she arrived, her mother's lips were pursed in a displeased line, but her father's beard was twitching, a sure sign that he was holding back a smile.

"Yes?"

"What's the purpose of this outing?"

"Socialization. It's good for primates."

"Honestly, Rhodie. Don't be crass." Just as she reached the doorway, she heard her mother's soft voice again. "Please don't use the bathrooms. You'll get hepatitis."

Rhodie smiled as she stalked down the hallway toward her waiting carriage. After a short ride, during which she doubted this decision about fifty times, she stepped out onto the street and into the warm night in downtown Barrowdon. Garrett, Jacobs, and several other soldiers she recognized waved when she walked in, and she beamed at them.

"I don't know what I'm doing here," she admitted to Garrett as she slid into the booth.

"You're having fun, Doctor." She grinned. "Let's get you a drink."

"Or twelve!" Jacobs called, and she chuckled as the rest of the soldiers applauded the suggestion.

The waitress put a half-empty mug and a full shot glass down in front of her. "On the house, Your Highness."

"Thank you," she said, lifting the glass to sip the amber liquid.

"Wait, wait, wait," Garrett said, putting a hand over the top of it. "You didn't put the shot in!"

Rhodie crinkled her nose. "Is mixing types of alcohol advisable?" She drank, of course, but usually just half a glass of white wine at palace functions to make them more bearable.

"It's advisable." Jacobs smirked. "It's definitely advisable."

It didn't take long before Rhodie was forced to agree: the garish decorating at the Rusty Nail didn't seem nearly as offensive as it had when she walked in, and the music selection seemed to be more to her liking as well. She still didn't want acquaintances putting their hands on her body, so she declined the invitations to dance, but she enjoyed watching the others and analyzing their technique. But dancing made her think about James, and thinking about James led to talking about James, and before she knew it, she was outside the bar, climbing back into her carriage, with Trosen hurrying to keep up.

Before she knew it, she had directed the carriage to a building across from Grammarless Park, to a penthouse suite she'd never actually been inside. She knocked, and a few moments later, the door opened.

"I'm here," she sang. "Hellooooo, Arron."

His face looked stunned. "Rhodie, are you . . . drunk?" He peeked out at her security, which was lingering nervously behind her. "Trosen, what the jack?"

"I'm sorry, man, she's a force to be reckoned with when she's like this. Wouldn't listen to a word I said."

She wobbled and broke their eye contact. "Yep. I am drunk. It's Friday. I just dropped by—oh, hello, Edward! Hello, Francis, hello, Sam and—is that Tezza? Hello, Tezza! I just dropped by to—say, are you having a party? Do you mind if I join you? And where's my sweet sister-in-law, have you left her—oh, there she is, hello, dear . . ."

James took her firmly by the shoulders to reclaim her wandering attention. "What are you doing here?"

"You," she said, sticking a finger in his face, "said you would have dinner with me tonight." She threw out her arms. "So here I am."

"It's nearly ten. Dinner ended a few hours ago."

"I got distracted," she said, pushing her dreads out of her face. "Goodness, it's terribly warm in here, don't you think?" Rhodie began to shed her coat as the other guests sprang into action.

"I'll take her home," said Edward. "We should be going along, anyway."

"Noooo," said Rhodie. "I just got here, I can't go home yet." She plopped her purse by the door unceremoniously.

"I'll make her some coffee," said Abbie, slipping into the kitchen.

"See, James?" Rhodie said, pointing after her, "now that's hospitality. That's the kind of welcome one expects when one comes calling."

He was shaking his head . . . but he was smiling. He wasn't angry. She patted herself on the back for such an excellent idea in coming here. Perhaps her evening of indulgence wasn't so ill-advised after all.

"Come on in and tell us all about where you've been. I'm sure there's a charming explanation for your inebriation." He put an arm around her waist and led her over to the kitchen table, then helped her sit down, which was very convenient because her legs weren't being as helpful and responsive as they usually were.

"As a matter of fact, there *is* a charming explanation for my inebriation. Have you ever had a boilermaker?"

His eyes narrowed. "Who gave you a boilermaker?"

"Not one," she said, holding up two fingers. "Three. His name was Kevin."

"Kevin at the Rusty Nail?" asked Saint, arms crossed.

She nodded and immediately regretted the quick movement. "I was, and it was a lovely establishment. Kevin was just a doll. Didn't even take my picture."

"But I bet someone else did," Saint muttered, getting out his phone. "Oh, look: 'Royal Rhodie puts on the Ritz at Rusty Nail.'"

"Oh," she said, looking down at her blouse, "was I overdressed? I didn't notice. I did remember not to use the bathroom, though." Abbie put the coffee in front of her. "Oh, bless you. Abbie, remind me to tell Mum that I didn't use the bathrooms." Rhodie clasped the mug with both hands and sipped the black liquid.

"Well, we'll be taking off," said Sam.

"Sam, wait!" They all turned to look at Rhodie. "Have you ever tried a boilermaker?"

"I can't say that I have, no," he said, his lips twitching with amusement.

"You should," she said, drawing out the second word. "James, do you have any whisky?"

"Yes," said Tezza, grinning, "let's ply Sam with whisky and see what happens."

"You'd like that, wouldn't you," he muttered as he helped her into her coat. "Apologies, Your Highness, but I despise vomiting. Also, it's late, and we need to get home; our home study is tomorrow, for our adoption."

"Oh, what a shame. Perhaps next time. I'll show you how to do a depth charge . . ." She mimicked dropping the shot glass into the beer and made soft explosion noises.

James was massaging his temples. "Drink the coffee, love."

"Is it wrong that I'm kind of enjoying this?" Abbie asked, sitting down next to her at the table.

"Says the woman who isn't going to have to field a bunch of questions about this on Monday," Saint said, shaking his head.

"No," Rhodie said somberly, patting her hand. "Life is made for living. Enjoy away! You get it, girl!" She turned back to James, the reason she'd come here. "I told my new friends about what happened between us, and they said I should 'Go get it, girl.' Their words. I thought it was sage advice."

"It might not feel that way in the morning," James said softly.

"Give me your phone," Rhodie said, holding out a flat hand.

James scowled. "No."

"Give me your phone. Gimme, gimme, gimme."

"No," he said, backing up when he saw that she was rising from her chair. Her steps faltered as her whisky-wobbled legs failed her, and he lurched forward again to catch her before she fell.

"Aww, you catched me," she said, resting her head against his shoulder. "Just like on the slippery river rocks. And now we're on the rocks in another way. That's . . . that's . . ." She lost her train of thought as she groped him for his phone.

"Rhodie . . . are you really going through my pockets?"

"Still here, by the way," Edward said from the couch. "If things get frisky, I will leave."

"She's *your* sister."

"She's *your* ex-girlfriend . . ."

Even in the state she was in, Rhodie noticed that James seemed troubled by the term, but then her fingers closed around cool metal. "Ha! Found it." She slid out of his arms down to the hardwood floor and tried to unlock it. "How does this open? Phone, open. PHONE, OPEN."

"Good grief, stop yelling," James said, leaning down to press his thumb to the sensor.

Rhodie wasted no time. Things may have been a bit woozy, but this was no time for her brain to let her heart down. "Rhodie, Rhodie, Rhodie," she said, scrolling, looking for her own name. When she got to "Saint" without finding herself, she felt tears coming. "You deleted me?"

"No, no," he said hastily, trying to take the phone back. "Just . . . look under *M*."

She scrolled so quickly, she passed it. "Ah. Here I am. You tricked me, it was under *M* for 'My Princess.' That's right, though. *I'm* your princess. Me." She turned the screen so he could see it. "And this is probably my number . . . I think. Not so sure about that, but I'll check and see later. Unblocked." She handed the phone back to him. "You don't have to answer, but don't block me."

He was staring at her. She couldn't read his expression, but it was an intense one. After a long moment, he reached out his hand to help her up, and she took it gratefully. It was good to be on her feet, especially because her stomach took the opportunity to eject everything it contained.

CHAPTER FORTY-TWO

AFTER SHE THREW UP, the events of the evening got even more blurry. James helped her into her coat (maybe), Edward helped her into his carriage (she thought), and the next thing she remembered was getting into bed after a maid (*Which one? Who knows.*) helped her remove her vomit-stained clothes.

Now, in the pale light of dawn, she groped around for her phone and her glasses.

Rhodie: Are you awake?

Abbie: Yeah. I mean, it's like 9.

The pale light of midmorning, apparently.

Rhodie: What did I do.

Abbie: Oh, honey. I feel like we should get you some coffee first . . .

Rhodie: Abbie.

Abbie: Seriously, though. Come to our place, I'll make you something strong . . .

Rhodie: ABBIE.

The phone rang shrilly, and Rhodie winced so hard, she strained muscles in her face she didn't know she had. And she was a doctor.

"Hello? In soft tones, please."

"Hi," Abbie whispered. "How's your head?"

"Attached. Throbbing. What did I do?"

"Let's start with what you remember . . ."

"I went to the Rusty Nail. I became very inebriated. Then I went . . . home?"

"Nope."

"But you made me coffee."

"You crashed our video game night at Arron's. You were super drunk. You stole his phone. You threw up on his Pyetian wood floors."

Her horror grew with every sentence out of her sister-in-law's mouth. In fact, horror overtook her completely, rendering her speechless at her own lack of decorum.

"Rhodie?"

"Yes?" she squeaked.

"It'll be okay. Weirdly enough, I don't think he really cared. He kept staring at you. I think he was actually really happy to see you, even though you were drunk and gross."

Her phone pinged with a message. "Just a moment, Abbie . . ." She blinked hard, trying to focus on the small type on the screen.

Arron: You threw up on my floor.

Arron: I believe some light recompense is in order.

"He's texting me! He's texting me!" Rhodie sat bolt upright, and her stomach lodged a formal complaint in the form of dry heaving. She wiped her sweaty palms to try to write back. Being hungover was really putting a damper on her ability to multitask. "I'll call you back!"

Rhodie: That seems fair.

Rhodie: What did you have in mind?

Please say a date. Please say a date. Please, please, please . .

Arron: Edward mentioned you have *NeverMind: A Brief Primer on Psychiatry* by Gordon Waffle.

Rhodie: Yes. Would you like to borrow it?

Arron: Why else would I ask?

Rhodie: Who knows? Everything out of your mouth is the setup to a joke . . .

Arron: Yes, well . . . I'm working on that.

Arron: Hence the book.

Rhodie: I see. Well, as your friend, I would be happy to assist your emotional education.

He was quiet for a long time after that. Was that the wrong thing to say? She was aiming for supportive, friendly. Maybe he'd taken it wrong . . . Rhodie voided her bladder and brushed the nastiness out of her mouth. She stood naked, staring at the scale. She really wanted to get on it. Gordon had said she could, once a day. It would probably be low, deliciously low; if she'd thrown up, she'd be at a good number today.

All the numbers are just numbers, Rhodie. They're not good or bad. Assigning a moral value to them might not be helpful. She stretched out her foot and tapped the scale so that the display blinked on. She watched it flash "0.0" until it blinked off again. She tried to breathe deeply and really think about what *she* wanted. She could always get on tomorrow. She would go and eat breakfast . . . She could always do it later. *The number won't be as good!* her mind argued, but it was interrupted by her heart, leaping like a lamb in a spring meadow, at the sound of another text message.

James: You've already done that. Leave it at the gate, I'll come get it.

The heart-lamb froze mid-bounce. Was that a good thing or not?

James: For which I'm very grateful.

Rhodie: Me too. I'll give it to the gate staff.

She turned his words over in her mind as she turned on the shower and tested the heat level. It was a game of chess now . . . He hadn't thrown the board away yet, but he wasn't playing to win, either. They were at a stalemate, and she didn't know how to break it.

CHAPTER FORTY-THREE

IT WAS SEVERAL WEEKS before James and Saint were able to make the journey to his father's estate. He hadn't accepted anything yet except the invitation to visit. The duke sent a simple oak-and-iron carriage for him that was carved with a silhouette of the mountains that stood at the north end of the property, far less ostentatious than he would've imagined. Given the circumstances, he felt like it should be pulled by horses that had been transformed from mice, changed by a fairy godmother's intervention. Sadly, they seemed quite normal.

As they came to a stop at the gates of the duke's property, his book and overnight bag slid out from under the seat. The idea of sleeping under his father's roof was strange, but he didn't want to make the six-hour journey twice in one day.

James felt like throwing up, and it wasn't due to the bouncing of the carriage, which actually had surprisingly good shocks. *Why am I considering this again? Why don't I just go back to my regularly scheduled life and forget about the duke?*

"Hey." Saint was watching him. "Don't throw up on me. Please."

"Helpful, thanks. Why did I bring you again?"

Saint cocked an eyebrow. "Because Sam's special brand of social awkwardness would just make things worse, bringing Edward would seem like a power play, Abbie hates travel, and because, unlike you, I can keep a secret."

"There aren't any girls here. I mentioned that, right?"

"No, you told me this place would be packed with chicks I could show my medal to."

James stuck his head out the window to breathe deeply of the fresh early-summer air. "This is the world's longest driveway. Why is his driveway ten miles long?"

"Privacy. This is the way to live, mate. If you don't want it, maybe I'll take it."

James wasn't listening. He was staring at the stone mansion they were quickly approaching; it sprawled across the estate, nestled amid rose gardens, rows of thick hedges, a labyrinth, patios, and gazebos. He wondered if it was all for show or if the duke liked to be outside. *I don't know anything about this man. I don't know why I'm doing this.* But suddenly, the feeling of holding Emma, his newborn niece, a few days ago came back to him, and he did know. This was for Cora and Brighton and Emma and Ivy and his mum. *His mum.* He hadn't told her he was coming up to Greenmeadow Downs, and the guilt was eating at him like a parasite. They'd had a few cordial but cold interactions since their argument, and he didn't like leaving things to fester. He needed to make time to go up and see her, too, have it out in person, hug and make up. If this worked out and he could quit his job . . . Nope, he wasn't ready to go there yet.

"I'm freaking out," James breathed as the carriage rolled to a stop. "Talk me down, Francis."

"Stop freaking out."

"That was perfect, thanks."

Saint slid on his sunglasses. "You're welcome."

It felt more like they were arriving at a hotel than a home; they were shown to their rooms to have the opportunity to freshen up and dress for dinner, which would be served in an hour in the lilac dining room.

James wasn't normally much of an exercise hound, unlike his friends, but he found himself doing jumping jacks next to the ornate four-poster bed just to burn off some nerves.

THEY WERE ON THE FOURTH course of their seven-course meal when the duke transitioned from pleasantries to business.

"When you're ready," the duke said, signaling for a refill on his wine, "I'd like to introduce you to some young ladies who would make an excellent choice for duchess."

Not an excellent wife, nor an excellent life partner. An excellent duchess. A business transaction. Someone to make an heir with and throw dinner parties.

"What makes them so excellent?"

The duke swirled his wine, watching the pattern as it slid down the glass, checking its quality before he took a sip. "They come from wealthy families, they have the right education. Any of them would be useful to you as you transition into the role, help you meet expectations."

Yes, but would they risk outing our secret relationship and damage their own reputation to save mine? Will they chance going into the river headfirst, or just stand by and watch as I fall? For the hundredth time since Petros told him the truth, he wished he'd been there to hear Rhodie fight for him. He wished he'd just believed her, asked what happened. Been a grown-up instead of acting like a teenager when his feelings were hurt. Woz, he'd been so stupid. But that didn't mean he needed to be stupid about this, too.

James grunted noncommittally. "Give their numbers to Saint. I'll choose my own spouse."

"Just make sure you're investigating any potential partner thoroughly. I know what you're up against, I've taken advantage of the line of beautiful women anxious to catch a wealthy duke's attention myself..."

"Hence my existence," he said, gesturing to his chest. In his peripheral vision, James saw Saint wince, and he knew he'd gone too far.

"No. That's not how it was with Aideen. She didn't..." He trailed off, staring down the table. "She didn't know who I was."

Interesting. He'd like to get his mother's side of the story, someday. Probably on her deathbed. Her chatty nature didn't seem to extend to that chapter of her life.

"Anyway," the duke continued, regaining his composure, "you must be very careful whom you allow into your life from now on. There are many women who would like to claim the other half of your title."

And yet, there's only one I want to give it to... This is pointless, he chided himself. *She's stopped texting, calling, coming by. You pushed her away and she went. Stop fixating.* He wanted to. And yet... the largest part of his heart wondered if she might give him a second chance if he groveled hard enough. Despite appearances, maybe she hadn't moved on yet. Maybe if he asked her, she'd—

"Arron? Are you listening to me?"

James bristled at the fatherly tone, but nodded. "Yes, you're concerned for my virginity. I'm afraid it's a foregone conclusion."

Saint choked on a bite of roasted potatoes, and James whacked him on the back to help clear it until he was breathing normally again. The duke seemed mildly amused, which was lucky.

"Listen," his father said, leaning forward. "In one of my newspapers, they had a picture of you with Princess Rhododendron somewhere downtown." James met his hazel gaze, waiting for him to go on. "They never printed it, as I wanted to maintain your privacy and the royal family's."

"And?" he prompted, impatient. "We're friends. Are we not allowed to be photographed together?"

"Certainly, certainly you are. She just doesn't make many appearances in such publications, and I wondered what the circumstances were."

He threw his napkin onto the table and sat back. "My sister Cora was getting married at the courthouse. I invited the princess to come, and she did." *With thirty minutes' notice. Yes, she was pissed with me later because of that photograph, but I bet she'd still do it again.* He swallowed hard. "They know each other from when I was shot. Why do you ask?"

The duke's tone was surprisingly soft. "Because I'm curious about you, about your life." The staff were quietly serving the salad course.

"Sorry," James muttered, leaning back so they could clear his plate.

"What would you say to a trial run on the dukedom? Come live here with me for a few weeks, see what it's like. If you hate it, turn it down. Otherwise, we'll at least have more time to get to know each other."

Forgetting his manners, James put his elbows on the table. "Forgive my directness, but do you have time for that?"

The duke shifted in his chair and sighed. "I don't rightly know. But you're the only person I want filling this role. I'd bet my right ear that you're like me: you love a challenge, get into trouble when you don't have one. And I know from your grades that you've got the intellectual capacity. It's a lot to juggle, and there's lots of judgment calls, but if you commit yourself to the role, I think you might be surprised how you might benefit society. We don't just sit around playing croquet. Well, some of us do, but . . ."

"And if high society sneers at my dockside humor and bird's nest hair?"

The duke clasped his hands high behind his head, smiling. "Then you won't have to attend their charity balls and you'll have more time for video games or whatever makes you tick."

James laughed, shaking his head. "It can't be that simple." *Can it?*

"Why?" The question came from his side, from Saint. "Why can't it be that simple?"

"Whose side are you on?" James joked, but Saint didn't laugh.

"You'd be good at this. Jersey, maybe you'd shake things up a little, get people to think a little harder about their own lives. Maybe you're just the cherry bomb those traditionalists need."

"Is that a hair joke?" he quipped, and Saint did grin then. "Yes."

James sighed. "Okay. I agree to the trial run. I may need your help in procuring some extended leave. I'm not on my CO's good side right now."

"Have you ever been?"

"No," he laughed. "Never."

"That's why you should just become the boss."

CHAPTER FORTY-FOUR

"THIS IS THE STRANGEST family reunion in the history of our nation," Edward murmured as he spread his legs to receive his pat-down at the prison gates.

"Or any other nation," Rhodie agreed, still feeling a bit green around the gills from the sail to the island; the water had been choppy. It mirrored her mood: no progress toward a reunion with Arron, coming to grips with her eating disorder, meeting with Gordon, who excelled at turning her world upside down. And now this, visiting her eldest brother for the first time since he'd been hauled away in Trella. She gripped the brown paper bag she'd brought more tightly. Maybe she shouldn't have come with Edward. She'd promised she would. And she did want to see Lincoln, but she wanted the boy who used to tease her mercilessly and boast about how wonderful his reign was going to be, who used to splash her in the sea, race her on horseback along the cliffs, beg her to play strategy games with him. She wanted the old Lincoln; she didn't know this man.

The brown-haired guard passed them off to the warden, a white man with black hair salted with white at his temples, who led them down a narrow, windowless corridor. The warden opened a door at the end of the hall into a room that had clearly been converted for their purposes: someone had covered the dirty, skid-marked gray floor with a large, smooth silk rug in calm shades of blue and green. Three armchairs in

a matching shade of teal sat in a circle with a low tea table between them, each perfectly equidistant.

"Will this suffice, Your Majesty? We'll try to prepare
something more appropriate next time, but this was the best
we could do on short notice."

"It's fine, Warden," Edward assured him, taking the seat
nearest the door. His leg was bouncing, vibrating like a harp
string, and she parted her lips to chide him when the metal
door buzzed, then swung open. Lincoln entered, head down,
wrists cuffed, wearing an orange jumpsuit, led by the same
guard who'd patted down Edward. The king stood up, and
Rhodie had the sudden urge to grab his hand. She knew why
he hadn't brought Abbie; she was still far too shaken by her
attempted kidnapping last year. Still, she felt that she wasn't
the right person . . . She lacked her sister-in-law's spunk. Abbie would probably spit in Lincoln's face.

Her brothers stood like statues, watching each other, as
the guard unlocked Lincoln's handcuffs. They stayed that
way until the guard and the warden closed the door behind
them.

"Your Majesty," Lincoln's quiet voice was gravelly, "I just
want to thank you—"

Edward was across the room in a flash, embracing his
brother before Lincoln even got the chance to open his arms.
Lincoln stared at her over Edward's shoulder, his eyes misty.

"Hi, Rho."

"Hello, First Brother." The First Son of Orangiers
choked out a sob and tried in vain to return his younger
brother's ardent hug, but it was no use. The king was pinning
his arms to his sides relentlessly.

"Edward . . ."

"Woz, I'm so glad you're okay. You're so stupid," Edward said, his voice thick.

"Now, now," Rhodie chimed in, "Rutha used to say that there were no stupid people, just stupid decisions."

"Rutha was wrong. I was stupid. But at least I put an end to it."

Edward let out a shaky sigh, and she knew he was close to crying, too. A strange feeling came over Rhodie: she wanted to join their hug. She wanted to feel their big, stupid arms around her, too; she wanted to be in the sandwich. Shuffling over, she ducked under Edward's arms and wedged her way between the two men.

"I felt very left out over there," she explained, her voice muffled. "You were having a moment, I know, but I couldn't help it." What started as a guffaw quickly built into chuckles, which built into belly-laughing. Tears streamed down her face in relief: they had made it. They'd all made it through this nightmare. Yes, Lincoln was in prison, but by all rights, he should be dead.

"We should have tea," Lincoln said, taking charge as usual, wiping the tears from his face that they were all pretending were from laughing so hard.

"It's getting cold, I'm sure," Edward agreed, and they all sat down. An awkward silence descended as she poured for the Duke of Darlington from the angular white teapot.

"So, Rho," Lincoln said. "What's new?"

"I have an eating disorder."

Both men's hands froze midair. Edward set his teacup back down.

"You do?"

"Yes," she said, sipping her own tea. "I'm seeing a psychiatrist. It's helping."

"You are?" Lincoln asked, the tea in his hand forgotten entirely. "Since when?"

"About six weeks, I think." She crossed one ankle behind the other beneath her chair. "It's been good."

"That's . . ." Lincoln and Edward shared a perplexed look before the prisoner went on. "That's great, Rhodie. And things with Arron are going well, I assume?"

Rhodie saw Edward wince in her peripheral vision.

Lincoln saw it, too. "What? Don't tell me you're not together? That man was 100 percent in love with you."

"I know." She nodded. "I know he was. Maybe he still is, but . . ."

"But what?" Edward asked, grabbing a shortbread cookie.

"But I don't know how to get him back to the chessboard, so to speak."

"That's an easy one," Lincoln said, sitting forward in his chair, elbows on his knees.

"Oh, really?" Rhodie said, raising an eyebrow at him.

"Sure. You want to get him back to the chessboard? Start a game with someone else."

"That's an interesting idea," Edward said, reaching for another cookie.

"Wait, wait, don't fill up on those. I brought something." Rhodie reached under her chair for the brown paper bag. "And they tested them for poison on the way in, so they should be safe for both of you." She carefully put two pastries on napkins and passed them to her brothers before claiming a third for herself. Lincoln sniffed at his, while Edward popped the whole thing in his mouth. *They're just the opposite in normal life, but not when it comes to dessert,* she mused, grinning.

"Orange? Anise?" Lincoln asked, taking a bite.

"It's called a derbyhorse cake. I can't fathom why, but it's my favorite."

Edward grinned at her. "You do have a favorite."

"I do now." She smiled back.

As time often does when spent with people we love, the time together went too quickly. Edward was needed back on the mainland; Rhodie needed to get back to the lab, too. They promised to come back again soon, and bring their parents next time.

"Have you heard from your contacts in Trella?" Edward asked, as they stood leaning over the railing of the ship, watching black clouds gather as a storm started toward the tiny prison island.

Rhodie nodded, pushing the hair out of her face the wind had tossed there. "Yautia actually emailed me. I'm sending her some rare ivy species that she's interested in comparing to the vines she has there. She's sending me more tea; I'm dying to know if it will make our magic visible as well. If it doesn't, it may indicate the existence of 'species' of magic."

Edward frowned. "Is that possible?"

She shrugged. "It's been theorized, but since each magic user experiences their relationship with the magic slightly differently, it's very hard to prove. If it's visible, it wouldn't disprove it, but if it isn't visible, it will be imperative to find out why."

"Fascinating." He looked out to sea. "I can't wait to hear your update."

It wasn't the right time, after such a good visit with Lincoln, but . . . she had his undivided attention. It was too rare an opportunity to let pass by.

"Something else I spoke with Dr. Waffle about . . ."

"Yes?"

"Would you consider not arranging marriage contracts for your children?"

Edward frowned. "What do you mean?"

"I mean, doesn't it seem strange to you that we're asking our royals to know themselves so well at such a young age?"

The king was silent, but he didn't turn away. "I'd never really thought about it. It's just . . ."

"The way things are. I know. But it doesn't mean that's the way they have to be, does it? That's something I'm realizing. This next generation, it's in our hands. We can do things differently. Give our girls more options. Let our boys grow up a little more before we thrust such heavy responsibility on them."

After a long pause, he nodded once. "I will think about it. There may be other solutions."

The knot of tension in her stomach started to unwind. "That's all I ask."

Edward turned back to the rolling waves. "Now, about getting James back to the chessboard . . ."

"I'm listening . . ."

CHAPTER FORTY-FIVE

EDWARD: You're coming on Friday, right?

James: How could I miss my best friend's birthday?

Edward: I know things have been awkward around here for you . . .

James: It's my own fault. Don't worry about it.

James: I'll be there.

Edward: Good. It wouldn't be the same without you.

Edward: Come a bit early and hang out.

"I should warn you . . . ," Edward said as they walked toward Beverly Hall.

"You got anchovies on the pizza again?"

"No, mate. It's . . . Rhodie. She's with someone else tonight. I've helped her to connect with an appropriate suitor."

"Oh." James tugged at his earlobe. "Fine, good. That's good."

"I'm delighted that you feel that way, and I agree, it is good. You're both getting on with life, right?"

He was quiet for too long . . . He wasn't getting on with life. He'd spent all day planning out what he was going to say to her, how he was going to find out if she was still interested at all. But he couldn't admit that, not when her brother had basically just announced her engagement to someone else.

"James?" Edward had the same pinched look around his eyes he'd had when James had first admitted his mother's financial situation was less than stellar. "Are you all right?"

"Yes, of course." He wanted to make a joke to reassure his friend that he could give him this gift, do him this service . . . but he couldn't think of a single one. Dr. Waffle had been encouraging him not to lean on humor in difficult moments, but he didn't realize it was going to feel so terrible. He opted for sincerity. "You have my word. I'll behave."

"That's what you said before you went to Trella, too," Edward joked, and James elbowed him.

Everyone else was already seated when Rhodie and Grayson Cross, Duke of Grabbleton, came in. The duke pulled out her chair for her, and she smoothed her modern mauve dress as she sat down. *Look at me,* he thought in her direction. *Just for a moment.* He certainly hadn't come to watch her flirt with her . . . her . . . *boyfriend.* Except, since it was arranged, perhaps "boyfriend" didn't quite work. *Intended? Fiancé?* James shook his head without meaning to. *How could she want that after what we had?* He'd had a lot of time to think over the last few weeks . . . too much, probably. But it had solidified in his mind that his time with Rhodie was the deepest, warmest relationship he'd ever had. Probably because in her purest form, she was the deepest, warmest person he'd ever known. And now this guy might get to know her that way. He knew he should be happy for her, but he couldn't muster it just then. He'd blown his chance. He'd screwed up royally.

Edward would "get to" have a fancy ball thrown by his mother and his wife on his actual birthday, attended by foreign dignitaries and ambassadors and mayors and governors and other stuffy people that neither he nor Edward would ever want at a party. This wasn't that. This was the family party, the inner circle.

"Beer, mate?" Saint offered, and James accepted it gratefully. He'd limit himself to a couple; Saint, Sam, James, and Edward were going to take the king's ketch out sailing after this if they were sober enough to keep it away from the cliffs. If they weren't, they were going to play video games. Crashing those vehicles had fewer consequences.

"What, no salad? No appetizers, no wine?" James joked.

"There's lobster on one of the pizzas," Sam said. "That's as close to fancy as this gets."

Someone bumped his shoulder, and he turned to see Abbie grinning at him.

"Hey!" He gave her a tight hug. "Haven't seen you in a bit. You all right?"

She nodded, sipping her sparkling cider. "I'm better. Back to school for the summer, trying to get caught up from all the time I missed."

"Well, take your time. There's no rush. You're the grand duchess, after all . . ."

She scowled. "You know I don't like to play that card . . ."

No, but she could. They'd welcome her back whenever at the university, just like his friends had let James take his time in coming back to the palace. He was glad he had; it was good to be with them again, despite the pain of also being without Rhodie. Even that was fading somewhat . . . though sitting there listening to her laugh at Grayson's jokes was not helping. He wasn't even *funny*.

Luckily, most of the focus was on Edward. He opened his presents after dinner, and unsurprisingly, he got some good stuff: *Rogue Knight 6* from Andrew, which wasn't supposed to be out yet, several new nonfiction books that James was already planning to borrow, a wireless fitness tracker from Abbie—the man had an undying love for gadgetry. The duke and Rhodie had gone in together on a gift (already?), and it was perfect, of course: a solar-powered waterproof speaker Edward could take on the boat, already charged for tonight.

"So," James said across the table. "How goes the duking these days?"

"Just fine," said Grayson, wiping his mouth. "Arron, isn't it?"

He ignored the spike of irritation at the use of his first name. He'd been casual with him, this was a casual setting. He let his emotional porcupine quills resettle before answering. "Yes, Arron's fine."

"Yes, Rhodie's told me about your—"

Please don't say "nasty breakup."

"—voyage to Trella. It sounded like a fascinating trip."

"Our voyage, yes. It was. Have you been outside the Veil?"

The man furrowed his eyebrows incredulously. "Never. I see no point to it, really."

"Exploration, adventure, greater cultural understanding. Those are a few possible points." Seeing the man's confusion, he plowed ahead. "But getting back to your duking, how do you spend your days?"

"Spend my days?" he asked. "I'm afraid I don't understand."

"Do you play croquet? Bridge? Practice your harpsichord, what?"

"I spend time with my financial advisors. I meet with people who are interested in contributing to the foundation or presenting a plan to receive from it. I host other dukes and duchesses who are touring the nation for various reasons. I attend social events in order to network."

"I think I'd prefer the harpsichord," he mumbled, but Grayson didn't hear him, because he was looking at his phone.

"Please excuse me, I need to return this call."

"I guess he doesn't know about Ignatius and his 'no phones at the table' rule," Sam whispered, and James smirked. Rhodie's chair was blocking his, so she pushed back from the table, then she turned toward Grayson. He whispered something in her ear, and James had a front-row seat to watch as his hand slid down her back. Lower. Lower. Lower . . . until his giant, veiny hand rested on the curve of her backside and *squeezed*. Rhodie's mouth dropped open, and she looked away, her cheeks pink. The duke chuckled.

James saw red.

CHAPTER FORTY-SIX

HE SAW SO MUCH RED, James was sure rage had burst a blood vessel in his eyes to make his vision turn that color. He tried to jump to his feet, when he felt a firm hand on his shoulder, shoving him back down.

"Easy, mate," Saint said.

"But he—" he sputtered.

"Not now."

He seethed quietly as Rhodie gave the dead man a chaste kiss. Technically, of course, he was not dead yet, but James would remedy that soon. Very soon. It was the only thought that comforted him. No one was going to touch Rhodie with anything less than respect, especially right in front of him. She had clearly not been expecting that, and it was never going to happen again. Not ever. He felt someone at his elbow and looked up. Ignatius stood over him.

"How are you, son?"

"Fine, sir, and you?"

"You don't look fine. You look upset."

What is it with this family and telling people they look like fish guts? First Lily, now Ignatius?

"Do you want to talk about it?"

"No, sir," he forced out, "I'm fine. Everything's fine."

"Mmm." Ignatius leaned over. "They make a beautiful couple, don't they? Handsome. Their children will be good-looking, too, I suspect."

"I suppose so." The idea of Rhodie not only having sex but having children with someone else was so abhorrent, James wanted to throw up. "Would you excuse me, sir? I'm not feeling well."

"You do look a bit green," Ignatius commented as he continued down the table.

"Yeah, with envy," Saint muttered. James kicked him under the table as he got up to leave. Once in the bathroom, he surveyed himself in the mirror; overall, he looked better these days. Not so pale, not so unkempt. He was sleeping better since he'd started meeting with Dr. Waffle, so the shadows under his eyes were receding. They had started talking about the shooting but ended up spending more time on his father. Forgiveness was hard. It was easier to be angry. With Rhodie, with Grayson Cross, with Lincoln, with his father, with the guy who took the last seat on the train. . . almost anyone. But anger wasn't getting him anywhere; it was keeping him stuck. It was keeping him alone. Yes, it kept him warm, but so does lighting yourself on fire.

James splashed water on his face and dried it on their soft towels. *I can do this. I'm going to set aside my anger and be happy for her. I let her go; I lost my chance. If this is what she wants, then I'll support her.* He pointed at his reflection sternly and spoke to himself.

"Go out there and act normal. Don't ruin Edward's party with your petty jealousy. Come on."

He passed Ginger as he went back to the hall. "All right, love?"

The teenager gave him a skeptical look, glanced up and down the hallway before she leaned in a little. "I put my money on you. Don't make a fool out of me."

"Pardon?" he asked, but she was already continuing toward the bathrooms. James shook his head, still trying to make sense of the odd comment, when a pale-purple blur moved in the courtyard.

It's her. This is my chance. I won't profess my love, I just want to feel her full attention on me again. James opened the doors to the garden and stepped outside. Rhodie turned.

"Step outside for a smoke?" he said, smirking.

"I hardly think so." She turned back to what she'd been staring at: the moon.

"This isn't what I meant, you know," he said, sidling up behind her, resisting the urge to touch her bare arms.

"I beg your pardon?"

"When I told you to move on. I didn't mean for you to ask your brother to find you a socially appropriate husband. I meant for you to fall in love with someone else."

She turned to face him. "How do you I know I haven't?"

"Because I have twenty-twenty vision." He crowded her space, but she held her ground. "Find someone else. Please. Just not the Duke of Grabbington."

"Grabbleton."

"My appellation suits him better . . ."

"You'll forgive me for pointing this out, but you have no say in the matter."

His temper flared. "You don't even like him, it's so obvious it might as well be stamped on your forehead with ink. Woz-damn-it, Rhodie, couldn't you have just resigned yourself to spinsterhood? Taken up some sort of pathetic hobby that would bring you no contact with the males of the species? Cross-stitch, for instance?"

"That's rather selfish. Also, my uncle cross-stitches."

"In a group? Doubtful."

"Perhaps I'd run into a suitable man while picking up more string at the sewing store."

"It's so adorable how you think life works," he said, never breaking their eye contact. He stepped closer. "How much would it take to bribe you to become a nun? Ten thousand? Twenty? If I sell off some investments, I think I could have it for you in a few days."

She crossed her arms. "But as a nun, darling, wouldn't I give up all my worldly possessions?"

"Damn, you saw right through my ploy. You always were too smart." He sighed. "Well, I guess there's nothing for it. I'll have to marry you myself."

"How do you know I'll take you back?"

CHAPTER FORTY-SEVEN

HE COULD HARDLY BELIEVE his ears, and his stomach clenched uncomfortably. "Pardon?"

"All along, you've implied how unworthy you are. I never agreed, but then at the first sign of my own unworthiness, you dumped me like yesterday's pH strips. Didn't you want me to move on?"

"That's . . . that's . . ." He wanted to deny it. He wanted to tell her how much it had meant to him that she'd tried, that she'd kept trying to apologize. "That's right," he said softly.

"So help me understand what changed. Because I'm no man's prize."

Anger flared hot in his chest. "If by that you mean that you're a person and not a trophy to be won, then I agree. But if you mean that you're not a treasure, then we've got a problem."

"I meant the former," she said, a small smile playing at her lips.

"I do love you," he said. "You know that."

"Indeed I do. But I don't wish to marry just because you're jealous that someone else played with your toy."

"It's more than that." He turned away, tugging at his earlobe. "I just needed time. I had some things to work through . . . most of which had nothing to do with you, honestly." He turned back to her. "The counseling is helping. That's part of what's changed. Now that I've forgiven you, I just . . . miss you."

"I miss you, too," she said, and he could hear in her wavering voice the tears she was holding back.

"I was also given some missing information from Petros. It seems he chose to omit the part of the story where you begged Weathers not to discharge me dishonorably."

Her eyebrows rose momentarily. "I see."

"I'm sorry that I . . . jumped to conclusions. Didn't let you share your side. Didn't make sure I had all the facts." James mentally summoned his courage and fought the urge to throw up. "And I have something important to tell you, something I've omitted as well."

Her expression lost its placid neutrality. "What is it?"

"I'm the next Duke of Greenmeadow Downs." He held his breath.

She brightened, and he thought she outshone the moon. "Oh, how lovely. I've always admired that region."

He blinked. "That's it?"

"Yes?" Rhodie looked perplexed. "Should there be more?"

"Nothing about our improved financial compatibility? Nothing about my apparently blue blood or the court of public opinion or your brother's acceptance?"

She brought her hands to his cheeks. "You're a fool," she said tenderly. "There are, of course, logistics to be worked out regarding your new role, but 'husband' is the only title that ever mattered to me, and I can give you that one myself."

He felt tears stinging his eyes; he wanted to tell her it was more than he'd dared to hope for, but his voice was too rough to make work. He just covered her hands with his; maybe she would absorb the sentiment through diffusion or osmosis. Was love a solvent? If so, he felt permeable enough for it to pass through.

Through the patio doors, James could hear them singing "Happy Birthday," and he was glad they'd decided not to wait for them. When he turned back to her, her eyes were lit with excitement.

"Sounds like cake time. Shall we go in?"

"Who are you, and what have you done with Rhododendron?"

She laughed. "I'm right here, love."

"You are, aren't you?" he murmured, his gaze falling to her lips. Woz, he wanted her. The real her, not the picture-perfect princess he'd imagined her to be. He wanted her cheesy jokes and her late-night hair and her angry chess and her book discussions and her haughty sniffs.

"Yes," she whispered. "I always was. I always will be."

"Don't say things like that when I can't kiss you . . ." He caressed her arm. Without warning, she turned them so that James's back was against the wall and began kissing his neck. Desire pulsed in his belly, and he shuddered.

"Rhodie," he said, his voice cracking, "I can't kiss someone else's fiancée."

"You're not," she murmured between gentle presses of her lips. "I'm kissing *you*. It's completely different."

He let his hands fall to her sides and instantly regretted it; the thin fabric masked nothing of her hips underneath. *She has curves now. She's gained weight, she's eating, getting healthy . . .* He loved the feel of her new shape, couldn't keep himself from running his hands over her, getting to know her again.

"Am I going to have to duel him for you? I'm crap with a sword."

Rhodie straightened up to look him in the eye. "Now, see here, everything in your lead-up can be a joke, but not the proposal itself!"

"Oh, I'm sorry," he said, one hand to his chest. "Did you think I was proposing?" She nodded ardently, and he chuckled. "No, princess; not tonight." He kissed the tip of her nose. "Get rid of Grabbington officially, then we'll talk."

"He'll be heartbroken, you know. He really loves my backside."

James felt his breathing speed up again, and she rubbed his back. "A joke, darling. A joke. Relax. My goodness, you're going to burst something." She paused. "Do you hate the idea of me with someone else so much?"

"Yes," he erupted immediately, pulling her close. "I hate it with my whole being. You belong with me. I've known it since I met you."

"I wish I'd known then, too."

"Doesn't matter," he said, pulling her into his side, kissing her temple. "You've come to the same conclusion. That's good enough for me."

"Mr. James." They both turned to identify the speaker, and James stiffened at the sight of the Duke of Grabbleton. How long had he been standing there? Nerves melted into straight-up fear as the duke stalked toward them, stern-faced.

"Listen," James said, guiding Rhodie behind him with one hand, holding up the other in a show of innocence, "I'm sorry, I shouldn't have—"

The larger man stopped three feet from them, right hand outstretched, and James stared at him. Looking around as though trying to find the trap, he hesitantly took it and gave him a firm shake.

"I know when I've been outmaneuvered. Congratulations to you both. I hope to be invited to the big day."

"Please contact me if you need a date," Rhodie chirped from behind him. "I have a few appropriate candidates in mind."

The man chuckled. "I may do that. At least I got to have birthday cake with the king, eh?" The duke was smiling as he headed for the many-paned doors, and James pivoted slowly to face Rhodie, arms crossed over his chest.

"He's taking this very well," he said suspiciously.

"Hmm? Oh, I suppose so, yes."

"A little too well, perhaps?"

"Whatever do you mean? He's just being a gentleman."

"You set me up."

She was as unrepentant as an atheist in church, grinning at him, but she began to back up slowly. "Well, I don't think I'm entirely to blame. I never said he and I were engaged. You simply assumed . . ."

"No, no." He pointed at her, closing in on her. "You tricked me, and you're going to pay for that."

"Really?" she asked, interested. "How?"

Pulling her close, he nuzzled her behind her ear, then whispered, "I'm going to make you dance with me."

Her laughter rang in the courtyard as he made good on his promise. When they finally went back inside, everyone at the table fell quiet, watching them. He pulled out her chair for her, then took Grayson's former seat beside her.

After a few moments, James finally broke the tension. "You laid it on pretty thick with that 'they'll have beautiful children' bit, sir." Grinning, Ignatius leaned across the table to shake his hand. Everyone burst into laughter at that, chattering to one another excitedly. Ginger smugly collected money from Dahlia and Andrew.

"Sorry about that," Ignatius called over the din. "Couldn't resist. I thought you were going to explode when he grabbed her."

"Ginger's passing comment didn't make sense until Grayson offered his congratulations so readily . . ." Her two closest siblings rounded on her, and Ginger huffed her discontent at being outed.

He took a breath to say more when he felt Rhodie's hands on his face, turning it to kiss him. She planted one on him, not nearly as chaste as the one she'd given Grayson earlier, to very vocal approval.

"Guys, I'm going to have to take a rain check on our sail," he murmured, kissing her again. "Something's come up."

EPILOGUE

The Duke of Greenmeadow Downs was reading *My Practice, My Promise*, his legs stretched across the silk seat of an armored carriage as it bumped along a long cobblestone road through the dense redwood forest that surrounded his property. He leaned back like he was at ease; in reality, he'd read the same page six times and still hadn't absorbed a word of it. Reading his wife's favorite book often brought him comfort when they'd been apart a long time, and this had been the longest stretch yet. Ever since he'd been appointed ambassador to Gratha, he'd done a lot more travel . . . and so had the duchess. Her latest expedition had taken her to northern Brevspor for six weeks. He'd meant to be home first to welcome her, but due to weather, his flight had been delayed two days, meaning they'd lost their chance to spend a lazy weekend catching up. *No matter,* he told himself, *we'll be together now.* Together with all their friends and most of their family. Not exactly the kind of welcome home he'd wanted, but it would have to do.

And truthfully, he liked it when they all came up; it would be fun to celebrate the twins' birthday all together. Edward and Abbie liked to get out of the city, and his estate was one of the few places with enough privacy and security for them to relax. It wasn't like it wasn't big enough for all of them. He peered out the curtained window . . . Looking at his massive stone manor was still strange after living here eighteen months. It still felt like his father's house.

The carriage rattled to a stop under the portico, and James jumped out before the footman could descend to open the door for him. A dark-haired girl with tawny skin held a chubby black baby on her hip, both looking at the fading white roses that flanked his front door, and the girl grinned upon seeing him.

"Hello, Uncle James!" He wasn't her uncle, of course, but that didn't seem to matter to Sam and Tezza.

The baby pointed her cookie at him and said, "Da."

"Child, I look nothing like your father," James chided gently as he kissed Raquel's cheek, then Lilac's.

"I think she just wants to share," Raquel explained, bouncing her like a pro.

"Well, in that case, my darling niece, I shall pass on the soggy offer."

"Da," she replied solemnly, taking a bite herself.

"Have you seen Aunt Rhodie?"

Raquel shook her head. Inside, something crashed and James could hear a group of boys laughing their backsides off.

"Oliver Charles Saint, that better have nothing to do with you!" a male voice bellowed, and James stepped out of the doorway just in time to let Olly, Simon, and Natan tear by. All three boys called greetings over their shoulders as they ducked into the gardens. Saint was hot on their heels, but paused when he saw James.

"Oh, hello, mate, welcome back. How was Gratha?"

"Hot as ever. Have you seen my wife?"

"Afraid not," he said, adjusting the green linen sling that held his sleeping daughter. "Sorry to run off, but duty calls. And don't worry, we'll replace it."

"Replace what?" James called after him, but Saint didn't hear. The staff was unloading his trunks from the carriage, and he strode into the foyer past them. He heard soft voices coming from the library, and he peered inside. Abbie was nursing a sleepy Laurel, her daughter's small hand clutching a gold locket around her neck, swinging it lazily. Tezza and Sam's newest daughter, Jacinta, was standing at her knee, watching.

"She's having the milk?"

"That's right." Abbie nodded. "That's her food."

"I think she likes it," the girl said, leaning even closer, and Abbie chuckled softly.

"Yeah, sure seems like it." She looked up to see James and smiled. "Welcome back, weary traveler."

"Thanks. Sorry to interrupt, but have you seen Rhodie?"

At the sound of his voice, Laurel sat bolt upright, and Abbie shook her head as she quickly covered herself. "You heard your favorite uncle, did you?" Abbie teased her. Laurel held out her hands to James insistently, and he went to her gladly. He blew loud, sloppy raspberries against her neck, and she cackled. He'd never tell Lilac, but Laurel was his favorite, too. The kid wasn't happy unless she was going Mach 10 with her hair on fire. "Parker's in the kitchen, last I knew—he might've seen her." He shifted Laurel to his shoulders, holding her ankles securely. She gripped his hair hard as he galloped out of the library, Jacinta chasing after them.

"Hey, look who's back!" said Ignatius, who was leaning on the marble island in the "upstairs kitchen" with Edward and Sam. It was really more for show and a midnight snack, as opposed to the commercial-style kitchens in the basement.

"Yes, and I picked these two pretty flowers somewhere along the way. Do you know whom they belong to?" Edward and Sam both automatically reached for their kids, though Sam did check his daughter's hands for stickiness first, much to James's amusement. They'd adopted Natan and Jacinta, who were siblings, only about six months ago, but James thought Sam was adapting to a three-kid household fairly well.

"Has anyone seen Rhodie?"

"She was right here a moment ago . . . ," Edward said, looking around as Laurel scrambled to get down. "Sorry, I'm not sure which way she went. The wives are out back, they might know."

He threw them all a tired salute, then passed through the back door onto the deck.

Sigh. Brooke, Lily and Tezza stood looking at the view, chatting, each holding a champagne flute, discussing the finer points of potty training, which apparently Jacinta was struggling with.

"Breaking out the bubbly so soon, are we?" he asked, kissing each of their cheeks.

"Have you arrived already?" Lily asked. "Rhodie wasn't expecting you until tonight."

"I caught an earlier flight; she didn't get my text?"

"I suppose not," she said. "But I've seldom seen her so anxious, so I'm sure it will be a happy surprise. She's inside, somewhere."

He smiled as he turned back to the house, but he felt a hand on his shoulder. "Hang on," Tezza muttered, waving her hand around his shoulders. "You picked up some Grathan magic. We don't need that hanging around." Despite not being in the protection business anymore, she'd become an even more powerful magic user since becoming a mother. James wasn't sure if the two things were related or not.

He was getting tired of asking around, and if he struck out again, he'd just start a room-by-room search of all twenty bedrooms until he found her.

Andrew passed him on the stairs, headphones on.

"Hello, young prince," James said wearily, and Andrew lifted one earphone to hear him better. "Have you seen my wife?"

"One of the babies spit up on her. She went upstairs to change."

"Thank you," he said, taking the stairs two at a time, ignoring the knowing smirk he was getting from his brother-in-law.

Lily's words echoed in his tired head. *Anxious? Rhodie?* That didn't sit well with him. She'd been a little distant on the phone the last few times they'd talked. He knew she was ready for him to be home, even though she had plenty of work to do without him around. James opened the door to their bedroom quietly, hoping to sneak up on her in the shower or in the closet. Thinking about how many people were in his house (twenty, thirty counting staff?), he locked it behind him in anticipation of a happy reunion with her . . . even if it was a quick reunion. But the sound of sniffling had him hurrying into the suite with a very different question in mind.

Rhodie sat on the edge of their bed, fingers pressed to her lips, reading something on her phone, silent tears streaming down her face.

"You're crying?"

She looked up sharply. "You're home?" He barely got his arms open before she was in them, giving him the type of bear hug he'd thought only his father-in-law was capable of. Rhodie was crying even harder now, and he stroked her back.

"I caught an earlier flight. What's wrong?" He kissed the top of her head.

"I won."

"You won . . . what?"

"The Kleitzman-Popperfield Prize for Scientific Impact. I won for my hybridization of the villania with the Orangiersian wild mint. They said it was 'ushering in a new era of magical exploration for the continent and beyond.'"

He pried himself from her grip to hold her out by her shoulders and look into her eyes. "Really?"

She nodded. "First, I was on the long list, and then I was on the short list, and then . . . I didn't want to tell you while you were gone, I didn't want to get your hopes up."

"Baloney. You didn't want me to tell anyone."

"That too." She laughed sheepishly.

"I'm getting so much better, though! I haven't told anyone about your embarrassing hair debacle."

She pointed at him. "And you'd better not, either."

"I'm insanely proud of you," he whispered, pulling her close again. "You're eight years ahead of my ten-year plan. We'll have to call Gordon, he'll be thrilled for you."

Rhodie laughed through her tears, shaking. "I still can't believe it. There were so many wonderful, talented applicants this year. I insisted from the beginning that Yautia be credited with me in the prize, and they agreed, but I never thought . . ." She gave a shuddering sigh.

"I did," James said, kissing her temple. "I knew. I'm not bragging, but . . . I absolutely knew."

"You're a very intelligent man."

"Tell me more," he said, tugging her toward their bed, and she laughed again.

"Now? Even with everyone downstairs?"

"Some of them are upstairs, I'm sure." James whipped his shirt off. "I'll let you look at my third nipple."

"I've seen it," she said, smirking, but he felt her fingers on his chest nonetheless as he angled his head to kiss her neck. She sighed happily. "I missed these freckles. I missed these lips . . ."

"They missed you, too. So very much." He backed toward the bed, drawing her with him by her rounded hips.

"I love you, One-and-Only Husband," she said softly.

"And I love you, One-and-Only Wife," he replied.

Would you please leave a review?

Whether the plot moved too fast or too slow,
Leave a review and let us all know!
Did Arron annoy? Did Rho make you snore?
Leave a review now; it's hardly a chore!
<u>Goodreads</u> and <u>Amazon</u>, wherever you bought,
Please take a minute and share what you thought.
Glowing reviews keep my business afloat,
And at parties, they give me a reason to gloat.
Thanks for reading my work!

Get the complete Borderline Chronicles!

The Ex-Princess (Abbie and Edward, HFN)[1]
The Un-Queen (Abbie and Edward, HEA)[2]
The Almost-Widow (Sam and Tezza)[3]
The Jinxed Journalist (Saint and Brooke)[4]
Magicology (The Warlord-in-Chief of Gratha and Frieda, coming summer 2020)

---

1. https://amzn.to/35tjrbi

2. https://amzn.to/35r9o6U

3. https://amzn.to/31agadE

4. https://amzn.to/2VzN32d

Bonus scenes and discussion questions available at fionawest.net!

WANT TO READ THE EX-Princess or The Un-Queen with your book group? We've got you covered: snag our free printable and a drink and you're ready to go. Or maybe you're just curious what happened when James hit on Rhodie at Edward's wedding...stop by my website[5] and check out all the fun extra scenes!

Acknowledgments

TO MY FAMILY: THANK you for listening to me whine about how much revision injures my soul, thank you for eating dinner much later than planned, thank you for funding my endeavors and believing in me more than you probably should. And especially to Mr. West, who is unequivocally the best.

To the whole crew at Salt and Sage, but especially Erin (communication conqueror), Mandy (editor extraordinaire) and Veronica (sensitivity reading superstar): you have each elevated my work far above what I could achieve on my own, and you've done so in a spirit of cooperation and encouragement. I appreciate you.

To my copy editor, Jessica Gardner: Thank you for keeping me from looking like an idiot who can't spell. You do such a wonderful job of polishing my work.

To my sensitivity reader, Stephanie Lucas: Rhodie would be lucky to have a counselor like you. Thanks for helping me make the experience authentic and compassionate.

To my writing group in Haiti: I am actually tearing up thinking about how you've kept me sane these past few years. None of this would've happened without you. You mean more to me than you know.

To my beta readers and critique partners, Angela Boord, Rebecca Hopkins, Liz Schandorff, and Lila: I know what a big job it is to read someone's work with a critical eye without coming off as discouraging, but you each do it so well. I'm so thankful that you keep coming back for more!

To my cover artist, Steven Novak: your artistic work is the only reason anyone sees my artistic work. Thanks for putting up with all the little tweaks I always want.

To Roll for Fantasy: thanks for creating an awesome free map program. You rock.

Connect with Fiona!

Thanks so much for taking the time to sample my work. I hope you enjoyed reading it even more than I enjoyed writing it, though I doubt that's possible. Being an author is a dream come true, and getting to share my books with delightful, thoughtful readers like you just adds to the sweetness. Drop me a line and let me know what you thought or leave a review on Goodreads[1]!

Sign up for my bi-monthly newsletter, The West Wind, for freebies, deleted scenes, book reviews, and insight into my writing process at https://www.subscribepage.com/west-wind.

On Twitter as @FionaWestAuthor[2]

On Facebook as @authorfionawest[3]

On Instagram as fionawestauthor[4]

On Goodreads as Fiona West[5]

Or email me at fiona@fionawest.net. I love talking to fans!

---

1. https://www.goodreads.com/book/show/42446823-the-streetdweller

2. https://twitter.com/FionaWestAuthor

3. https://web.facebook.com/authorfionawest/

4. https://www.instagram.com/fionawestauthor/

5. https://www.goodreads.com/author/show/18433825.Fiona_West

CPSIA information can be obtained
at www.ICGtesting.com
Printed in the USA
LVHW010315020920
664772LV00005B/554